No Defenses

Faith McCarty stood with her dress torn, her flesh bruised, her back against the wall of the crude cabin where she had been taken.

Before her stood her two abductors: one—a brutal, squat figure of pure animal strength; the other—thin and wiry, with eyes that gleamed with weasel-like cunning, and a grin that seemed to split his death's-head face.

They said that they were holding her for ransom—and that her husband would pay whatever they asked to get her back alive.

But now they had time to kill—and Faith shuddered as she thought of the days and nights to come, when she would be the sole source of these men's amusement . . . the one outlet for their lusts . . .

THE RAVAGERS

The West was no place for fairy tales . . .

Also by Arthur Moore and available in
Popular Library editions:

THE RAIDERS
THE RIVALS
THE BURNING SKY

THE RAVAGERS

A NOVEL BY ARTHUR MOORE

John Q. Ross II
311 Cummings Ave.
Buffalo, Wyo. 82834

POPULAR LIBRARY • NEW YORK

Published by Popular Library, CBS Publications, CBS Consumer Publishing, a Division of CBS Inc.

December, 1977

ISBN: 0-445-04126-9

To Maria and Alf Harris

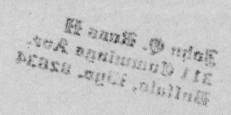

PRINTED IN THE UNITED STATES OF AMERICA

There is a tide in the affairs of men,
Which, taken at the flood,
  leads on to fortune.

                              Shakespeare

There's a fortune in that bank.

                              Jesse James

Chapter One

Bucky Jordan stumbled out of the Roseberry Saloon on Fifth Street, mumbling to himself. He had run through his money, discovered his credit was nil, and small gusts of anger were rumbling in his throat. He turned to wait for Johnny Fuller and Tim Newton, yanking his revolver out and spinning the cylinder.

"I got no use f'this town anyways," Bucky said. "Where you want t'go, Johnny?"

"I don' give a damn . . . let's head south." Johnny bent over the hitchrack, picking at the reins, and Tim pushed him aside.

"Lemme do that. You're blind drunk, f'crissakes."

Johnny, lean and tall, bristled, shoving the other back. Bucky pushed between them and fired the revolver recklessly. He yelled at them to mount up. Instantly Johnny laughed, drawing his own pistol, shooting into the air with a whoop.

The horses pulled at the reins, prancing and stomping, but the three danced, holding onto the pommels and mounted clumsily, and dug in spurs. Bucky led them down the narrow street toward the River Road and, as he turned the corner, fired into the air again. Johnny and Tim came whooping after, firing pistols at the signboards hung out over the street.

A dozen people crowded to doors and windows, gazing at the galloping trio, and someone yelled, "Get the sheriff!"

A signboard came crashing down and swung crazily by one end as a bullet cut one of the small chains that held it. Several saddled horses broke loose from a hitchrack and loped away down the street, heads tossing.

A light wagon, coming from Fourth Street, wheeled in a tight circle. A woman sawed at the reins as the team was spooked by the shots. She was stout, dressed in blue calico and a short bonnet; there was a small boy beside her, white-faced and clinging to the seat. The woman screamed as the wagon teetered on two wheels. Then she was thrown out, shrieking, as the wagon overturned and slewed sideways.

The boy was dumped out and the wagon-bed came down atop him. A broken wheel spun into the street. Halfway into the next block, Bucky reined in and pulled the horse's head around. They were heading away from the bridge, and he yelled to the others, pointing back. Johnny had emptied his pistol and was trying to reload, holding it high, ramming out brass. Someone in a window sent a shot over his head and he ducked and glanced around in astonishment, then spurred the horse to follow his friends.

None of them noticed the crowd running to the overturned wagon. But two men hurried into the street and emptied pistols after the galloping horsemen.

One of the horses reared, back legs giving away, and it fell, throwing Tim Newton. His companions ignored his yells and ran full tilt for the bridge.

As Tim got to his feet, staggering and limping, the pistol still in his hand, a rifle bullet cut him down and he dropped forward onto his face.

Frank McCarty rode into town on his sorrel horse late in the afternoon, dressed in jeans and an old shirt and leather jacket, a six-gun about his middle. He had been out on the prairie practicing with the revolver and rifle, as he did at every opportunity. He stepped down in front of the livery stable and old Sam got out of his chair with a grunt.

"Howdy, Frank. You-all missed the doin's. We had us quite a time couple hours ago."

"What happened?" Frank gave him the reins and stretched.

"Three fellas started shootin' up the town. One of 'em's over at Doc Litchfield's place now, layin' on a slab. Name of Newton."

"He's dead? Who shot 'im?"

"Don't rightly know." Old Sam scratched his white head. "Two-three of the boys took shots at the cuss. He overturned Miz Byer's wagon and her boy was kilt."

Frank sighed and let his breath out. He vaguely recalled the boy, a three- or four-year-old towhead. "Where'd the other two get to?"

Sam shrugged. "Went off across the bridge. There wasn't a damn lawman in town either. We ought to have us some town law, Frank. Folks is mighty riled about that boy."

"Yes, I expect so."

He walked to the office, considerably subdued. It was the second or third such incident—though without tragedy until now—that had occurred in the last month. Roseberry wasn't a cow town, but it sometimes seemed like it when wild spirits let off steam and shot up storefronts. In the last year or so a line had been established near the edge of town, mostly behind the new stage and freight yards. There were five houses to his knowledge, each with three to six girls; there were also two dance halls across the street from each other on Fifth Street. It

9

was the seamy end of Roseberry and every weekend it attracted a great number of footloose men from the surrounding ranches.

The town was growing up, and these were the usual growing pains, like them or not. A few times he had suggested at town-council meetings that they make an effort to curtail the saloons and the girls, but it met with little support. The members of the council were merchants; and even Noah Applegate sided against him, saying it was the right of people to let off steam now and then.

It was inevitable that the McCarty grasp on the town would loosen like a knot in an old rope, and there wasn't a damned thing he could do about it.

He read the letters on his desk, talked with the office manager, Ken Larkin, and went home to a busy house. Faith was getting ready for one of her semiannual trips to Ironton, making lists and preparing. It was a period he dreaded because the house always seemed so empty when she was away. And little David seemed to feel, despite his single year of life, that he was an abandoned child too, though Mrs. Steen, the housekeeper, was as much of a mother to him as possible. Mrs. Steen had taken the place of Mrs. Barber, who'd returned to Tennessee when her husband died. She lived in while Faith was away, in a small apartment behind the dining room, an addition tacked onto the house after it had been rebuilt.

Fitting the Winchester into the hall gun rack, he hung his pistol and belt behind the door for the time being and went into the kitchen, where Faith had laid out supper.

He kissed her and sat down.

"Billy Quinn said there was some excitement in town today," she said, sitting opposite.

He told her about the three men and the death of the Byer child. "Karl was out of town on business and there wasn't a deputy close by, either. The two, whoever they were, got away clean."

10

"That isn't right." Faith shook her head sadly. She was a beautiful woman, with brown hair gathered at the nape of her neck, lustrous dark eyes, and jet lashes. It was a constant source of amazement to him how she had transformed herself from a gawky farm girl into the poised and thoughtful woman who was his wife—and the managing owner of the largest women's shop for five hundred miles in any direction. Looking at her, he recalled the first time he'd seen her at Webber's Station years ago, wearing a faded and patched ill-fitting dress, riding in a dirty farm wagon pulled by mules, as her parents came to the territory to scratch out a bare living from the earth. There had been something instinctive inside her even then, longing and struggling to free itself; and when the first breath of opportunity came along, she had grasped it and her progress had been meteoric.

She echoed old Sam's opinion that the town needed local law.

"It's a question of paying for it," he said. "Everyone wants the benefits but no one wants to foot the bills. It would require three town marshals at a bare minimum, and that's something like three hundred dollars each month for salaries."

"Couldn't they make their salaries in fines?"

He smiled. "Maybe. But if the salaries depend on fines, then we'd have police arresting people for borderline law-breaking. We'll have to hire a justice of the peace too, and he'd let most of them go—unless his salary depended on—"

Faith laughed. "The cares of government don't become you, Frank. Sometimes I wonder why you stay on the council."

"To keep an eye on things." He sipped coffee, then changed the subject. "Have you arranged passage yet?"

"Yes. I considered taking Margaret along, but now I've

11

changed my mind. It's an unnecessary expense, hotel and food, and I can do all the note-taking myself."

"She'd be company for you. It's a damned long ride to Ironton and back."

Faith shook her head. "I've thought it over. There'll be company on the stage. Anyway, have you read the St. Louis papers lately? They're talking another panic in the East. We should save our money, dear." She patted his hand. "You have a tendency to indulge us all, and I think you should change your ways."

"I'll try," he said dryly, aware again how much she'd changed hers.

Frank took the envelope the delivery boy offered him, fished out a short dime and said, "Thanks." The boy went out, whistling on the steps to the street, and Frank tore the envelope open. It was from the stage line super in Ironton, Angus Williamson.

Another group of women, Angus wrote, headed by someone known locally as Gertie de Vere, was on the way to Roseberry. There were four in the group, including Gert, and Angus stated from impeccable sources that all were "cyprians." "Just thought you'd want to know," Angus said, probably tongue in cheek.

Frank glanced at the hollow-ticking Seth Thomas on the wall and took a cigar from a box on the desk. Girls and dance halls contributed heavily to the petty troubles in town, no doubt about that. He knew that Sheriff Welch thought most of the town's crime came from that district—and most of the killings, like that of the Byer boy.

Of course, closing down the line and the saloons would make the fur fly. And he was not at all sure they *could* close them down. People were apt to take the law into their own hands when they came up against an unpopular decision from a couple of the town fathers. Ramsay Hamer once said he didn't fancy having his store shot up because he'd said the wrong thing or voted the wrong way in the council. It could happen.

Frank leaned back and put a booted foot up on the desk edge. He'd never heard of a western town successfully banning girls and gamblers. It would be as bad as trying to close up the saloons. *That* was probably impossible.

He lit the cigar and puffed, scratching his brown hair. Noah talked a lot about freedom, how they'd fought a war to get it not so damned long ago. Freedom to live and work—and get drunk and play cards and indulge in all the other petty sins. How did you give a man freedom and take it away too?

Frank cared a lot about Roseberry, and there were others who cared too; the town was no longer just a wide place in the trail. It was no longer a frontier town catering to mule skinners and travelers. It wasn't a cowhand's town either, or a farmer's town. It was rather like a small city with a great many diverse elements and no single preponderance, although farmers were scattered throughout the county in large numbers, mostly close-in. There were a dozen small ranchers; the McCarty holding was still the largest, but the others were shipping more beeves every year. Roseberry might play host to fifty or sixty cowhands of a Saturday night; and most of them welcomed the girls.

The town was still growing; it had a telegraph to Darnley and Ironton and south to Hatfield. There was even talk of extending the line to Santa Fe. There were two weekly newspapers, the largest, the Roseberry *Courier*, run by sharp and caustic Noah Applegate. The second, the *Advocate*, had been started only a month past and had put out only a few poorly printed issues. And someone had once proposed at a town council meeting that horsecars be established along Front Street.

13

Frank examined the end of the cigar. It was important for him to hold onto his council seat, if for nothing else than to safeguard his own interests, but the days were gone when his word was law. He glanced at the clock on the wall; fifteen minutes to the council meeting. He got up, a big, restless man with broad shoulders and small waist; he had the squarish McCarty face with a slightly aquiline nose and a firm mouth. He'd worn a moustache for several years, but had shaved it off last year about the time David was born. Faith said she liked him better without it.

Taking his Stetson off the peg, he went out to the hall, calling to Ken Larkin that he was on his way. He ran down the steps to the street and stood a moment to finish the cigar. Main Street faced on the river and, by an act of the council years ago, no buildings had been allowed on the river side. As a result every building on the main street had a river view; trees, shrubs and grass had been planted on the strip between road and river bank to create a very pleasant park.

He walked east toward the bridge, nodding to a half-dozen people; he knew every merchant in town and a great many others by first names, though hundreds of new families had moved in of late on both sides of the river. One of these days they'd have to make a population count. It was probably nearing the four thousand mark including those at the Bend.

Old Sam was sitting in a tilted-back chair in front of the livery stable, soaking up the sun. "Howdy, Frank," he said.

Frank greeted him and paused a moment to gossip. Sam learned everything that was happening in the county sooner or later. Between Sam and Jake Netter, owner of the Silver Spur Saloon, one didn't have to bother with a newspaper. Charlie Larson, the town drunk, had sobered up enough to ride a fast mare in a race a few days past,

14

Sam said, and had fallen off and wrenched his arm. He'd have made it fine if he'd been drunk. One of the Litchfield girls was getting married, and there had been a horrendous flood near some eastern city.

Frank clucked his tongue and went on, passing the newly painted hotel where a sign stated one might take a room for a week for five dollars, which seemed a mite high. He glanced at Faith's two story Women's Center, sniffing the perfume that wafted from the open door. The store was a success; it had started as a dress and milliner shop, but when Ethel Harris had retired, Faith had remade it. The store catered to women but sold children's clothes and toys as well. A woman could buy a cotton bonnet or the latest fashion from New York, if she could afford it. There were perfumes, colognes, and cosmetics, every kind of accessory, and clothing. Faith's inventory was huge, because she also supplied dry-goods stores for hundreds of miles around, and employed a number of men with wagons who called at distant houses and ranches with her goods.

Karl Welch had asked to attend the town-council meeting. As sheriff of the county he was always welcome, but for him to ask meant he had a piece to say. Frank met him downstairs in his office; Karl was a stocky, quick-eyed man with dark hair beginning to show a dusty gray at the temples. He dressed carefully in a broadcloth suit and black string tie, his star badge peeping in a glint of silver from under the edge of his coat.

Frank asked if there was news of the other two men who'd hoorawed the town.

Karl shook his head with a wry face. "We'll never see them again. Dead gent is Timothy Newton, according to a letter in his pants. Nothing else says a thing. He's a drifter like his pals and didn't have a dollar on him. The county will have to plant him."

They went upstairs together. The council maintained an

office and a conference room over the sheriff's rooms and jail. The outer office was a small, square room with a desk, several file cabinets, a table and three straight chairs. There was a lantern on the desk and two flower pots in the window, which had chintz curtains drawn back.

Amy Gordon, a tiny dried-up woman with gray hair and pale eyes behind steel-rimmed glasses, smiled at them and gathered up her notebooks and pencils, tucking one behind her ear. She followed them into the larger room, where the others were waiting. There was a long table in the center with chairs around it, a sideboard, a bar with a row of bottles and glasses, and a desk. On the wall were framed pictures, one of President Grant, who was in his second term, one of J. McCarty and Amos Van Borcke together, taken ten years ago, and a small, fixed-smile portrait in a gilt frame of Dr. Nichols, who had saved Roseberry from a diphtheria epidemic.

Noah Applegate was already there, with Seth Potter, the postmaster. They were of a size, the postmaster gray and balding with an almost unhealthy white skin peppered with liver spots, the editor brown and hairy. Noah was swarthy, with tufts of gray-black hair growing at all angles from his head; he wore a brownish moustache and his brows were bushy, hanging over sunken eyes. He smoked a huge carved pipe and looked small and delicate. They were poring over a copy of the *Advocate*, which was spread open on the table, discussing some item or other as Karl and Frank entered and hung their hats over the sideboard.

" 'Lo, Frank. Howdy, Sheriff."

Ramsay Hamer entered a moment later to shake hands all round. Ramsay looked like a merchant. He operated the mercantile store near the east end of town and was portly and red-faced, always rumpled, always needing a haircut.

16

"Sorry I'm late," Ramsay said. "The latest Monkey Ward catalog came in and I was leafin' through it."

"When'll Faith be going, Frank?" Noah asked.

"In a few days, I suppose." Frank took his regular place at the head of the table, Amy Gordon at the far end. "If nobody minds, we'll let Karl have his say right at the start. Then he can stay afterward as he pleases."

"Fine with me," Seth said genially.

"Where were you yesterday, Sheriff?" Noah asked, in a schoolmasterish voice.

Karl sat down gingerly. "I was about twenty miles south at Milkweed Crick." He glanced at Noah. "Somebody fed an old renegade Indian named Tom One-Eye a couple bottles of home-made rotgut and he went out and massacred two gents who were campin' by the crick."

"What happened to the Indian?" Noah said with more interest.

"Don't rightly know. Sleepin' it off, likely. Look behind your printin' press when you get back."

Noah cocked an eye at the stocky lawman, not sure he was being joshed.

Frank said, "You've got the floor, Karl." He sat down and fished for a cheroot.

"I've said this afore," Karl began, glancing at each of them in turn. "I've got four men and a hell of a big county. With things as they is at present I can't see to policing the town too. You saw that yesterday—though I can't promise we could have stopped them hellions if we *had* been here. It only takes a minute for some hombre to cause a damn lot of trouble." He seemed to notice Amy for the first time. "Excuse me for swearin', Miss Amy."

She murmured something, writing busily.

"So you want us to provide our own town policemen," Ramsay said.

Karl nodded. "I think you ought to. You can use the jail, of course. I've got four cells that'll hold five-six at a

17

crack if they have to. You should have a town marshal who knows ever'body. He can make rounds ever' day and be seen all day long—and night too. You can pay for the men partly by taxin' the line and the dancehalls and saloons. It seems t'me that sin ought to be taxed."

Ramsay chuckled. "I don't see why not."

"There's gambling too," Karl continued. "I can't stop it—even if I was ordered to. Let it come out in the open and tax it."

Noah said, "Every preacher in town will castigate us."

"Castigate 'em in your newspaper, Mr. Applegate," Karl said. He glanced at Frank. "But get the taxes first." He pushed back his chair and stood. "Talk's cheap, but money will get you some town law and we need it."

Frank stood and shook hands with Karl when he rose to leave. "Thanks for coming, Karl." The others echoed his sentiments; Karl winked at Frank and went out, closing the door.

"All right," Seth said, "we know we need town law. Who'll we get?"

"Joel Beale?" Ramsay said.

Frank shook his head. "Let's sit on it for a day or two, so we can all think about names." He eyed each of them. "Are we voting for three town marshals?"

They nodded, as Ramsay sighed. Frank said to Amy, "That's an official 'yes' vote, Amy. The council is unanimous."

"Taxing sin won't be enough," Noah said. "Not in the long run. We'll have to get up some new taxes and shove 'em down folk's throats."

"We know that," Frank agreed, "but there's one more thing. It's also time we had our own town judge. The police can arrest but they can't police *and* judge at the same time."

"No, they can't!" Noah said, rapping the table. "That's unconstitutional."

18

"So we need a justice of the peace."

Seth's eyes grew round. "Do you mean build a courthouse?"

"No, a J.P. can hold court in his own house for the time being. Later on we can get him a building somewhere."

"Dammit," Ramsay said with asperity, "we've got along in Roseberry for a lot of years with the circuit judge. Why do we—"

"Frank's right," Noah said. "We can't hold a few drunks over for two months waiting for some circuit judge to get around to us. Things have to be settled right now. Swallow it, Ramsay. We need our own police and judge." He knuckled the table. "I move we appoint a justice of the peace for Roseberry."

"Second it," Seth said.

Frank put up his hand. "All in favor—" He looked at Ramsay, whose hand went up reluctantly. "Motion carried unanimously, Amy."

"Who'll we get?" Seth said instantly. "Will Amos serve?"

"I doubt it." Frank shook his head.

Noah puffed blue smoke and looked at the bowl of his pipe. "We've got some lawyers in town, but I'm damned if I think any of 'em's worth a damn as a J.P., especially not Schuyler Wood."

"We don't have to decide it this minute," Frank said. "But a J.P. doesn't have to be a law-school graduate. Keep that in mind. We need someone with good common sense."

"That'll rule out *all* the lawyers then," Noah said. "I never saw a lawyer or a politician worth his—"

"Hell, *we're* politicians, aren't we?" Ramsay said in a higher voice than usual. He pulled out a turnip watch and looked at it with lips puffed out.

Noah stared at him, then looked at Frank. "What

19

about the railroad, Frank? You feel like going to Ironton to have a heart-to-heart talk with some of those officials?"

"Hell no," Frank said at once. He had no intention of making *that* trip, to hold a probably fruitless conversation with John Hightower. He'd met the man once and come off second best. The railroad held all the trumps. They could build tracks or not as they chose, and he was convinced that to talk to them was like shouting in the wind—and he would not beg, for all the good it would do.

Noah grumbled but did not pursue it. Noah's cross was the railroad; Ramsay Hamer had said many times that if Noah would stop lashing the T&T in his editorials, they'd get a depot in Roseberry within the month. Noah took sides on almost all questions of the nation, let alone local problems. He frequently ran editorials condemning members of congress in acid terms, as well as big business, such as that run by the Goulds and Vanderbilts. Noah was for the little man, he declared, on the side of the farmers, who were all too often at the ferocious mercies of the railroads and the urban workers.

Noah was erratic, but he was genuinely interested in progress, and he did care about the town. The composition of the town council had changed in recent months; Frank was the only one remaining of the original four. J.M. and Amos had both resigned, pleading retirement, and Jake Netter had run into a four month siege of sickness and, though he was now recovered, had withdrawn in favor of Noah. Seth Potter and Ramsay Hamer had been asked to serve. Frank thought them both men who cared.

Caring was an important factor, which was why he had rejected Schuyler Wood's bid to sit on the council. Schuyler made an issue of the matter, writing editorials in the new paper, the *Advocate*, insisting that the council seats be elective.

20

Noah, bless him, had supported Frank's view, that the council was composed of fine men and did not need change.

There were times when Frank wished he was more like his father. Schuyler's editorials sometimes got his goat, but when he'd shown them to J.M., the old man only laughed. Such talk rolled off J.M.'s back like chaff. J.M. cared nothing about what anyone said, unless it was to his face and he happened to take exception to it. Then things happened swiftly.

But Frank wasn't his father. He was like the old man in looks but not in disposition. He cared what his neighbors thought, and he tried to do the right thing, even though some thought him high-handed—like Schuyler.

The railroad was another matter, and he had not discussed his thoughts with Noah or the council. He was the only cattle rancher on the council, of course, and as such might be expected to want the railroad even more than the rest. There had been a time when he would have financed a spur track to Roseberry, but no longer. It was only ten or twelve days' drive to Jackson with a herd, and there was water all the way; hardly a hardship at all. To the old timers it was a lark.

There was also another reason. When the railroad came to Roseberry, passenger service on the stage line would probably disappear. Who wanted to ride in a jolting, dusty stagecoach when he could take a more comfortable and faster train? The freight business would remain, but new lines would have to be instituted so they would not have to fire a lot of people. He'd talked to Luke Dobbs about it several times and plans were being made, just in case.

"If there's nothing else," Frank said, "let's adjourn."

"Just as soon," Ramsay said, getting up. Amy Gordon folded her notebook and gathered up her papers, and they all stretched.

21

Frank walked along the street with Noah, who chewed his big pipe as he talked about the fiasco of the eastern firm, Jay Cooke, deploring the fact that a few unscrupulous men could plunge the entire nation into panic.

"Money will get tight in a few months," Noah prophesied, "and business will stagnate. See if it doesn't."

"In the East," Frank said, but he sighed inwardly, knowing the little editor was probably right. Money was already scarce here in the West; most folks bartered for goods, and seldom saw hard money year in and year out.

"It may not touch us directly," Noah said in his pompous manner, "but we'll feel it. Your wife will notice it in her dress business because she orders from the East."

"Yes . . ."

"We need laws against such practices by big business." Noah gestured with the pipe. "Those men think themselves above the law—and I'm damned if they aren't! But it's wrong. They're humans like the rest of us, not gods. They should not be allowed to corrupt the nation for private gain."

They paused in front of the *Courier* office as Frank agreed with the editor that politicians should be made of sterner stuff.

"They receive too many temptations," Noah said, "it's a wonder there's an honest man left among them." He sighed. "Look at what's being said about President Grant right now, poor fellow."

Frank managed to excuse himself and continued toward his office, wondering how soon the effects of the panic would be felt in the West. If business stagnated in the East as Noah feared, then they would all suffer in various degrees, probably. He knew they had overdue accounts on the books, and made a mental note to consult

Luke about them too. Luke Dobbs had assumed the duties of general business manager for both stage and freight lines, while Quincy Beale was in charge of rolling stock, hostlers, drivers, guards, and all the vast equipment of the lines, housed in dozens of stations over a thousand miles.

He knew it could be considered self-serving that he did nothing to encourage the railroad but, he told himself, it was not the worst chasm he would ever cross.

As he halted at the entrance to the bank, his eye was caught by a colored poster in the window. "Centennial Anniversary!" the sign proclaimed. "To commemorate the signing of the Declaration of Independence an Exhibition of the arts and industries of all nations will be held in Philadelphia during the summer of 1876 on the beautiful fairgrounds of Fairmont Park."

Frank rubbed his chin; that was next year, and he had thought many times of taking Faith to see the once-in-a-lifetime experience. He read the poster again, wondering if there was any reason why he and Faith should not take a month off. He had never taken her on a real vacation. . . .

Chapter Two

Schuyler Wood came out of Jake's Saloon and walked toward him, pulling on gloves, a tall, distinguished-looking man, dressed to the hilt as usual in a frock coat, diamond stickpin in his cravat, a dazzling white shirt, and top hat of dyed black beaver.

He saw Frank and put out his hand, "Well, Mr. McCarty, what a pleasant surprise."

"You're formal today, Schuyler." Frank shook hands, smiling. "I read your latest editorial in the *Advocate*. I'm afraid you credit me with too much power."

"It's the power of money, Frank, something that people can understand. Fanciful arguments are all very good for the ladies' teas, and even for Congress, but I believe in getting to the heart of things." Schuyler Wood smiled winningly. "You're the shark in the Roseberry pond. No one else."

Frank made a face. "I've been called a lot of things, but never a shark."

"The year isn't over."

"It's drawing to a close. We'll have a new year soon, a time to reflect on the old and change our courses in the new."

"Very poetic, Frank. I expect you mean me. But I

never change, year to year." Schuyler tipped his hat and walked away.

Schuyler Wood walked back past the saloon and got into a light buggy drawn by one black horse. Turning the buggy in the street, he drove east to the toll bridge and went across, pausing to pay his fare, then driving quickly to the converted stable where Cole Stedman had set up a pressroom. Tying the horse to a hitching post next the building, Schuyler squinted at the front. Cole had very recently painted a sign there: *Roseberry Advocate*. Underneath was a smaller notice: *Job Printing*.

Inside, Cole had the iron stove going, and the single room smelled strongly of coal oil and ashes. The stove was in the center, with the job press to one side and the type cases on the other. Cole was standing in front of the composing stone, tapping type in an iron chase. He glanced around. "Oh, hello, Schuyler. Didn't expect you."

Schuyler removed his hat and looked about the room. Cole had dressed it up considerably in the last several weeks. The two previous editions of the paper were pasted to one wall, along with a Confederate flag and a number of framed pictures. One of the walls had been painted white and over the desk were a calendar and an ad for stomach bitters which depicted a scantily clad young woman holding a glass.

"I brought my editorial." Schuyler took a folded sheet from an inside pocket and handed it over. "I thought you were going to get someone to help you here."

Cole sat down with a sigh and unfolded the sheet. He was a thin, worried-looking man, clean-shaven, with bags under his eyes and sparse blonde hair. He took a pair of spectacles from a vest pocket and put them on, tilting his head back as he read.

26

"Still attacking McCarty, huh?"

Schuyler found a cigar and smelled it. "I can't drop it abruptly. You know that."

"Hmmm." Cole read the sheet through and put it down on the chase. "McCarty's not going to hold elections and you know it."

"Yes, I suppose so. He's in the catbird seat."

"You're barking up the wrong tree, Schuyler. This is McCarty's town and you can't change it in six months, or maybe not in ten years. The fact of the matter is, McCarty's been good to most of 'em."

"He owns most of 'em, you mean."

Cole shrugged. "That's true too. You want a drink?"

Schuyler shook his head. He watched Cole take a bottle from the desk and pour a generous amber-colored dollop in a tumbler.

Cole said, "I don't have help because I can't find anyone who ever saw a press before, let alone a composing stick."

"Teach them."

Cole sighed and drank half the liquor, smacking his lips. He eyed the other almost malevolently. "Yes, Your Honor." He took off the spectacles, folded them, and tucked them in the vest pocket. "This edition will be a day late."

Schuyler frowned. "You were a day late last week."

"It might even be two days late. Hard to tell yet." He drank the rest of the liquor and gazed at the empty glass. "I know what you're thinking, Schuyler, but it's not because of this." He put the glass down on the desk.

Schuyler made a noise in his throat. He took a turn up and down the room, hands deep in his pockets. He'd set Cole up in business with the idea of swaying public opinion and forcing McCarty and the others of the town council to open council seats to free elections. So far it had been a disappointing campaign. The *Advocate*, with

27

two editions out, had been a voice crying in an uncaring wilderness. No one seemed to listen. Of course they'd been able to print only a few hundred copies, and had distributed them free; Cole came into the deal with the understanding he could use the press for job printing or any other kind of printing that would make him money for his own profit. Schuyler had financed everything, including enough to keep Cole in victuals; the editor slept on a cot behind the type cases.

He hated to give up the fight, because there was so much at stake, but he was beginning to have second thoughts about his real chances of success. McCarty *was* well entrenched, as Cole said. Maybe too well set to pry out of office; thus far the council had rejected or ignored the suggestions that it be elected. He himself knew the power of the incumbent, or had known it once, but he had been out of office too long. A grand jury looked into some of the business arrangements he'd made in an eastern city—which arrangements had later been characterized by a local newspaper as "shady"—and he'd been forced to resign. But that was a long way away, and this was a new land and a new opportunity. He'd come west with the idea of becoming a big fish in a small pond, only to discover that the pond already had a big fish in it. As he'd said to McCarty, a shark.

He left Cole to his work, climbed back into the buggy, and moodily drove into town, giving over the horse at old Sam's livery. His office was around the corner in the next block, and he walked the distance, chewing on a cigar. By rights he should long since have become an alderman or councilman—a good many others thought so too, or at least expressed the idea to him. But he could not get past that one obstacle—this was McCarty's town.

McCarty's town.

Schuyler slowed his pace, took the cigar out of his mouth, looked at it, and threw it away. This was

28

McCarty's town . . . because old J. M. McCarty had founded it.

What if *he* founded his own town? He hurried across the street and unlocked his office. Inside, he took down several volumes from the neat rows behind his desk and leafed through one. The Townsite Act of 1844 provided . . . that a group could stake out 320 acres, purchasing it from the government for $1.25 an acre, and sell it for any amount!

The act had been amended in 1867, making it necessary for the group to contain one hundred members to qualify, but that was a technicality that could be gotten around.

Schuyler left the volume open on his desk. He sat down, selected another cheroot, and leaned back in his chair, thinking.

After a bit, he lit the cigar and unlocked the desk to riffle through the drawers, until he found a battered red-bound book of names and addresses; he opened the book to the Ts, and set it aside. Taking a sheet of foolscap, he wrote a letter, with many pauses and much lip-biting, and signed it with a flourish. He addressed the envelope to Mr. Horace Gromley in Ironton, care of the Tascosa & Tahlequah Railroad.

He wrote a second letter, only a paragraph, and signed it "S.W." On the envelope he wrote: "Mr. George Kilburn, Esq., 15 Hillrise Street, Kansas City, c/o Mrs. Nell Gammell."

Then he put on his coat and walked around to Second Street and slipped the letters into the post-office slot.

The scheme to discredit McCarty came to him that evening as he sat in Jake's Saloon and watched a pretty girl in rose-colored tights and a loose, low-necked shirtwaist sit on a cowhand's lap and run her hands through his hair as his companions whooped and egged her on. McCarty had never been involved in scandal of any kind,

29

and it might well turn the scales overnight if Schuyler could stage the right scene. The girl got the cowboy on his feet after a bit, and led him away to what was transparently a guilty appointment—as it was called by the press.

Schuyler gazed after them and thought of Gertie de Vere's establishment on the other side of town. Maybe he could interest her in a little business. . . .

As soon as he received a reply to his letter, Schuyler took the eastbound stage to Ironton, arriving four days later. After registering for a room at the Cattleman's Hotel, he went immediately to the offices of the Tascosa & Tahlequah Railroad, where he was expected.

He had supper in the hotel with his old friend Horace Gromley, and they talked far into the night. The next day he spent several hours closeted with Horace and Mr. John Hightower, superintendent of the road. The meeting went well.

Horace Gromley was a man with expensive tastes. His position with the railroad allowed him to meet numbers of people in influential circles, and he was accustomed to receiving information from them concerning the stock market, in which he dabbled. But he did not confine himself to one facet; he had made a pile of money five years before, buying and selling land on the basis of confidential information supplied by Schuyler Wood, who then occupied a high county post in the East. Horace was always hungry for money.

Horace and John Hightower had held their own private meeting without Schuyler. The railroad, Hightower told him, had decided to build to Roseberry the next spring. It was a logical extension, since Jackson was not a town for business; it had become the railhead only because the late

Clark Otey had paid for the rails, and because the McCarty ranch kept it in the black with cattle shipments.

However, there was no money in the move for any of them if the T&T built to Roseberry, but Glover was another thing. There was plenty of land at Glover, land that would quickly increase in value when the railroad came. Men could become wealthy that way. Hightower was amenable to the change, with one proviso. There must be a town. Glover must be a fact, not merely a plan on paper.

Horace Gromley relayed this to Schuyler, who instantly agreed. "The first sale of lots will provide the capital to build at Glover," he promised.

"And when will that be?"

"I've already set in motion the first plans. I will have an exceptional salesman in Chicago or New York within a few months."

He had a drink with Horace, then packed his bag to catch the stage back to Roseberry.

When he returned, there was a letter waiting for him from George Kilburn. George was on his way and would arrive in Roseberry as soon as travel accommodations allowed.

He arrived three days later.

George Kilburn was a man six feet tall, broad shoulders, light brown wavy hair, which drooped over his forehead in an engaging manner, and the steady, honest gaze of a peddler of suspect merchandise—which he was. He was getting on, a trifle past fifty, waist thickening, eyes not what they used to be, occasioning the use of spectacles—which he hated—and lines of worry had begun to erode the fine features that had in the past so impressed a number of wealthy widows. His well-modulated voice had convinced them of his sterling qualities and of the soundness of the stocks he was pushing, and his nimble fingers had deftly transferred large sums from their pockets to his.

But the time had come when women did not respond to his advances as they had once, and he was forced to cast about for other forms of gainful enterprise that did not require arduous toil. Naturally, salesmanship was one of the first ideas to enter his mind, since in one way or another he had been selling all his life. He considered taking orders and down payments for catalog goods—for a non-existent company. Or perhaps peddling mining stocks with no mine attached, at which he once spent much time . . . and a little time in jail, to boot.

Neither of these greatly attracted him, perhaps because they were old-hat and provided no challenge, and not a great deal of money either. And then, while he was seriously considering his future, the letter from Schuyler Wood arrived.

At once he purchased a ticket, got on the train and hurried west.

He took a suite at the Roseberry Hotel, a small sitting room and bedchamber on the third floor, and sent a boy with a message to Schuyler. He had time for a bath and a shave before Schuyler showed up, a package in his hand. The package turned out to be a bottle of whiskey.

"To celebrate the occasion," Schuyler said jovially. "How are you, George?"

"Excellent, Schuyler. Couldn't be better." He provided a corkscrew and two glasses, and they toasted each other. Schuyler also gave him a cigar and they seated themselves in the sitting room, which had a view to the south over the river.

"Your letter said you were involved in a business proposition that needed my talents," George said for openers. He lit the cigar and puffed contentedly.

"Let me bring you up to date." Schuyler launched into

a discussion of his fight to gain prominence in Roseberry and of the McCarty clan.

"I've heard of them," George commented.

Schuyler concluded with a quick résumé of Cole Stedman's printing press, and how he had decided to cut his losses and begin again elsewhere. He explained the Township Act and how he had hired two men to make a survey of the territory along the Roseberry River.

George Kilburn sat entranced as the plan unfolded. This was certainly what he had been searching for—a scheme with vision, and one with unlimited possibilities for profit. His quick mind leaped ahead to those possibilities, but he kept his expressions under control. Schuyler might well have stumbled onto the greatest money-making game in the country!

It was easy to see Schuyler was wrapped up in the idea, eager to make a go of it, eager for reality. He wanted to found a town and make it grow to rival or surpass Roseberry.

"With the money we gain from the sale of lots, George, we'll build at the townsite. It takes no time at all to put up buildings. The town can be a going concern in weeks!"

This realization surprised George. It was the first time in his experience of Schuyler Wood that the man seemed strictly on the level and serious. He regarded Schuyler narrowly. The lawyer still dressed exceedingly well, appeared to be at ease, but underneath he detected a feeling of something George could not define. Maybe it was that Schuyler wanted this particular thing even more than he admitted to himself.

Schuyler wanted to use Kilburn's talents as a salesman to sell lots or shares in the new town. "You'll go back east with the printed brochures," Schuyler said. "There's ready money in the East—not much out here—and by the time those eastern folks come west to see for themselves, there *will* be a town to see."

"Brochures?" George asked. "You have a brochure already printed? Can I see it?"

"No, they're not printed yet." He showed George a few sheets of paper. "I've been writing down a selling message. And of course there'll be a picture of the town—"

George blinked. "A picture of a non-existent town?"

"We'll have an artist draw it for us."

"I see." George smiled. Schuyler hadn't changed so much after all.

"For the time being," Schuyler said, "I must not be connected with the proposition. You are the only one to know, George."

"Why?—if it's legal?"

"I have my reasons. But I can tell you the main one is that I fear McCarty's interference if my name is involved. He may do his best to scuttle the scheme, just to keep me from success."

George nodded. "It's a good enough reason. All right, we won't tell anyone. What about finances?"

"I'm willing to put up six hundred dollars in hard cash."

"Is that enough?" George sounded surprised.

"It should be ample—do you expect me to furnish you with room and board?" Schuyler glanced about the hotel room, obviously not the cheapest.

George, who had taken the suite for the occasion, shifted uneasily in his chair. He had only a few hundred in his kick and had counted on a better deal from Schuyler. The man was proving to be a tightwad. "How do you figure it?"

"You'll need to purchase the land, then stake it out. That will cost about five hundred dollars. Printing the brochures will be a smaller cost—I expect the artist will charge less than forty dollars."

"Have you been to a printer?"

Schuyler smiled. "I have a printer here in Roseberry. You may have to go to Ironton for the artist."

George nodded, frowning at the glowing cigar. He was thinking of various mining stocks he'd had made up in the past, in two colors on good paper. "I would suggest you add a hundred dollars to your total. If I'm to do all the work I think you should bear the expenses."

Schuyler hesitated, then sighed. "Very well. Seven hundred dollars, but don't ask me for more, George."

George regarded his visitor silently. If the money ran out he damned well would, but he said no more on that subject. "What about the land? You say you have a plot in mind? Does it make a difference where it is?"

"It makes a very great deal of difference! I must impress upon you, George, this is a strictly legal enterprise and I expect the town to take root and grow. When you purchase that land it will be a matter of record, and you are required to stake it. If you don't, and some local official decides to investigate, then we're both in serious trouble."

"No cause to get upset, Schuyler. It will be done your way. Where is the land?"

"It's a large meadow about twenty-five miles west of Roseberry. The land is level, bounded by the river and a stream, an ideal site for a town—especially when the railroad builds to it."

"The railroad?"

Schuyler smiled. "That's my trump card. Yes, I've already arranged for the railroad."

George whistled. That *did* make all the difference in the world. He knew Schuyler had highly-placed friends, but it had not occurred to him the scheme was as sound as that! Such a fact would make selling the lots a foregone conclusion and send their price up.

"There's nothing there at all now," Schuyler went on. "And nothing near it. The River Road stops about twenty miles away, so you'll have to follow the river west. It isn't difficult, and I have a map for you, of course." He laid the surveyor's drawing on the table.

George leaned over and studied it. The drawing showed the river and the winding creek and also contained exact situation data. There was an indication of the proposed railroad route coming from a town named Jackson.

Schuyler said, "The land is used at present by the McCarty herds as a grazing area, but McCarty doesn't own it."

"Will I have trouble with the McCartys?"

"They won't know a thing about it. Besides, as I said, they don't own the land." Schuyler smiled. "It would be fair to say in the brochure that the town will adjoin the great McCarty ranch. If people assume the McCarty employees will trade there, so much the better."

George nodded. Better and better. He glanced up as Schuyler handed him a document. He read it quickly, a document in legal language for him to sign. It gave Schuyler three-quarters of the profits to be realized from the sale of land in the new town of Glover.

George signed it quickly. "Why call the town Glover?"

"It's the name of a thief I knew once."

George laughed. Schuyler had more of a sense of humor than he'd thought.

Chapter Three

Dressed in jeans and canvas jacket, Frank sat across the breakfast table from Faith the morning she was to take the stage to Ironton. Little David had been fed and put into his play area, and Mrs. Steen was fussing in the kitchen. He had looked forward to this day, but not with any enthusiasm, though it was easy to see that Faith was keyed up at the prospect.

"I'll write you from the hotel in Ironton," she said, "and I'll wire as soon as I arrive to let you know I got there safely."

"You'll be gone a week?"

"No more, darling. I want to be home for your birthday on the 16th . . . that's twelve days away." She finished her coffee and rose, hurrying upstairs to return with a small traveling bag.

Frank went out to the buggy, where Billy had already tied on her valises. His sorrel horse was saddled and tied to the rear of the buggy, with a Winchester in the boot. He thrust hands in his pockets and looked at the gray, overcast sky; it smelled a little damp but the mists would probably burn off before noon. He could hear Faith and Mrs. Steen conferring on last-minute details, then she came out, still talking, and he helped her into the buggy. Mrs. Steen waved, and they were off.

37

The town was still mostly asleep as they clattered down the River Road to the east end. The driver was just bringing the battered red-and-blue Concord around from the yard when they arrived. Luke Dobbs was standing in front of the depot, fingers in his vest pockets, his graying hair falling over his forehead as he watched Frank wheel the buggy and stop. He snapped his fingers and a husky boy ran out to unfasten Faith's bags and carry them to the stage boot.

Luke came over, grasping Faith's hand. "You got a nice day for traveling, Faith. Not likely to stir up much dust for a couple hours." He grinned, showing picket teeth. "Hullo, Frank." He glanced at the holstered pistol on Frank's hip. "You ridin' along, are you?"

"No, Gus's starting a herd along the river this morning. Thought I'd go look 'em over." He glanced at the several passengers who were lining up for the stage, two older women and four paunchy men. "Have somebody take the buggy over to Sam's, will you?"

"Sure," Luke said. "You have a good trip, Faith."

"Thank you, Luke."

She kissed Frank, then climbed into the stage and settled herself. The other passengers clambered in, huffing and murmuring as the agent yelled, "All aboard . . ."

Faith leaned out of the window and waved as the driver kicked off the brake and shouted. Frank lifted his hat, smiling but feeling glum. He watched the coach clatter eastward and Luke said, "Don't stand there lookin' like a man who's lost 'is last corn dodger. She'll be back."

Frank sighed and nodded. He fished out a coin for the boy who had toted Faith's bags, thanking him. Luke took the lad aside, pointing to the buggy. The boy untied Frank's horse, looped the reins about the nearest hitch-rack, got in the buggy, and drove off in the direction of the livery stable.

The Roseberry River took a slight swing northward after leaving town, then slowly turned back southeast. Jackson, one hundred and fifty miles distant, was on the eastern side of the river, so the McCarty cattle drives to railhead never crossed the river, although crossing it for more than half the journey and recrossing it would have saved at least two days.

On the sorrel horse, Frank hurried east, cutting the broad cattle track within the hour. Gus had driven the herd to the river the day before and held them there that night. He had two thousand head and would have them penned in Jackson in about ten days.

Frank skirted the track and came upon the tail end as the sun was beginning to break through the misty layers overhead. The cattle were red and spotted shorthorns, the Durham breed, strung out in a long, snaking line more than a mile long. He found Gus sitting a black horse on a low ridge, one leg curled around the horn, as he puffed contentedly on a corncob pipe and watched the chuck wagon bump over the uneven ground; pans rattled and the cook swore.

He waved when Frank appeared and leaned over to shake hands. "Didn't expect you-all, Frank. You must of got up b'fore breakfast."

"Saw Faith off to Ironton." Frank nodded toward the herd. "Fine looking bunch of critters."

"They'll do." Gus was a big man, as big and heavy as his father, with level gray eyes that seemed to study everything about him. He wore jeans, a checked wool shirt, and a heavy brown coat; there was a six-gun in a shoulder holster under the coat and a carbine in the boot under his leg. Gus Kramer was an old-timer, nearly as old as J.M., and had worked for the JM brand as long as Frank could remember.

They discussed prices for a bit; Gus had been in communication with an agent at Jackson, and cattle prices were holding fairly steady. He would take the best figure he could get. Frank offered no advice, knowing Gus expected none. Gus was in charge and would do what he thought best. Though Frank could overrule him, he would do such a thing only as an extreme. To step in and supervise Gus's actions would be tantamount to dismissing him. And dismissing Gus would be about the same as firing J.M. himself.

The sun began to flush the sky as Frank rode to the head of the long column, yelling greetings to several of the hands, exchanging banter. This was an easy drive compared to the harried and dangerous trails of eight years past, when a herd might be on the move for three months, fighting elements, Indians, and disease. These men would have water in sight most of the way and would barely need haircuts by the time they reached town.

But it was exhilarating just the same to get away from the town, listening to saddle leather squeals and the bawling of cattle and smelling the fragrance of sage and grass. Even the faint raw odor of a far-off disturbed skunk was welcome. One day, he was sure, the railroad would come to Roseberry and then the cattle drives, for them at least, would be over forever. They'd take the herds to cattle pens at the edge of town, chouse the beeves aboard, and that would be it. Frank reined in and watched the shambling cattle. Probably to men like Gus and his father, not having to drive would be a welcome luxury. But to men like himself, the newer generation, some of the fun would go out with the churning wheels of the engines. He had made eight or ten long cattle drives, and he was young and strong enough not to have been enormously inconvenienced by the hardships.

But maybe he tended to recall the fun times and not the stampedes at night in the rain, or other disasters.

He turned the sorrel in the pale lemon sunlight and went back slowly, wanting to make the outing last as long as possible. He'd be sitting in the office soon enough.

The remuda was off to his right, a bunch of perhaps eighty horses, with a rider sitting his mount languidly as they grazed. Frank turned toward Gus to bid him good-bye when his eye was caught by several fast-moving shadows in the direction of the river. Three riders lying along their horse's backs were running flat-out toward the remuda. In that first startled glance, Frank recognized them with astonishment as Indians—Indians were raiding the horse herd!

He slid the Winchester from the boot, levered it, and fired at the leading brave.

The shot brought a yell from behind him. He dug in spurs and the sorrel horse jumped forward, head down. The remuda guard came to life, snatching out a pistol, but almost instantly the horses engulfed him. The Indians were screeching, waving lengths of cloth, and the remuda was in full stampede in seconds.

Frank fired at the second horse and saw the animal stumble and go down, throwing its rider. The Indian scuttled away, an angry face turned toward him, but Frank ignored the man. Anyone afoot would be easy to run down later.

The remuda horses were scattering. Two men could not drive them all in one direction. The two Indians were concentrating on about twenty horses, yipping and screeching, running them directly eastward over the prairie. It was a desperate attempt, Frank thought, with only a slight chance of success. The Indians would count on their ability to outlast and outmaneuver the cowhands who came after them. He fired again and again, hoping to bring down another Indian mount, but it was damned hard to hit anything from the deck of the hard-running sorrel. He caught sight of two of Gus's men galloping toward the remuda from the right, but they were a long way off.

The Winchester clicked empty and he shoved cartridges from his belt, managing to reload as the sorrel settled down to a steady pace. In another moment he saw that he was gaining on the herd. The two redsticks were chivvying them desperately, constantly glancing back at him. One thrust his arm out and snapped off four shots from a pistol, but all went wild.

Frank closed the range to a hundred yards and began firing again. At the eighth shot, he hit a horse and the Indian instantly turned, jumped free when the mount collapsed, and ran toward his companion. The third brave whirled his mustang, ran to the downed man to pull him up behind. The two gave up the herd and rode toward the northwest as the downed brave popped shots at Frank.

Reining in, Frank aimed carefully and knocked the man from the horse. The remaining Indian ran off to the skyline and disappeared.

When he came up to the man, there was nothing he could do. The bullet had gone in under the arm and the Indian was dead, a not-too-young brave wearing whiteman's jeans, shirtless and barefooted.

He glanced back while he reloaded the rifle. Gus and two hands were bearing down upon him, and there was a scattering of shots from the direction of the river.

Gus said, "One got away?"

"Yes, and no chance of catching up."

Grunting assent, Gus motioned the hands toward the scattered horses and they galloped off. Gus leaned on the horn, looking down at the dead Indian.

"First one of them I seen in a coon's age. We ain't been bothered by Innans for years. Be sure to tell your pa about this."

42

"Is there a shovel in the cook wagon?"

Gus nodded. "I'll send one of the boys back t'plant 'im." He sat up straighter. "Sounds like they got the other one too."

Chapter Four

The Indian put afoot by Frank had offered fight when two of the cowhands closed in, had nicked a horse, so they shot him.

"He's a damn good Innan now," one of them said.

Frank got down and turned the dead man over. He was about the same age as the other, wearing an old pair of black pants and nothing else. His jet hair was braided, but there was nothing on him to tell his tribe. There was a knife in his belt and his battered rifle was a single-shot Sharps with a row of silver tacks in the stock. He had five extra cartridges in his pocket. Damned poor.

"Some wandering bunch," Gus said, "probably hungry as hell, looking to sell a few horses for grub."

"Hell of a long way off the goddamn reservation," someone said.

Gus pointed at the man. "You, go get a shovel from cookie."

The entire remuda was recovered, though it took an hour to round up the horses. The guard was unhurt; he took a good deal of hazing from his friends, but he was not blamed for not sounding the alarm soon enough. No one could reasonably expect an Indian raid at that time or place, and besides, it had come too suddenly.

Frank took his leave near noontime and rode back

toward Roseberry. The Indians had probably followed the herd hoping to luck into an opportunity to run off the horses. They might have done better to wait until nightfall, then cut out a cow, if they were after food. He sighed; no one had yet been able to get into an Indian's mind. What made sense to a white did not occur to the red man, evidently . . . or was it that simple?

The river was wide and shallow here, many miles from the town, flowing over sand and round rocks, leaving occasional flat islands, long strips of wet sand, often with weeds or willows garnishing them. The shorelines were dense green, unrelieved by blossoms or buds. As Frank's gaze swept the bank, suddenly something moved.

He slid his pistol from the holster instantly, clicking back the hammer. There was something in the brush ahead of him only a few rods distant. He checked the sorrel, searching with his eyes—and the thing moved again. It was a pony. The horse scrambled to its feet and dashed into the water, with an Indian boy astride its back.

Tapping spurs, Frank nudged the sorrel into a run. He held the pistol wide and fired a shot that splashed water in front of the pony. The boy looked back with eyes like saucers, then he pulled up the horse and sat apprehensively as Frank came up to him.

"You speak English?" The boy was only a child, five or six years old, half naked and scared to death, though he was doing his best not to show it.

"I speak," he said.

Frank pointed with the pistol. "Go back." He waited until the boy turned the pony and headed back to shore, splashing through shallow brown water.

"What're you doing here?"

The boy looked toward the distant herd, though it was out of sight.

Frank said, "They told you to wait here while they raided the horses?"

46

The boy nodded slowly.

"Who were they?"

The boy hesitated a half minute. "Uncle. Two brothers."

"Where'd you learn English?"

"At the mission school."

"What's your name?"

"At the school they call me Joseph."

Frank pointed toward the town. "All right, Joseph, let's go. You got any more family hereabouts?"

The boy frowned and gazed back toward the herd. "I heard shots."

"There was trouble." Frank sighed. "Did you know your uncle and brothers were going to steal horses?"

Joseph nodded again, eyes wary. He had undoubtedly been taught that stealing was a white man's crime.

"One of them got away. The other two are dead."

Joseph bit his lip and looked down at his brown hands. In a moment he asked, "Who got away?"

"I don't know. The dead ones were wearing black pants and jeans."

Joseph hugged his pony, head down. They had walked the horses half a mile when he said, "Uncle wearing black pants."

George Kilburn was vastly annoyed at having to make the journey to Ironton to find an artist. He had gone to Roseberry for the conference with Schuyler with no idea that he'd be turning around and going right back. He resented it; Schuyler was treating him as a flunkey, putting up a miniscule amount of money and taking the lion's share for it, while George did the work.

And on top of all that, he had to return to Roseberry again with the finished plates for the artist's rendering, so

47

Schuyler could save a few dollars by having the brochures printed on his own press.

On the long weary trip to Ironton, George did considerable thinking—there was little enough else to do. He had a detailed sketch in his pocket for the artist; the drawing might take three or four days to produce, and the making of the halftone plates for three colors another several days. The remainder of the brochure would be typeset. As the coach swayed and jolted eastward, George wrote out advertising copy, polished and refined it, and put it away in an inside pocket.

Then he turned his thoughts to the problem of the staking. Someone had to go to the selected plot, cut stakes and drive them, and George had no intention of doing it himself. It had been a damned long time ago since he had so much as cut a load of firewood, and the idea of cutting stakes and driving them to delineate lots for 320 acres positively made him shudder.

The second day out, he thought of T.E. Serly.

T.E. was a strong, husky man who would balk at such labor, but who would do it for a cut. T.E. was a gambler, salesman, and ne'er-do-well who was not the brightest, and who would make an ideal partner, especially when his eyes were dazzled by the prospect of the largest haul of his life.

George sent a wire that night, and when he arrived at Ironton there was a reply waiting. T.E. had taken the bait and would arrive by the next train.

Joseph was skittish about entering the white man's town, but Frank took the pony's hackamore to prevent him from bolting. He kept up a running conversation, mostly about the weather and the crops, assuring Joseph he would not be harmed and interjecting a question now and again. He discovered the boy had relatives, a mother and other kin, not more than eleven of them, holed up in the limestone caves near the Bend, waiting for the raiding party to return. Joseph avoided the subject, but apparently he had no father.

Frank had no idea what to do with the boy, save return him to his mother, and at the same time he felt a large measure of pity for the lad. Even though the Indians had been trying to run off a horse herd and had shot at him, it was a sad thing to kill two of them. The Indians were off the reservation; they might be running and they might be hungry enough to attempt something extreme, prompted by fear or despair.

A number of people stopped to stare as they moved down the main street. The boy's Indian heritage was apparent, and Indians were not generally loved—though few people in Roseberry could recall the last Indian raid in the area. The raids and massacres of less than a decade ago were still fresh in most minds, however. Newspapers and periodicals played them up in lurid fashion.

Frank reined in and got down in front of the sheriff's office, motioning Joseph off the pony. Karl Welch swiveled in his chair to stare in astonishment at the boy.

"Where'd you find *him*, Frank?"

Frank sat and related the story as the boy listened attentively, gazing at Frank with an unfathomable expression.

Karl heard the story through without comment, then fished for a sheet of paper and read it off. A band of Indians had left the Sandrock Reservation three days before and had not been seen since.

"They're southern Cheyennes," Karl said, looking sidelong. "What kind of redhide are you, boy?"

"I am Cheyenne," Joseph said, his eyes filming over.

"How did the agency feed you?" Frank asked.

49

"They fed us carrion," Joseph said. "My uncle said we must go away or we will die. You going send us back?"

Karl scratched his head. "I don't see how we can help it. What you think, Frank?"

"We can send some telegrams demanding an investigation, but I've got no idea if the bureaucrats will listen. Just holding office seems to tax some of them to the limit. But the first thing is probably to take this boy back to his people."

Karl got up and put on his coat. "I'll go with you."

It occasioned more stares as McCarty and the sheriff escorted the Indian boy through the town. No one made obvious remarks, not wanting to tangle with either man, but it was apparent to Frank that Joseph would have been run out of town promptly had he been alone.

They went out the River Road, past Frank's house to the Bend Bridge, and went across it. Frank glanced at Joseph and motioned the boy to take the lead.

Joseph said, "They will have a lookout. If white men come, they will shoot."

Karl said gruffly, "We'll take that chance. Go on ahead, boy." He snaked his rifle from the boot and put it across his thighs.

Joseph looked at it with an impassive expression, turned and rode off south, moving slowly through the cottonwoods. A light breeze came up, twinkling the leaves, green on one side, silvery white on the other.

But no shots came to search them out. Frank leaned forward in the saddle, going with the horse, guiding him without pressure, his head cocked to catch any sound. They came to the limestone caves and Joseph halted to look back at them.

"They are gone." He shrugged.

Karl said, "How d'you know?" He frowned at the jumbled hills. The caves were in a section of tiny badlands, deep arroyos and honeycombed earth carved by ancient water-action, which had dug a series of caves great and small. Karl and his deputies had been here before, smoking out cattle thieves and men of various stripe who ran from the law.

"I am sure," Joseph said, and Frank thought he looked very sad, forgetting for the moment he was in the presence of whites.

Frank nudged his horse. "Show us where they camped."

The boy went forward slowly, constantly glancing up toward the high rocks and ridges where a lookout would have been. He wended his way through a deep arroyo that smelled dank, and set the pony to a steep climb. They came out on a shelf of rock where Joseph slid down to enter a large rocky cave.

Karl got down and followed, but Frank sat the sorrel horse for a moment, looking round. He had not been here for years; he recalled his father saying that roving bands of hostiles had used the caves from time to time when the whites first settled Roseberry. It was a natural fortress, with so many openings and vantage points that a man could never be sure he was alone. This very minute, Joseph's entire band might be hidden away in any of the hundreds of fissures and seams of the limestone, watching.

Frank stepped down and ducked into the gloomy cave. It smelled of soot and ashes; the serrated ceiling was blackened by smoke and the ashes of a hundred campfires filled a rock-rimmed depression in the center. Joseph fingered a bit of worn leather as Karl picked up a discarded, worn moccasin from a corner.

"They've gone all right," he said. "I'd say yesterday."

Frank stooped and felt the cold ashes. He went outside, wondering what the next move should be. If they went after the Indian band there would be shooting. The Indians had no way of knowing he and Karl were not the law come to punish them. He studied the hard earth; on the other hand, how *could* they go after the band? There was no white within a hundred miles good enough to track Cheyennes over rock. Even another Cheyenne might fail. Neither was there any way he could send the boy out alone; he was too young; even if he wanted to go, it was far too risky.

He saw Karl studying the ground as if wondering which way the band had gone; then the sheriff shook his head, beckoning Joseph.

"Where'd they get to?"

"I do not know," Joseph said.

"They had another place figured out," Karl persisted. "When your kin run off the horse herd they would all meet, wouldn't they?"

Joseph was silent, glancing at Frank.

"Let's go back to town," Frank said, climbing on the sorrel. He could not imagine Joseph telling them, even if he knew.

A light drizzle was falling as they reached the Bend Bridge. Frank reached behind him, unfastened the poncho he carried there, and gave it to the boy. Joseph was visibly shivering and quickly thrust his head through the hole, gathering the too-big poncho about him. Karl smiled, seeing the child's head poke through the heavy folds.

When they reached his house, Frank reined in, motioning the boy through the gate. Karl said, "What you going to do, Frank?"

"First thing, feed him, then get him some dry duds."

Karl moved closer. "You can't keep that redskin in your house!"

52

"Why not?"

"You don't know what he'll do!"

"He's only six years old, Karl."

"But he's a Cheyenne! He's a goddam savage! You got a boy of your own inside there—and Miz Steen. This 'un probably never been in a house in his life!"

"He's been to the mission school."

Karl sighed. "Dammit, Frank, you're as stubborn as your old man." He pulled his mount's head around, glared at the waiting boy, and loped off toward town.

Frank led the way around the house, got down, and pulled the boy off the pony. Billy Quinn came from the stable, staring at them.

"Who *that*, Mr. Frank?"

"A friend of mine, Billy. Get these horses out of the wet." He took Joseph's arm and hurried him up the back steps into the house. He drew the poncho off over the lad's head and Mrs. Steen came to the door, her eyes huge with surprise.

"Ain't he an Indian, Mr. Frank?"

"Yes, and he's cold and hungry." He pointed to the woodburning stove. "Get over there, Joseph, and get yourself warm." The boy moved to the stove and put out his hands gratefully.

"Land o' Goshen!" Mrs. Steen said. "I never seen an Indian this close up before." She lowered her voice. "Is it all right, Mr. Frank? Does he speak English?"

"Yes. I'd be obliged if you'd fix him something to eat—and me too. Do you think you could find a shirt for him to put on?"

Mrs. Steen sighed. "I expect so." She moved to the cooler, eyeing the boy over her glasses. "His name's Joseph? My land, imagine him having a Christian name."

"He's been to school," Frank said. "Joseph, this is Mrs. Steen. You can say hello to her."

53

The boy turned, staring at her. "Howdo," he said formally.

"Oh my goodness," Mrs. Steen said. "He sounds just like Luke Dobbs."

Schuyler Wood waited till long after midnight to call on Gertie de Vere at her place of business. She met him in her private dressing room-office, shoes off and flopped in a comfortable chair with a bottle at her elbow. It had been a hard night, she said, and asked him to sit down.

Schuyler closed the door firmly and seated himself on a stool as Gert poured out a second glass of religion. "You come wanting something," she said. "What is it?"

"How d'you get along with the town council?"

"I get along all right." She shrugged. "They tax me a little, but they let me alone."

Schuyler changed his tactics. "It's worth money to me if McCarty is involved in a scandal." He saw her eyes glisten.

She asked, "The young one, Frank?"

He nodded. "Politics, you understand."

"I understand all right." She sipped the whiskey, regarding him with narrow eyes. "A scandal . . . something with one o' my girls?"

"That's good enough."

"How much money?"

"That depends on our success. I'd like something that can be written up in the newspaper."

She gave him a half-smile. "Are you a generous man, Schuyler?"

"I can be generous—and a good friend." He returned the smile with interest. "And a terrible, unforgiving enemy."

Gertie regarded him silently for a moment as she

sipped the whiskey. He knew that she was aware of his political aspirations in Roseberry, and she might want to ride with a winner. She said, "I own a house across the river. It's a—"

"Is it in your name?"

"Of course, my real name, Gertrude Turek."

"Do you live in it?"

She shook her head, with the same half-smile. "You don't know much about this business, Schuyler."

"Tell me."

"There are some men who don't like to come to a brothel. They're willing to pay well but they want more privacy—and sometimes want to spend more time, like several days. That's why I have the house. It's a quiet place, not too close to neighbors and screened by plenty of trees and bushes. Maybe you can get McCarty there— let him be found with a couple of undressed girls."

He gazed at her with no expression, thinking that no one would be able to pull that kind of trick on Frank McCarty, but the house might be valuable—yes, it might at that. An idea occurred to him, not full-blown, but he would mull on it. He said, "The publicity might run you out of town."

Her eyes narrowed. "Not if you're on my side." She made a greedy motion with her fingers. "How much do you want this McCarty smeared?"

Schuyler smiled and rose. "I'll see you're taken care of, Gert. Exactly where is this house?"

She wrote it out for him.

Chapter Five

T.E. Serly was a short, dark man who habitually wore a bland expression, since he considered himself a gambler. He got off the train in Ironton dressed in broadcloth pantaloons (tight trousers with a strap under each instep) and a brown sack coat with a flowered vest under it. He had a windup watch on a chain which was hung across his front, and he carried a carpetbag containing all his worldly possessions: a hairbrush, a second pair of pants, two white shirts, four pairs of socks, and two fresh decks of cards.

He had small brown eyes, a small mouth, and a pinched nose; his hair was brown and stringy under a gray felt hat, and he patted his breast pocket where there was a cigar case containing two cheroots he'd bought on the train.

T.E. was not in the chips, but then he seldom had been, in his life. He had sold whiskey by the barrel, a home-made product manufactured from an Indian-trader's recipe; he had been part owner in a sleazy hotel and dancehall, and had sat out the war in Nevada after deserting from an Indiana regiment in '62. He met George Kilburn when they shared a cell in Ohio for a month; the authorities had received a complaint that

57

T.E.'s whiskey caused the blind staggers—and so it had proved.

While they were being moved to a sturdier jail, T.E. and George had managed to slip away, thus the bond between them. That was eight months ago.

George came along the platform, extending his hand. "T.E.—damn glad to see you. How you been keeping?"

"Fine, George. You're looking well and prosperous." George always looked prosperous; the better one knew him, the more one realized that the more prosperous George looked, the worse off he was. T.E. carried the carpetbag and they went through the station to the street, where George hailed a buggy for hire.

George was staying at a boardinghouse only a block from the center of town, and he suggested T.E. move in with him. That was soon accomplished, and the rates adjusted by the landlady, Mrs. Pringle, who agreed to the arrangement. Then they went out to sit over coffee in a downtown café.

It was T.E.'s first journey west, and he was not impressed by the dirt streets and generally run-down appearance of the town. Few merchants, apparently, kept a decent coat of whitewash on their buildings, and dust was everywhere, even though it had been drizzling only the day before. T.E. had arrived with high hopes; George had one desirable quality—he thought big. T.E. prayed that some of whatever bonanza George was into would rub off. He had about eighty dollars total in his pants and was looking for more. That of course was a lifelong occupation, since he was seldom able to retain any of the funds that came his way. But he was determined to turn over a new leaf and resist calling for drinks for the house, as had been his wont. On the train west, he had told himself firmly that he had to count his chickens against the day when he'd need one as a broiler. He would never see forty-three again, and, according to the papers, times were getting hard again. He hoped George had something good for him.

It occurred to him that George might try to separate him from his scraped-together dollars, and he set a mental limit to the amount he would admit having. Thirty dollars, he decided. If George asked, he had only thirty dollars.

"It's good to see old friends, T.E.," George said as they were seated at a quiet back table. "The old faces are disappearing. Have you run into anyone I know?"

"I've been out of touch," T.E. said, "working along the river. Damn poor scratching, though. . . ." The café was small, mostly tables and straight-back chairs; a sign in the window advertised: Tables for Ladies. The ceiling was stained wood with a chained-up chandelier, and the walls were papered with stripes and roses. He wondered if he was buying or George was.

A girl in a starched dress came to the table and George ordered a pot of coffee and a spot of brandy each. He offered T.E. a cigar and they lit up. "I've run onto a proposition, T.E., and I know you'll be interested." He winked and smiled.

The wink made T.E. wary. George was a con man, after all, and personality was one of his trade tools. "I came to listen," he said.

"The best thing about this plan is that it's legal. It's the kind of thing to make a man rich, and no sheriff riding him down later on." George winked again. "That means a lot to the likes of us."

A legal scheme was not what T.E. expected, and his hopes began to fade. The girl came with the coffee and cups and went back for the brandy as they sat silent.

When she had gone again, George said, "We're going to found a town."

"You mean find one?"

"Found means to start, to begin. Let me lay it all out."

59

George leaned forward and talked steadily for ten minutes, explaining the plan, leaving out Schuyler Wood entirely. He presented it as his own. The two of them would carry it out, he said, and reap the rich rewards of honest toil. He dwelt on the possibilities and ease of operation. They would satisfy the law's requirements, and then they were on their own. The money would roll in, and all of it profit after the printing costs were deducted.

T.E. was astonished at the idea. He had thought towns just grew; the idea of building one from scratch was incredible, and yet George was obviously enthusiastic. George had been considering this scheme for months, he said, and had looked into all the facets. It had been done before and had made the founders rich. They would do it again.

George said, "We'll cut the three-hundred-twenty acres into small lots and sell them for as much as the traffic will bear. Hundreds and hundreds of lots." He beamed. "Did you ever hear of anything so magnificent?"

T.E. made rapid mental calculations. That meant a hell of a lot of money! Hundreds of thousands! He began to feel some of George's excitement.

George lifted his brandy glass. "Here's to a mighty prosperous new year."

T.E. lifted the glass, and hesitated. "This's going to need financing, George."

"I've got the money. Enough to do it. Are you with me, T.E.?"

T.E. smiled. "All the way, George." They clinked glasses and drank.

George put down his glass and smiled with relief. "I really hoped you'd join me, old friend. You're a man I can trust and I knew you were sharp enough to grasp the immense opportunity. We'll sell the lots in the East, maybe through a financial group, but that can come later." He waved his hand. "We may want to sell a number of them ourselves to people who're eager to come west, start a new life free of factory shackles and crowded cities, who—"

"Have you printed the brochures yet? Can I see one?"

"Not yet." He tapped his pocket. "I've got the message all worked out, and I've made printing arrangements and got the artist started. How much money have you?"

"Ah—about thirty dollars."

"Hmmm, not very damned much." He stared at T.E., fiddling with a spoon. "We've got to swing this proposition into action as soon as possible—before all our cash runs out. I've got money to finance the printing, a considerable amount, mind you, but there's hardly enough for the staking."

"What you mean, the staking?"

"The land has to be staked." George sighed deeply. "I was hoping that between us we could pay a man to do it." He appeared to worry over the question.

T.E. asked, "The land is near Roseberry?"

"A few miles west, yes. It *has* to be staked, else some officious inspector will call it all off and we'll have lost a lot of time and money. Actually, it's not that much work . . ." He looked hopefully at T.E.

"Well, maybe I could do it."

George smiled radiantly. "By God, T.E., that would take a world of worry off my mind! Could you?"

"I—I suppose so. What would I do?"

George produced a sheet of paper and pencil and began to draw. "Pace off each side of three-hundred-twenty acres—that's one-hundred-sixty square rods, or forty-eight hundred and forty square yards. Use a stake and a rope for measuring to lay out streets like this—" He drew rapid strokes. "Each street ought to be fifty feet wide. The thing doesn't have to be surveyor-accurate, but line up the stakes as best you can."

"Jesus Christ! Three-hundred-twenty acres!" The immensity was beginning to come clear. "Do we *have* to do it?"

"My dear old son." George's face was stern. "It may take months to sell off all the lots, plenty of time for some goddamn nosy official to go fishing and wander by Glover to see how it's coming. I impress on you this is a *legal* operation and we must keep it so at all costs. I assure you I'd one hell of a lot rather not do it, but we don't dare take the chance." He smiled winningly. "But it's a small price to pay for becoming rich, eh?"

"Yes, I guess so." T.E. sighed. He thought it over for a moment. "But is it legal to show brochures picturing a town that isn't even there?"

George winked. "Tush. The brochures are only a stratagem. Every business parades its best points, don't they? Besides, it's always necessary to tell a few innocent lies in any business enterprise."

T.E. nodded. That was certainly true. He bit his lips, thinking about doing manual labor. But then, hundreds of thousands waited just beyond reach—more money than he ever dreamed of owning. It would provide him luxurious living the rest of his life.

"You go stake out the lots, T.E., and I'll get the brochures printed. In less than a month we'll be seeing the first of the money rolling in." He swallowed the brandy. "When can you get started?"

George advanced him seventy dollars and a round-trip ticket on the Roseberry stage, and walked to the station to see him off. He cautioned his new partner about silence. "Say nothing to no one at all. Nobody!"

"Of course not, George."

"Pretend you're going hunting or prospecting, or just plain drifting. Anything but the truth."

"Dammit, George—"

"All right. Wire me when it's done and when you'll get back here." They shook hands and T.E. waved from the coach as it clattered out of town.

On leaving the stage depot, George went directly to the artist's studio. Amiel Ives had been recommended to him by a printer; he looked the part, a thin, pale man with un-rimmed glasses and delicate features, and he could show a number of beautiful colored plates that were exactly the kind of thing needed in the brochure.

Ives had the preliminary sketch finished, and George examined it, both hands clasped behind him, pleased at what he saw. Ives had nestled the town in surrounding hills, timbered, with a pleasant stream; there were com-mercial-looking buildings along the river front with a wharf or two, warehouses, and a sawmill.

"Put in several steamboats," George directed. "The Mississippi kind."

Ives was startled. "On the Roseberry?"

George smiled. "Just for effect. It's not impossible, you know. And letter the name: 'Glover,' at the top some-where."

"Glover . . ." Ives wrote it down.

"And put in under the name: 'Crossroads of the West.' " That was a nice touch. He was rather proud of it. "How soon can I have the finish?"

Ives hesitated. "In five days."

George turned about, startled. "Five!?"

"Well, four then."

"As quickly as possible, old son. I *must* have this right now." He pointed to the drawing. "Is that the latest model of a train?"

"Yes, I copied it from a railroad flyer."

"All right." George went to the door. "Put plenty of gold and red on it. I don't want anyone to miss it."

"They won't, Mr. Kilburn."

"Good." George smiled and went out. The damned art-work was costing a fortune, fifty dollars! He glanced at the sky and thrust hands into his overcoat pockets. But it was worth it. Nothing else would sell the lots like a smart picture.

He arranged for the plates to be made, then spent the next days doing little or nothing, hoarding his remaining cash parsimoniously. Schuyler Wood was a tight bastard, allowing him nothing for living expenses. After the costs were deducted he would have barely a hundred dollars for himself out of Schuyler's advance.

It had occurred to him a hundred times to cut Schuyler out completely, have the artwork made up, go east and peddle it. The brochures would have to have Schuyler's name on them, of course; so would the lot deeds, and that meant Schuyler would know, sooner or later, that he'd been crossed—he'd have *proof* of the double-dealing, not just a suspicion. And that in turn meant that Schuyler would have one hell of a good case against him if he was caught. If. George had to weigh very carefully his chances of staying out of the pen against the fact that this was the best scam to come along in a generation.

The deciding factor was that he'd have a big head start on Schuyler. He might easily sell a hundred lots before Schuyler heard about it. He could also begin sending Schuyler money from the sales to keep him quiet. He could say he was meeting more opposition than he expected, that the sales were going slowly but that he expected them to pick up—that sort of thing. As long as Schuyler was actually receiving money, he wouldn't panic.

Or if worst came to worst, he could always found his own town. There was room for lots of towns out there on the prairie. And he could always get someone like T.E. Serly to do the actual labor.

George went out to a nearby restaurant with his mind practically made up. He would play along with Schuyler for the time being, maybe get another hundred dollars from him and a train ticket east. It amused him that Schuyler was paying for his own downfall.

In the meantime he waited impatiently for Amiel Ives to finish the artwork.

A number of letters passed between Schuyler and Horace Gromley in Ironton relating to Schuyler's plan. At Schuyler's urgent request, Horace gave up a proposed trip to St. Louis and agreed to come to Roseberry for a week. Schuyler wrote back that he would meet the stage and provide a house for Horace in Roseberry.

He had to promise Horace a rousing good time, with all the liquor and girls he wanted. It was going to cost a pretty penny, but it was going to be worth it.

Chapter Six

Frank McCarty looked across the table at Preacher Logan Rossiter, a tall, rawboned man with an eagle gaze. Preacher was slightly younger than most men of his calling but he had the same intensity. He had come before the town council to ask for land.

"I got nothing," he said, " 'cept what you see before you, gentlemen, and a tired horse and wagon down on the street. But I can work." He showed them a pair of huge horny hands.

"What you going to work with, Preacher?" Ramsay Hamer asked.

"I'll gather a flock about me, devoted to the Lord." Preacher had no doubts. He looked at each of them in turn, a dog-eared Bible on the table in front of him. His brown, shaggy hair badly needed trimming and his beard was dusty.

"I mean," Ramsay said, "you come here askin' for land. Are you going to build on it—and if so, what with?"

"I'm going to build a church, sir. A place for folks to worship. I'll—"

"We already got two churches," Noah said.

"They's always room for one more," Preacher said, placing his big hand on the Bible. "My flock will donate

67

labor and material and we'll have us a church on that land before snow. I promise you-all."

Frank said, "How long've you been in town, Preacher?"

"I arrived yesterday, sir."

Frank got up and went to the front window. He looked down and saw the horse and wagon Preacher mentioned. It was an old buckboard, weathered and repaired, and the horse was a tired gray. There were belongings piled in the back behind the seat. Noah was questioning the man further about his intentions and desires. Frank thrust hands deep into his pockets and turned from the window, staring at the itinerant minister.

Roseberry had seen a number of fire-and-brimstone preachers; some were honest men doing their best to keep evil at a distance, even though their efforts were often inept. Others were out-and-out rascals, passing the hat after stirring up an audience with catch-phrases and shouting.

Preacher looked like a shouter to him, but no one had ever come before the council requesting land to build a church. That was a point in Preacher's favor because it intimated permanence. Of course it might be a clever ruse; there was nothing to keep the man from running out when the building was half finished. He saw Preacher looking at him speculatively, so he sat down again at the head of the table as the questions petered out.

"Suppose we have our discussion and put it to a vote." Frank stood up again and smiled at Preacher. "Thank you for coming, Mr. Rossiter. We'll get word to you."

Preacher got up quickly, smiling and bowing. "Bless you all," he said, gathered up his Bible and hat, and made his way out.

"I don't see that we've got anything to lose," Ramsay said.

Seth Potter shrugged. "I agree. He's got work hands, that one. What about you, Noah?"

Noah smiled, balancing the pipe in his hand. "Why not give him a piece of land down at the far end of town, by the line."

"By them whorehouses?" Seth was scandalized.

"Why not? If he wants to quarrel with the devil, seems to me that's a good spot to start trouble."

"*You're* the troublemaker, Noah," Seth said. "Damn me, if you ain't stirrin' up something you ain't happy. You can't put a man of God down there!"

"How the hell d'I know he's a man of God. He came in here with a Bible, but anybody can buy one. He wants to build a church, but how do I know he won't collect money for it and skedaddle?"

"You got no faith," Seth said.

Frank rapped on the table. "He won't collect money for anything, because there's not that much cash around. What he'll collect is lumber and nails. The main question is, will we give him land or not?"

"You want to vote?" Ramsay said, "I vote yes. But not land down by the line."

Seth nodded, "I vote the same."

"All right," Noah said, making a face. "Give him land. Now let's talk about the railroad."

"How d'you vote, Frank?" Ramsay asked.

"It doesn't matter. You three carry it. There's a corner lot opposite the corrals on First Street that we can let him use. It's in town where it'll be easier for folks to help put up the building."

"That's your land, Frank," Ramsay objected. "Let's give him something across the river."

"It won't hurt the land any," Frank said. "He won't get a deed to it, but he can use it as long's he wants. That's all right with everyone?"

They agreed it was. Frank rapped and Amy Gordon wrote it down and Frank brought up the next item.

"We've got to decide on the marshal," he said. "I suggest we call in Bill Spencer and see if he'll take the job."

"It's fine with me," Seth said. "But we'll need three men to do the job right. Bill got to sleep sometime."

"I agree," Noah said, fiddling with a pencil. "Leave it to Spencer to hire his own deputies. What about the money?"

"Fines, fees and taxes," Frank said, repeating what Karl had said about taxing gambling and prostitution.

They discussed it for a time; Amy reminded them they had applications for two more dancehalls to be built at the east end of town; they approved these finally, and then Frank brought up the matter of a judge.

Noah thought they should appoint someone with experience, but none of them wanted the lawyers in town.

Ramsay said, "What about Fred Ainger?"

"He's a schoolteacher!" Seth said.

"Yes, and a sensible man. Hell, a J.P. doesn't need to be a law-school graduate." Ramsay rapped his knuckles on the desktop. "I just want to put his name in front of you."

"Not a bad suggestion," Frank said. "What's your objection, Seth?"

Seth made a face. "None, really. I was surprised, that's all."

Noah said, "All right, Ramsay, why don't you approach him and see if he'll accept the job? We sure as hell need him." He sucked on his big pipe. "Anyone opposed?"

"So ordered." Ramsay nodded in a pleased way. "I'll see him right off."

A few days passed and the council interviewed Bill Spencer, a farmerish-looking man, young and strong, but with a steady eye and a good recommendation from Karl Welch. He had held a number of jobs, among them railroad fireman, cowhand, and surveyor's assistant. He appeared to have a fund of common sense, was unmarried and satisfied to work for one hundred dollars a month. He was hired for a term of one year, and they held a little ceremony as Ramsay Hamer pinned a badge on his vest.

Fred Ainger also came to the meeting, answered a hundred questions, and was appointed justice of the peace. The council agreed that he might use his own home as a court for the time being.

"Damn, this town is growin'," Seth Potter said.

A forceful man like Preacher Rossiter, who smiled with a great mouthful of white teeth, said appealing things to housewives, and presented in church a strong and energetic case against profligacy and the greater sins, and looked the other way when the smaller ones were mentioned, could not help but gather about him a flock. Preacher's flock saw in him the makings of a Savior. They cheerfully pitched in to build the edifice that was to become the Church of the Precious Blood. It was located on a corner across from the corrals on the last side street west, and could seat forty people on hard benches when it was completed.

Preacher had no wife and no ties to the Baptist Church. He was a freethinker, he said, calling himself a man-with-a-Bible. "If it ain't in the Good Book, folks, then it ain't what we need. 'By the sweat of thy brow shalt thou eat bread.' That's what the Lamb said, and, 'While the earth remaineth, seedtime and harvest and cold and heat, summer and winter, and day and night shall not cease.' A man ought t'listen to them words and not fall out by the way."

Preacher proved to be not only a shouter but a storyteller as well; he related incidents and amusing tales in a droll, penetrating voice and gradually worked up from stories to sermon, lathering his congregation with histrionics. He was a success from the start.

While the church was a-building—the plans called for a small apartment in the rear—he lived with various of his new flock, a few days with one family, a week with another. Most of the lumber and labor was donated, even the plans were drawn by Mort Cleary, the cabinetmaker, as a gift; Mort spent several afternoons each week supervising the construction. Preacher worked right along with all of them, sawing and nailing and spitting, his infectious good humor spurring them to greater efforts. When work was done for the day, Preacher went round to every man, shaking his hand and thanking him in the name of the Lord for the "good work you'all contributed today, friend."

One afternoon Preacher Rossiter happened to be passing the stage depot when the Concord from Ironton clattered into town. The arrival of any stagecoach was an event; people gathered, hearing the horn from a distance, everyone interested in seeing who stepped off the stage.

The coach was loaded, not quite to capacity; seven grinning men jumped down, a few cowhands with saddles atop the coach, a few drummers with heavy valises, and two men in frock coats.

As Preacher stared, four smiling young women were handed out with exaggerated gallantry and considerable laughter.

An undercurrent ran through the assembled group, all men—quick words and smiles, and a few invitations. The girls were pretty, wearing makeup and fluffy boas despite the rigors of the trip, and city dresses with frills, and were

72

traveling without male escort. They flounced and posed, bantering with the men as their luggage was carried off to a waiting mud wagon and stowed aboard by a thin, unsmiling man in a checkered suit.

Preacher's eyes fastened on a woman who met the stage and climbed aboard the mud wagon with the others, and he bit his lower lip as he recognized Gertie de Vere. She was clad in a pink wrapper, wore a broad-brimmed gray hat with bright flowers and silken ties. Gert had been born Gertrude Turek and had only assumed her "stage name" in Natchez, where he'd first encountered her. He had been starting his ministry then and they'd tangled over his denunciations—and he had been forced to leave town.

But he carried no grudge. The Lord was forgiving, and Preacher could not be less.

He was glad to see her—sorry that she still followed the sinful trade, but people seldom changed. Denouncing *her* from his pulpit would not effect a change toward God, he was sure. But he could rant against her profession, and the sale of whiskey, and the playing of cards and other gambling games.

For old times' sake, he went to see Gert. They were both older and perhaps wiser and, although she had called him some pretty scorching names once, he doubted she would refuse to see him. He waited till long after dark and made his way by a roundabout route to the line; how would it look to his flock if he should be seen in a house of ill-repute! He went to the back of the first house and rapped on the door. After a time a colored woman opened it and stared at him. "What you want, mister? Whyn't you go around to the front like—"

"I want to speak to Gertie."

73

"You got the wrong house, mister. She two down." The woman closed the door firmly.

Preacher went to the third house, rapped again, and repeated his request. Gertie came to the door, but she made him wait a long time first, and when she opened to him she had a revolver in his ribs.

"It's me, Gert! You forgot me already?"

"For God's sake—Preacher!" She dropped the pistol to her side and stared at him with round eyes. "I thought you were back in—where was it, Cairo?"

"Natchez. I want t'speak to you, Gert. You got a room we can talk in?"

She smiled. "It costs money to get into my room. You never did have a penny, Preacher. You still the same?"

"Don't josh me, Gert."

She frowned a moment, then motioned brusquely. "Follow me." She led him through the kitchen, into a small bedchamber, and closed the door. "All right, Preacher, what is it you want to say?" She put her back against the door.

He stood in the center of the tiny room looking at the cot bed. Was this what a den of iniquity looked like—a room with a cot off the kitchen? It looked to be a lumpy cot too. There were no pictures on the walls, a small chest of drawers with a basin and pitcher atop, several dresses hung behind a string curtain, and the room smelled of powder and perfume.

"I just wanted to see you, Gert. These here is all new folks, in town. It's nice to see somebody from—"

She laughed. "I didn't know you had all that sentiment, Logan. I'm just a whorelady who had you run out of town once."

"I don't hold that agin you, Gert. And it don't matter what you are, the Lord loves you."

Gert regarded him steadily. "You really b'lieve that, don't you? I mean, all that stuff in the Bible . . ."

74

"You got to believe, to preach. You're lookin' nice, Gertie."

"Thanks. But you came to tell me you're going to preach against me on Sunday, didn't you?"

He shook his head and smiled ruefully. "I guess I tried that once. Folks ain't perfect and they won't ever be. I know some of 'em comes to see you b'fore they comes to sit in my church, and that's just the way people is. A man has to accept it. He don't have to like it, 'specially if he's a preacher, but he damn well got to accept it."

She was silent. "I think I'd like to come and listen to you myself. . . . Of course folks wouldn't let me."

"They might not." He pursed his lips. "But we could fix up a little Bible reading class during the week—at night—if you was serious. I'd be happy to come an' hold it right here. Maybe one'r two of your girls might like to sit in."

Gert clapped her hands. "That's a hell of—I mean that's a fine idea, Logan! I guess whoregirls need the Bible just as much as any other sinners. Tell you what— Monday is our slow night, why don't we make it on Monday, say about nine o'clock?"

"That's mighty fine, Gert!" Preacher got to his feet and clasped her hands in his. "It makes me real glad t'hear you say it too. I'll be here on Monday night—but I'll come in the back way if you don't mind."

She laughed again. "I'll be looking for you."

He went out quickly into the night, exulting. He had never in the world expected that Gertie de Vere would be receptive to a Bible class! It filled a man's heart with the joy of the Lord! There was no way to tell what might come of it.

A half mile from the line, he paused by the river and gazed at the placid flow, listening to a night bird calling, to the soft chuckles of water in some hidden rill. He recalled the last time he'd spoken to Gert in Natchez. It had

75

been in one of the back rooms of a ramshackle house on the waterfront—he had no church at the time and was only a traveling preacher who had failed in everything else, farming, blacksmithing, keeping store . . . but his gift of gab had kept him in beans, and his strong beliefs had gathered crowds willing to listen.

Gert had been a hard-mouthed girl then, as bitter as anyone he'd ever seen. She'd sworn and spit at him when he suggested she turn away from whoring and give the Lord a chance. He said, "Gert, you're in an evil business!"

"It's all I know! I got a right to live same's you. You rather see me out stealing or doing something worse?"

"You're a pretty woman. You could get married like others."

She made a face. "I d'want to get married. Don't you think I see married men ever' day? I d'want none like that!"

"But the Lord wants something better for you—"

She screamed at him, "The hell He does! The Lord never lifted a damn finger when I was down an' out. He never got me a piece of bread—or a decent job. He let my old man beat the hell out of me, too. Don't talk t'me about your Lord!"

Logan Rossiter sighed; he stooped, found a pebble and tossed it into the dark river, listening to it splash. Maybe that was what had made him feel something special toward Gert. His old man had beaten him too. He knew exactly what it was like to live with poverty and hate. Those things had driven Gertie out where the devil's clutching fingers had torn at her and dragged her down. It wasn't really Gert's fault that she'd ended up a scarlet lady. Hate was a powerful force. Didn't he have to contend with it every day?

Sometimes folks told him he was an idealist, and he didn't quite understand what they meant. He thought of himself as a poor man serving the Lamb in whatever fashion he could. "The Lord works in different ways," he'd told Gert. "Don't harden your heart," but he doubted she'd heard him.

Sometimes it bothered him that evil was so attractive, and now and then he concluded that a kind of sham beauty was all that evil had . . . it had nothing underneath. Gertie Turek was such a one, especially in those days. She'd been a beautiful girl, with glossy copper hair, an oval face that seemed meant to enchant. The Lord made flowers to attract bees, and He had made Gertie beautiful to attract men; it was only another of the Almighty's incomprehensible ways that he had to put up with.

But tonight, Gertie had made him very happy.

It was the same week he met Schuyler Wood. Schuyler was a man nearly as tall as himself, distinguished-looking in a black frock coat and gray trousers.

Schuyler came round to see him, handing him a fat cigar. "Want to make your acquaintance, Preacher. I'm told you're a mighty good man with words." He gazed round the rough church admiringly.

"A man does what he can, Mr. Wood." Preacher smelled the cigar. A damned good one. When he put it between his lips, Schuyler scratched a match and held it for him.

"I've settled in Roseberry, Preacher, and I'm glad you've come here. We need a God-fearing man like you to keep the rest of us on the straight and narrow. And I know yours is not an easy task."

Rossiter nodded, blowing smoke, appreciating the gift. He had heard about Schuyler Wood, ex-judge and legislator; he looked every bit of it too. "A man don't expect the

Lord's work to be easy, Mr. Wood, but he got to do it. It brings a joy inside that ain't to be measured in dollars."

"No, of course not." Schuyler took a turn up the church aisle and back. "There are a good many sinners in town, I expect." He smiled. "Myself included."

Preacher waved his hand. "Them little no-account sins, they ain't the ones I'm after."

"Yes, you're right," Schuyler looked the other in the eye. "But the people who lead us, they should be clean, don't you think?"

"You damn right," Preacher said with feeling.

"They should indeed. A man needs leaders to look up to. A man's children should have examples."

"What you talking about, Mr. Wood?"

"Please, let's not be formal. I want to be friends, and my friends call me Schuyler."

Preacher smiled and nodded. "I haven't seen you here on Sunday, Schuyler."

"You will. I hear you preach a mighty interesting sermon." He looked round the interior again. "You've done a lot with very little, Preacher. Do you plan to stay on here in Roseberry or are you a rambling man?"

"I figger to stay on."

"That's good." Schuyler clasped hands behind him. "I hope we'll become better friends in the future." He made as if to go, then turned about and came back. "Something occurs to me, Preacher—"

"Spit it out."

"I have a friend, Mr. Cole Stedman, who lives across the river. He's a printer and is putting out the Roseberry *Advocate*. I will admit it's only a small four-page sheet at present, but it will grow."

"Yes, I seen it, Schuyler."

"Folks are eager for news and gossip of all kinds, don't you agree?"

"I certainly do."

78

"It occurred to me, Preacher, that you might be interested in writing an item for the newspaper each week, something related to your sermons—the word of God in print."

"By the Harry!" Preacher said, astonished.

"It'll carry the good word to all the outlying ranches and homes so that people who cannot get into town can read your words and receive the benefit of your sermons."

Preacher drove a great fist into the palm of his hand with an exclamation. It was a marvelous idea! Then his face clouded.

Schuyler asked, "What is it?"

"Well, I don't write very good, and that's a fact. I can talk all right, but when it comes to—"

"Don't give it another thought. I'll see that a very good secretary takes down your words. He'll read them back to you and you can make changes or additions. What do you say?"

"I think it's a purely wonderful thing, Schuyler. When d'you want me to start?"

"Any time you feel up to it. Come over to the *Advocate* office and I'll see that you get everything you need."

"That's a mighty kind thing, Schuyler, I surely will."

Schuyler put out his hand, smiled, and left. Puffing on the cigar, Preacher watched him out the door. Schuyler was a real fine man to go out of his way for folks like that; a man could be proud to live in a town that contained Schuyler Wood.

Chapter Seven

Joseph was only a child; he could ride a horse like the wind, and run faster than anyone Frank had ever seen; he was fascinated by guns, saying his people had only a few and no repeaters at all—they had stolen them, Frank surmised. And he was awed and baffled by the white man's ways.

Frank learned quickly that although Joseph had attended a school on the reservation for about a year, he had never been allowed inside any of the whites' homes. He had picked up English more from the white children with whom he'd come in contact than from teachers, and his vocabulary was more limited than Frank had first surmised. He did not know the words for most household things, and Mrs. Steen threw up her hands, trying to teach him to eat with a fork instead of his fingers.

He hated being indoors, spent all his time in the stable, but made no attempt at all to run away.

The very next day after Frank brought the boy home, he received word through Karl Welch that a small band of Indians had been seen in the vicinity of Bealer's Store, which was a collection of adobe and log huts on one of the old wagon trails about a day's ride west and north of Roseberry on the plains. When Frank heard it he saddled the roan, tied a poncho and food behind the cantle, put the boy, warmly dressed, on his pony, and they set out in the early morning.

The band was likely to be Joseph's kin. Frank felt it was worth the try to take the boy to his mother if the Indians would allow him to approach. Joseph understood that Frank wanted to return him to his people, and seemed relieved when they set out alone; the presence of the sheriff had made him uneasy. Frank explained that he had no interest in punishing the Indian band, and would not set the law on them. Joseph nodded but Frank could not tell if the boy believed him.

They rode across the undulating prairie for hours, flushing birds and scattering occasional bands of whitetail deer. The skies were lowering, curdled like milk, and past noon a breeze sprang up, plucking the loose soil and sage twigs, hurling them helter-skelter.

They stopped to eat near a sheet of smoky brown water, breathing the horses, then went on, with Frank using a pair of field glasses to search the horizons.

In the middle of the afternoon he spotted movement far to their left, and they turned toward it. When he halted on the next ridge to look again, Frank could see nothing at all and began to have misgivings. The Indians would certainly think he was hunting them and would probably melt away or scatter. The stratagem of scattering to the four winds, to meet later at an agreed-upon spot, had frustrated the cavalry dozens of times. It might well frustrate him now.

Joseph had nothing to say; his ebon eyes danced about the prairie, and if he saw more than Frank, he made no sign. It occurred to Frank that he might turn the boy loose to ride ahead. If his people were there, they would take him in. If not, the boy could always come back.

He was mulling this idea over when he heard the shout.

In another few seconds he and Joseph were half-circled by mounted Indians, none of them more than a hundred yards distant. Frank came to an instant halt, drawing the Winchester from its boot and levering it.

When he looked at Joseph, the boy was smiling.

T.E. Serly arrived in Roseberry tired and coach-bruised, glad to alight and claim his single carpetbag. He carried the bag down the long street to the hotel and inquired about a room and bath.

The room was one dollar for the night and the bath cost twenty-five cents including soap and a threadbare towel. He soaked in the bath then slept the clock round and a little more, and woke in the middle of the next evening. He went downstairs to the restaurant around the corner and ordered a beefsteak well done, followed by a slab of apple pie and strong coffee. After the meal he returned to the hotel and entered a game of pinnochle with several drummers who had a fund of risqué stories to tell.

In the morning he visited Sam's livery stable and asked about a horse and mule. Sam had a number of animals for sale, he said, and took T.E. out behind the stable and they leaned over a corral pole.

"Got them two sorrels, that there black, the roan t'other side of him and the two mules," Sam said. "What you think?"

"I think them sorrels is high priced."

"You're right," Sam grinned, showing scrag teeth. "Let you have the black cheap, though."

T.E. climbed through the poles and looked the black over. He was sound, not very young but strong. "I need the animals for a week'r two, that's all. How about you rentin' them to me?"

Sam was astonished. "Rent! I never rented an animal in my life!"

T.E. bit his lip hard. "Tell you the goddamn truth, I

haven't got the money to buy 'em. I got a hundred dollars—" He turned out the money to show it—the remaining fifty he had concealed in his shoe at the hotel. "You give me the two mules and you hold the hundred. When I get back you take what I owe you. That fair?"

Sam scratched his head. He could understand a drifter not having the price of an animal; times were not that good. But he was leery of renting to a stranger. "Where you going with my mules?"

"Down the river . . . maybe thirty miles." T.E. pointed.

Sam said, "Hell, there ain't nothing down there!"

"I—I'm thinking about taking up land." T.E. was desperate; he could see old Sam's reluctance, but he had to have the mules. The story about land was the first thing he could think of.

Sam's expression said he was crazy to do any such thing.

T.E. found himself explaining to the older man how much he'd wanted to own his own land, how his people had always been farmers, and now that he'd come this far it was impossible to go back without looking the land over. He had a right to file on 160 acres, and if he could find good soil—

Sam gave in at last. He put a worn saddle on one mule and a pack tree on the other, accepted the hundred dollars and wrote out a rental paper, which T.E. signed.

T.E. settled for the room and rode down the street to the Van Borcke store where he bought gloves, an axe, camping gear, and food. Otto Vrooman produced a gunny sack and put into it coffee, dried beef, hominy, a sack of flour, corn meal, beans, sugar, salt, lard, sowbelly, crackers, and tobacco. He also lugged it out to the mule and tied it on. As he accepted T.E.'s money he asked, "Goin' campin'?"

"Just heading west," T.E. said noncommittally. He got on the mule and headed down the River Road west.

Otto went back inside the store shaking his head. "N'other damn fool gone prospecting," he said to Amos. "There ain't any gold out there."

"He didn't buy a shovel," Amos observed, fingering his watch chain. He was a big, portly man, gray and slightly stooped. "You can't prospect without a shovel."

Otto went to the door and gazed westward, pawing his chin. "Wonder what the hell he *is* a-doin' then?"

Chapter Eight

Frank sat perfectly still on the horse, his finger on the trigger of the rifle. There were only five braves. The rest were women, and three of the men looked to be elderly. He could see only two rifles, but the others had bows strung.

He said to the boy, "Are these your people?"

Joseph rode forward without answering. He put his arms out, and there was a yell from one of the women. In the next second Joseph galloped the pony forward, jumped off, and three of the Indians surrounded him.

It was a nervous situation. He could probably hit three or four of them before they closed in—if that was their purpose. But if they killed his horse, it might be all over. It would be little satisfaction to take a number of them with him, but if they came for him, he would damned well do his best.

Then suddenly they were talking, jabbering one to the other, and in the next moment they were withdrawing. Frank sat the roan, watching them with the boy, the faces turned toward him no longer as hostile as they had seemed. He took a long breath and began to relax, conscious that he had been wound tight as thread on a spool. He let the hammer down on the Winchester as Joseph appeared from the group.

He rode the pony forward a few yards from the others, raised his hand and grinned. Frank lifted his hand in reply.

In the next second Joseph turned and the Indians closed about him again and began to move off in the opposite direction. Joseph was home.

T.E. followed the river the rest of the day. The road petered out a few miles past the Bend bridge, but there was a good enough path for another mile or so, then he had to make his own. George Kilburn had said there was only one good stretch of meadowland west of the Bend on the north side of the river. "You can find it in the dark."

George spoke as if it were a morning's work to find the meadow and stake it out. Of course *he* was back in Ironton, sleeping in a good bed and eating from china plates.

He came on the meadow as the light was fading and was surprised to find it so exactly like George's description. It was a large, level grassy area flanked by a stream and fronting on the river. The stream had rushing water in it, gurgling and splashing over rocks and cold as ice. He made camp back from the river in a little glade only a few yards from the stream. Cutting saplings with the axe, he fashioned a shebang and roofed it with a tarpaulin. He built a fire in front of it in a circle of rocks and began to feel more comfortable.

With the mules picketed in grass, and with a meal of beans and sowbelly inside him and his pipe lit, he put his back to a tree and contemplated the shadowy meadow where he and George Kilburn were going to make their fortunes.

The sky was misty and mysterious and a coyote yipped somewhere across the meadow. When George said there was nothing here, he was right. No one in his right mind would buy a lot in this wilderness, but George said there were plenty who would buy a pig in a poke; all you had to do was shade the truth a little. T.E. had confidence that George could shade the facts. It occurred to him then that he was trusting the con man a long way . . . but he remembered that George had advanced seventy dollars of his own money in order to get the meadow staked. That reassured him. What he was doing out here in the sticks was very important.

He finished the pipe, knocked out the bowl, and turned in, letting his mind wander over the things a man could buy with a hundred thousand dollars. He would never have to take a pair of shoes to be half-soled again.

In the morning he rolled out and began the task.

He cut down a large number of saplings and branches, trimmed them, and cut them to length. It took most of the day and he knew they weren't enough, but he began the pacing anyway. He set up stakes, paced off distances and drove more stakes.

Now and then he glanced around the horizon. If a drifting pilgrim came upon him, what would he think? A man driving stakes in a meadow in the middle of nowhere! The idea made him laugh and he decided to manufacture an excuse for it all, then couldn't think of a thing.

He had told George he would measure and set the stakes accurately by means of a carpenter's rule, but he found that too much trouble, and George was hundreds of miles away. He paced off, as nearly as he could, sixteen and a half feet, one rod, marked a length of twine and used that as his measuring stick. There were 160 square rods in an acre, times 320.

It took him a week to lay it all out; it took nearly another week to set stakes to lay out streets fifty feet wide. Then he sighted down the stakes and spent a day

89

straightening the lines. He could easily have spent three more days doing that, but he was about out of food. He had worked hard, and he had eaten more than ever before in his life.

He drew a crude map showing the exact relationship of the town plat to the stream and the Roseberry River. When it was all finished he was rather pleased with himself. The job was not as precisely done as a surveyor would do it, of course, but it was done. Even a government official would be able to see the work that had gone into laying it out.

The next morning he broke camp and hurried back to Roseberry.

Old Sam charged him twenty dollars for the use of the two mules and equipment; he sent off a wire to George Kilburn saying the job was done and he was returning immediately; within three hours he had an answer from George: "Well done, hurry back."

Two days later, near the middle of the day, some distance past the Gap, T.E.'s stagecoach passed another coming from Ironton. The drivers blew horns and yelled, the passengers waved. Then the other coach was past.

T.E. frowned, craning his neck to look back. There'd been a man in that stagecoach who bore a remarkable resemblance to George! But George was waiting for him in Ironton, so it could not be. There was no earthly reason for George to go to Roseberry anyway. With some difficulty he put the idea out of his mind. George *had* answered his wire, after all. It had simply been someone who looked like George.

When he received the finished artwork from the artist, Ives, George went immediately to one of the three printers in town and ordered color plates made. He gave the printer the copy he had written and helped plan the layout for the brochure and select the type before going back to the boardinghouse once more to wait.

In four days he received a telegram from Schuyler asking about his progress; he wrote a letter back delineating what he had done, explaining that he'd sent a man to stake out the lots and that the plates for the brochure would be finished in a matter of days, certainly no more than a week, and he would come to Roseberry with them.

A wire arrived from Schuyler: "Excellent. Am expecting you."

On the fourth day the printer had the plates ready and proofs had been pulled. George examined them, made a number of small corrections, then ordered five hundred brochures printed.

These would be his own. He would see to it they were printed as well as humanly possible, in bright colors—with Schuyler's name as promoter. But Schuyler wouldn't hear of them until much later when the buyers came to claim their lots on the meadow. George would be a thousand miles away by that time.

It took another three days to print the pirated brochures. As soon as he received them, George tied them into a neat bundle and arranged with the stage-line super, a Mr. Williamson, to place the bundle in the safe for a fee paid in advance. He then bought a ticket on the morning stage to Roseberry and went back to the boardinghouse to pack his bag, placing the carefully wrapped color plates at the bottom.

When he stepped off the stage, Horace Gromley was whisked away in a shiny buggy driven by Schuyler Wood. Horace was a natty man, middle height and balding, with a wide mouth and an easy smile. He had started life as an advance man for a traveling carnival and had worked his way up through salesmanship, joining the railroad during the boom years after the war. Not a great deal escaped him and nothing surprised him.

But he was curious about Schuyler's hasty retreat from the depot. "Someone after you, Schuyler?"

Schuyler laughed. "It's the other way round, Horsy. I'm after someone."

"Oh, you mean McCarty?"

"That's the one." Schuyler turned onto the bridge and fished in a vest pocket for the toll. He reined in to drop a coin in the caretaker's hat and slapped the reins. "You may think me petty, but it's a matter of getting even."

"I didn't know you felt so strongly about him."

"He and his kind have made this town impossible for me to live in." Schuyler growled the words. "So I'm getting out, as you know, but when I go I'd like to see McCarty stewing."

Horace chuckled. "You make quite an enemy, Schuyler. Have you figured a way to do it?"

"Yes, with your help."

Cautiously, "Within reason, partner."

"You'll be completely in the clear, as long as *you* don't say a word. I want you to talk to McCarty about bringing a spur track to Roseberry. A legitimate talk—but just talk. Will you do that?"

"A smokescreen?"

"Exactly."

"McCarty and no one else?"

"Yes. No witnesses. He must believe the meeting is confidential, a sort of preliminary, and I think he'll fall for it, especially if you invite him."

Horace nodded, "I see."

He let Horsy think it over and changed the subject, remarking on the countryside and the new houses and barns going up along the road. Roseberry was growing, and every time he noticed it, it rankled. There were street markers at the corners now and people had begun to number their homes to make it easier for others to find them. He turned the buggy onto Meadow Street, went down half a mile and slowed to turn at Gertrude Turek's house.

It was a well-built cottage with a large fireplace in the parlor and three bedchambers, one very small, a kitchen, and a woodshed. There was a stablehouse behind with a built-on room occupied by a slim, unsmiling man, an employee of Gert's. He was a driver, caretaker, and bouncer, and spent his days doing the hundred and one things Gert found for him. He was not in evidence as Schuyler halted the buggy in the drive and they carried the luggage inside.

The cottage interior was tastefully appointed; the wallpaper was not the cheap kind with red roses everywhere, but had silver stripes, or mauve geometric patterns, or hunting scenes. There were framed black-and-white prints on the walls, and comfortable furniture. Schuyler could see that Horace was pleasantly surprised; he probably expected less comfortable accommodations than a hotel room.

Schuyler had stocked the liquor cabinet with good whiskey, two bottles of gin, one of rum, and one of brandy. There was mocha coffee and other provisions in the kitchen, and Union Leader pipe tobacco near the fireplace. Gert had promised to send over two girls to keep Horace occupied and entertained on the night of his arrival, and would only charge Schuyler half price.

He made drinks while Horace stretched in front of the fire, and they talked. Horace was willing to talk to McCarty once or twice, without witnesses, to discuss a railroad spur to Roseberry.

"I'll promise nothing," he warned Schuyler. "We can talk about profits and costs—"

"Let him think you're here at Hightower's request."

Horace nodded and made a face. "I'll give him that impression. What happens when I leave?"

Schuyler smiled. "You don't really want to know."

"No, I guess I don't. As long as my talks are legitimate, don't tell me any more."

Schuyler smiled and held up his glass. "Your very good health, Horsy. I'll do the same for you one day."

"God forbid!"

There was a rap at the door and both men turned; Schuyler strode across the room and clicked back the bolt. When he opened it, two girls hurried in. He saw the slim man outside with a team and raised his hand. The man nodded and disappeared into the gloom with the buggy.

The girls were both blondes, Daisy and Sophie, bundled up in heavy coats against the chill. Schuyler hurriedly finished his drink as Horsy helped the girls with the coats, tossing them over chairs and hugging the girls, giving his name as Bill Clark. The girls were kissing him and calling him Billy as Schuyler let himself out.

Faith McCarty completed her business in Ironton, which had taken longer than she'd supposed, arranged for her various shipments to be delivered to Angus Williamson for reshipping, wrote a number of letters, sent a wire to Frank, and took the next stage for Roseberry.

She wore a traveling dress of dark blue with a high bodice and loose-fitting waist, with the skirt cut high to clear the instep. Her hat was small, of the same blue, and she wore her hair in braids, turned up and pinned close to the head. She had discarded the small reticule and for her journey carried a large black handbag of coarse-woven cloth which she found indispensable for combs, brushes, toilet articles, and handkerchiefs. Traveling by stage was a hot and dusty experience—when it was not cold and wet—and she steeled herself to accept the inconveniences; in a few days she would be home, with no need to return for another six months.

Two sunburned drummers, a young cowhand with a saddle on his back, and a good looking middle-aged man in a frock coat and duster whose name, he said with a bow, was George Wilson, were waiting for the stage. When it was brought round, the baggage was stowed. Angus handed her up, making sure she was seated next the window facing forward, and wished her a pleasant trip.

George Wilson and the drummers got in, the drummers striking up a conversation with her at once as the cowboy's warbag and saddle were secured. The drummers were brash as preachers, asking every sort of question, obviously titillated at the chance to travel with a very pretty young woman, ignoring George Wilson's remonstrations. Their attentions became so earnest that she was forced to speak to the driver, Billy Jack, at their first comfort stop, a meadow guarded by low hills dotted with blackjack oaks.

Billy Jack thereupon buttonholed the drummers. "You fellers got any idee who that there young lady is?"

The salesmen, rawboned and assured, only smiled. "She's a gal like any gal. You strip 'er down and she's—"

"She's Frank McCarty's wife." Billy Jack's finger poked at the man's chest. "And Frank is the onriest sonofabitch this side of the Mississippi, so if I'se you I'd shut my trap and give her no more trouble or you could wind up with your head blowed off."

"Mc—McCarty?"

"I told you," Billy Jack said, turning away. "Don't say you wasn't warned."

They spent the night at Somers Station, where the young cowhand left them. He hauled his saddle off the top of the coach and they watched him from the veranda, riding into the saffron dusk bound for his ranch somewhere out on the limitless prairie.

The second night was spent at the Gap. Billy Jack, skinny and whiskery, told them again how he and Frank McCarty had come up to the Gap to find the Ritters dead of diphtheria, and how Frank had burned the station down around the bodies. It was a story he told with relish, heightening it when he saw the shocked reaction of his audience. Faith had heard the story too many times and walked away from the group, locking herself in her room. Billy Jack's present version only faintly resembled the truth as she knew it from her husband.

Later she had a quiet supper of boiled pork, greens, warm corn bread, and milk. George Wilson came in while she was eating and ordered coffee. He had been to Roseberry once before, he told her, and thought it a charming town. He was traveling for his health, he said, but was looking for investments at the same time.

Faith assured him that Roseberry was a town with a future and that a man could do worse than invest there in a good business. When he asked about the railroad, she informed him that it had built to the town of Jackson about a hundred and fifty miles away, but their expectation was that it would have to build to Roseberry in the near future.

"If only to make sure of the cattle-freighting business."

"Railroads frequently disappoint us, in the matter of their right-of-ways," George Wilson said.

She wondered about that later on, as she was getting ready for bed.

That same afternoon Frank received a letter from Mr. Horace Gromley, on official Tascosa & Tahlequah Railroad stationery. Gromley stated he was visiting Roseberry as the first leg of a vacation trip, and would be pleased to see Mr. McCarty at his convenience, if Mr. McCarty was interested in talking about a possible spur line to Roseberry.

He wrote in the address at the bottom of the letter, and Frank sent a note in reply saying he could call on Mr. Gromley that evening.

After the reply was sent, Frank put his feet up on the desk and gazed at the far wall, lost in thought. The letter surprised him considerably; it was totally unlike a railroad official to initiate such a proposal, especially the T&T. He called in Ken Larkin and verified Gromley's position with the company. The man *was* a vice president, as he claimed.

Larkin, fussy and pot-bellied, with ink-blotched fingers, took off his spectacles and beamed. "It may be the first step in bringing the spur line here. It is inevitable, of course."

"Please say nothing about it," Frank cautioned. "Not even to your wife. We don't want to raise anyone's hopes, then let them down again."

Larkin's brows climbed. "You think there's something odd about the request?"

"It's peculiar," Frank admitted.

He rode across the bridge that evening on the sorrel horse and found the house on Meadow Street. Gromley was apparently staying with friends, a very usual circumstance.

He rapped on the door and Gromley opened it himself, a smiling, pleasant man. "Come in, come in, sir . . ." He took Frank's hat and ushered him to the parlor where a fire was leaping in the fireplace.

"Please sit down, Mr. McCarty. We've never met, but I've heard a world about you."

"Kind of you to see me, Mr. Gromley."

"Not at all. Would you care for a drink?"

Frank assented, watching his host tip up the bottle and bring two glasses, handing him one. They made small talk; this was Gromley's first trip to Roseberry and he found it a larger, more bustling town than he'd thought.

It was easy then to tip the conversation toward the volume of business a carrier might expect and its year-round probabilities. Frank had come prepared with figures and they spent an hour discussing them, with Gromley getting up and down, poking at the fire and tossing on new logs.

When he left, Gromley promised to talk with him again before leaving town. He gave the impression that he'd talk with his superiors about the conversation.

Riding away under heavy skies, with mist thick on the river, Frank could come to no conclusion at all. Was it possible the T&T officials were disagreeing on the line to Roseberry and had sent Gromley to confer with him in hopes of coming closer to a decision? Gromley had given no hint at all.

Chapter Nine

Ira Jalder was a skinny, almost wizened man, with a deeply lined face and narrow shoulders. He was in his middle thirties but looked older, squinting from under a brown felt hat at the Pettis Bank across the street. He wore a blue worsted suit with a red vest, pants tucked into brown boots. Leaning against a Conestoga wagon, he picked his teeth with a little finger and read the folded newspaper, bobbing his head up and down.

Several people came out of the bank and Ira studied each one, following them with his eyes as they went about their business in the little town. He was looking for a man named Emory Ledwidge and he had a good description. There had been a small crowd about the doors of the bank at opening time and it was possible Ledwidge had gone inside then.

The paper discussed the financial panic in the East. Jay Cooke & Company, of Philadelphia, having engaged too extensively in railroad schemes, had failed. Hundreds of prominent firms all over the country were involved in ruin.

Ira clucked his tongue over the news and stiffened as a portly man came from the bank, stood for a moment while he clicked open a watch, glanced up and down the rutted street, and made off away from Ira with a leather satchel in his hand. That was Emory Ledwidge, no doubt about it. The man stopped at a dusty buggy, put the satchel inside on the seat and untied the horse.

Ira slipped the newspaper into the Conestoga. He stretched and went along the street to a hitchrack, untied a roan horse, and mounted. Willie had given him correct information. Mr. Emory Ledwidge had been in the bank the week before, on his way to Darnley. Willie overheard Ledwidge say he would return the next Tuesday and close out his account. Ira smiled, watching the man slap the reins. This was Tuesday.

Willie said that Ledwidge had recently been involved in the sale of property and the odds were good that he'd have a great deal of money in the satchel. Willie was to get ten percent for his information.

Ira Jalder walked the roan along the main street, nodding to Bull Delling who was leaning on his saddle, watching the buggy take the road north out of town. Bull mounted and tailed him and they walked the horses like two men who had all day to get wherever it was they were going. Scratching a match, Ira lit a cheroot, slouching in the saddle and allowing the horse to make its own pace. He knew where Ledwidge was bound and he knew every foot of the road. The buggy had to take the winding road, but he and Bull would cut across country. They had timed it yesterday. Even if they walked the horses all the way they'd be at the road in the woods before Ledwidge got there.

Past the end of town he turned left, following a faint trail in the weeds, with Bull's horse grunting behind him. It was a long time before noon and big dumpling clouds were scattered across the heavens and the cottonwood leaves were twinkling. It had been a terrible summer, almost profitless, and with a month spent in a louse-ridden county jail to boot. He would never go near that particular county again. A week later he'd run into Bull and

100

they'd drifted to Darnley, talking prospects, and came upon Willie, an old accomplice, in the little crossroads town of Pettis, a day's ride southwest on the Roseberry Road.

Ira looked over the bank and thought it could be busted. But Willie got lucky overhearing Ledwidge. "Why bust the bank," Willie said, "when you can bust Ledwidge?"

So they had to wait the week out. But it was going to be worth it.

They crossed a wide stretch of prairie with a soft wind making patterns scurrying before them in the grass, went down a steep bank into a sandy wash with the sun glittering on the pooling water, and splashed across it. Ira squinted north; Ledwidge had to go another mile or so to the bridge. They went up the far side, with the horses scrambling and snorting, and across another grassy slope to the woods.

The road came twisting through the woods, over a few hills to the west, to the Ledwidge farm. Ira walked the roan down the road to the turn and got down, leading the animal into the trees. He stretched again and looked at the sun. Bull tied his horse, yanked out his revolver and twirled the cylinder.

"No sense shootin' him if we don't have to," Ira said. He'd never been on a job with Bull, a big, slack-mouthed man. Bull looked at him under bushy brows and spat. His eyes brooded, but he put the pistol in his belt.

"What you going to do afterwards, Ira?"

"Don't know. Maybe go back to Darnley and take the stage east."

Bull nodded, fished out a chunk of dull brown tobacco and worried off a bite. Ira stepped into the road, fingers in his vest pockets. Ledwidge wouldn't see them until he was right at the turn, and then it would be too late. A handful of birds scolded and chattered overhead and a squirrel

101

ran down the side of a tree two rods away and stared at him intently. Ira made a quick motion and the squirrel flipped its tail and disappeared.

He moved back and leaned against a tree, squinting at Bull. The big man was no thinker and likely to do anything if excited. He'd seen that in the county jail. Bull tended to roar and use his strength in brute fashion. He was sorry now he'd teamed up with Bull, especially since this job was going to be easy and he didn't need anyone along. It was going to cost him a half share, but it was too late to cry over spilt milk now; he'd have to make the best of it, send a cut to Willie, and light out.

He'd go back to the big river and down to New Orleans for the winter—no matter what he told Bull. There was a girl in the French quarter who—

"He's comin'," Bull said.

Ira pulled his thoughts back to the present. He could hear the hard tires of the buggy rattling on the roadbed, and the clip-clop of hooves. He glanced at Bull. "Let me do the talking."

With his hat off, he peered around the tree. The buggy was rocking steadily toward them, the horse's head bobbing. Ledwidge was sprawled in the seat, his eyes half-closed.

Ira pulled his own pistol, glanced sidelong at Bull, and stepped out into the road as the buggy rounded the turn. The horse saw him and shied; two wheels of the buggy bumped in the weeds and Ledwidge grabbed at the reins to haul in.

"Pull up!" Ira said loudly, holding the pistol so Ledwidge could see it.

The victim's face blanched. His eyes popped and he jerked his head around as Bull came into the road pointing the revolver.

"What is this!"

102

"It's a stick-up," Ira said, motioning to Bull to grab the bridle. "Get outa the buggy."

"But I haven't got anything to steal!" Ledwidge's voice was suddenly shrill and squeaky. His mouth dropped open as Bull cocked the revolver. "All right—all right—don't shoot!"

He climbed down from the buggy, puffing slightly, his hands trembling and his face very pale. Staring from one to the other of them, he licked his lips. "I've got a few dollars in my pocket . . ." He followed Ira with his eyes as the skinny man went around to the far side of the buggy and rummaged for the satchel.

Seeing it, Bull bared his teeth and took his eyes from Ledwidge for a second.

In that second Ledwidge jerked into action. His hand shot inside the frock coat and came out cocking a revolver. Bull heard the sound and yelled as he fired a shot over Ledwidge's head, too hastily done to aim.

Ira pointed his pistol and shot Ledwidge through the body.

The portly man grunted, dropped the revolver, and fell to his knees. Bull fired two shots into him as fast as he could work the hammer, then scampered around, cocking the pistol to fire again.

"He's had it," Ira said. "That's enough noise."

"That sumbitch tried to shoot me!" Bull yelled.

"Well, he didn't," Ira said. "Calm down." He had the satchel unbuckled and looked inside. Papers, it was full of legal-looking papers! He pulled them out and dropped them on the floor of the buggy; Bull was on one knee, searching Ledwidge.

Under the papers was a small packet of greenbacks and a leather pouch.

Ira snatched up the pouch. It was the kind a man might put jewelry into, and it felt like jewelry inside. His eyes on Bull, he slipped the pouch into an inner pocket

103

and went around the buggy holding the satchel in one hand and the money in the other.

"Not very damned much money," Ira said. "What'd he have on him?"

"Eight dollars," Bull said, holding out his hand. He looked at the packet. "Is that all?"

"Every damned bit." Ira tossed it to the other. "Count it."

Ira bent down and looked at the portly man. Dead as a fish. He'd put the bullet right through the ticker all right. Damn. He swore aloud. "They'll be after us for this, Bull."

"Hell, we had to do it!"

Ira chuckled, reloading his pistol. "You tell that to the posse. How much money?"

"Three hunnerd and fifty-six . . . and eight more. That makes—"

"Three-sixty-four."

"That goddam Willie!" Bull took the empty satchel and looked inside. Then he leaned into the buggy and pawed at the papers. "There oughta be more."

Ira sighed, nodding. There never was enough. "That's one hunnerd eighty-two for each." He took the money from Bull and divvied it up. Bull counted his and put it away moodily.

"We been diddled, Ira."

"Yeh, I hate to shoot a man for a piddling few dollars. . . ." Ira shrugged and looked down the road. "Let's drag him back into the trees. Give us a little more time if they don't find him right off."

He took the feet, Bull hefted the big man's shoulders and they heaved and tugged, dragging the body off the road and back under the trees, twenty or thirty feet. Ira kicked weeds over the frock coat and then they went back and frowned at the buggy.

"Unhook it," Ira decided. "We'll run it under the trees too."

It was a very light rig and it was easy to pull and push it a hundred feet into the brush so that it couldn't be seen from the road.

"Times is hard, Bull," Ira said. "Damn if they ain't. I figger we'd best split up here, what you think? We'll be harder to catch that way."

"They're not catchin' me," Bull said growling.

"I hope not. Me either. Well, we got a little eating money anyhow. Damn small pickin's, but better'n we were this morning, huh?" He slapped Bull's heavy shoulder.

"Some better," Bull admitted.

"No telling if anybody heard them shots, so let's make tracks. What if I go south and you go north—that all right with you?"

Bull nodded. He went into the trees for his horse. Ira untied the roan and mounted. "So long, Bull—and good luck." He took the reins of the buggy horse. "I'll leave this animal down in the wash there by the water. He'll stay there all week."

Bull nodded again, gloomily, and turned his horse.

Ira left the horse by the pools of brown water, crossed the wash, and circled the town. The Ironton Trace was south and he could decide what he wanted to do when he reached it. Probably Bull hadn't even thought about the Trace—and the stage line—but that was like Bull. Stupid. Ira laughed and felt the leather pouch.

He glanced back as he took the pouch out and reined in. He untied the string and poured the contents into his hand, two small sparkling rings and a black-rimmed brooch with the largest diamond he'd ever seen.

"Holy Christ!" he said aloud, then looked around hurriedly.

It was a huge diamond! He'd had some truck with jewels in the past and this was the McCoy—no doubt about it. No wonder Ledwidge had kept it in a bank vault. It was clear white, sparkling with a million dancing colors, and he turned it this way and that, astonished at his luck. It must be worth a fortune! He turned the brooch over and frowned at the fancy monogram on the back and made it out as "EL." That must be Ledwidge's wife.

"This's my day," Ira said softly, his heart hammering inside his shirt. The biggest haul he'd ever made! The two rings were diamonds too, but smaller stones. He put them all back in the pouch and went on.

His luck had certainly changed.

Five days later in Flatrock, north of Darnley, Bull Delling pored over a newspaper someone had discarded in the saloon. On the front page was a story of a holdup and murder near Pettis. Emory Ledwidge, well-known merchant, had been foully murdered and robbed on a lonely road as he was making his way home. The body had probably lain in the woods for a full day before discovery. Ledwidge's wife declared that her husband had been carrying a small amount of money and her diamonds, valued between thirty-five and forty thousand dollars.

Bull was startled. He read the item again with mounting anger. Forty thousand dollars in jewels? It was a fantastic fortune!

He put the paper down. Ira Jalder had cheated him! No wonder Ira wanted to split up so suddenly! Bull had thought it odd at the time, but hadn't objected. Ira found the jewels in the satchel while he was relieving Ledwidge of eight dollars. Eight damned dollars!

Bull got up and went outside unsteadily to lean against his horse. Ira had headed south. He hauled out his revolver and twirled the cylinder, looking at the brass cartridges. Ira had double-crossed him, and nobody did that to Bull Delling!

He put the pistol away and mounted, turning the horse south to the Darnley road. Ira had probably gone across to the Trace and south to Roseberry. That was where he'd start looking.

Chapter Ten

They reached Epps Station late the next afternoon, with its greatly enlarged rooms and new dining hall. Now that there were two stages each day along the Trace, the station had been rebuilt from the ground up. F.L. still ran the place, with his grown son Jud, and recent wife, presiding over the dining room. Jud was a paunchy young man, not at all like his lean father, and eager as a puppy to please. He gave Faith a separate table, fussing over her like royalty, returning when she'd been served, "Is ever'thing all right, Miz McCarty?"

"Of course, Jud, thank you." She sipped her coffee as he went off to serve a new customer, a thin, tired-looking man with a deeply-lined face. The stranger had come in from the hitchrack, swatting dust from his clothes; she'd heard him say at the doorway that he'd ridden in from Jackson and was there any news?

The man sat at the counter and Faith listened idly as Jud rattled off the latest from the telegraph. There had been a shooting in Darnley: A citizen had become riled at the impossible decisions of a politician and had fatally centered the man—and a jury had upheld the action. There had been a flash flood or two. "And I expect you heard about the shootin' at Pettis?"

"No, what was that?"

"Somebody stuck up a gent there and got thirty or forty thousand in jewels."

"Jewels!? You don't say." The newcomer was astonished. "What was anybody packing jewels for?"

"They were his wife's. He took 'em out of the bank that very day. When'd you leave Jackson?"

"Couple days ago. Did they catch this feller?"

"Nope, not yet. You want the dinner, mister?"

"Well, I come to get the Roseberry stage. How much time I got?"

Jud looked at the clock. "About twenny minutes."

Faith finished the coffee and got up to walk outside. It was a lovely crisp morning with ragged wisps of cloud sailing along the hills to the north; the skies had an emerald cast and there was no wind at all. The stagecoach had been brought to the door, wiped down, and hostlers were hooking up the lead team while the driver poked around underneath, testing and spitting.

She strolled out to the Trace and back slowly, swinging her tiny parasol, thinking about the decision she'd finally come to concerning the yard goods from Granbeck & Laurie. Perhaps she should have doubled or tripled the order, in view of the news. The Ironton paper emphasized the coming financial panic. If the editorials were right she might have trouble with reorders . . . and that kind of yard goods was a staple. She looked at the telegraph office, bit her lip and started toward it.

At that moment the driver blew his horn and someone yelled, "All aboard, folks. All aboard that's going to Roseberry."

Faith frowned and went to the stage, glancing at the boot to see that her portmanteau had been loaded. Billy Jack nodded to her, seeing the look. "All took care of, Miz McCarty."

He held the door open and helped her up the iron steps. She arranged herself in the corner seat; she'd wire

the company from Roseberry in the morning and triple
the order. The two dusty drummers piled in, followed by
George Wilson and the skinny man from the restaurant
who hurried through the door, still chewing. He tied his
roan horse on behind the coach and clambered in beside
her, nodding to all of them, tipping his hat to Faith.

When the horn blew again, the shotgun guard strolled
out, ignored everyone and settled himself. F.L. Epps
came to wave and the driver bawled, "We's on our way,
folks." He climbed over the wheel and took up the long
reins.

The skinny man lifted his hat again. "You're Miz
McCarty, ma'am?" He bowed from the waist, squinting at
her. His hair was dusty, lightly streaked with gray.

"Yes, I am," Faith said. She held on as the coach
jerked and swayed, clattering out to the Trace and turning
with a jingle and rattle of doubletrees.

"One of the Roseberry McCartys?"

Faith smiled politely.

"Well, ma'am, I heard of you-all clear to Kansas City.
You one of the daughters, are you?"

"I'm Frank McCarty's wife." She thought the two
drummers grinned opposite her but did not look at them.

"Nice to meet you," he said. "I'm Ira Brown, your ser-
vant, ma'am."

She nodded again, hoping to discourage conversation,
and gazed out the window, trying to bring her thoughts
back to business, but the two salesmen were chattering
immediately and it was impossible not to listen. One had
been at the telegraph office the moment before the stage
left the station and there was news, he said. The police at
Pettis were of the opinion, because they had followed certain tracks, that there was only one robber and he had
come toward the Trace. They had also found a red vest
discarded in the hills, and someone in Pettis recalled

seeing a slender man wearing such a vest on the very day of the murder.

The coach buzzed with chatter and speculation, the skinny man, Ira Brown, as voluble as the others. He was astonished to hear of such a huge robbery and declared the man would be caught, and asked if there was a reward. The drummer didn't know.

Ira then related a number of incidents that had happened at Jackson, saying he'd been there for almost a week because his horse had gone lame.

Faith asked him if he'd heard any talk of the railroad building west along the river and he said, "No, there wasn't a breath of anything like that in the saloons."

She returned to her thoughts and the chatter gradually died. It had been a long journey and they lolled on the cushions, getting what rest they could as the coach jolted and swayed.

The drummer's news from the telegraph had shaken Ira, though he gave no sign. He had thought the red vest well hidden and never supposed anyone would be able to track him across country. Why hadn't they tracked Bull too? At least no one on the stagecoach suspected him, thanks to his quick and ready tales of Jackson—a town he'd never seen. *That* was a chance he'd had to take; someone might have been familiar with it and asked questions, but they hadn't.

Late in the afternoon, at the last stop before they reached town, a horseman came along and halted to pass the time of day. He told them the sheriff had set up a roadblock at the edge of town and was searching everyone hoping to find the robber-murderer from Pettis.

Ira Brown, behind the coach looking his roan horse over, listened to the conversation and chewed his lip. He moved to the far side of the animal, pulled out the small leather pouch and fished in it, removing the brooch with the huge diamond. He slipped the jewel into his pocket and stared into the pouch with a sigh. Then he fastened the thong, tossed the pouch far into the weeds beside the road, and kicked a number of small rocks together into a pile as a crude marker. He was throwing away about a thousand dollars, but it was the only safe thing to do. If he was lucky he would return to this spot one day and find the rings.

He joined the others casually, clambering into the coach as Jack slammed the door. "Roseberry next stop, folks . . . we'll be there in 'nother hour or so. . . ."

The conversation soon died again and the passengers dozed in the warmth of the slanting sunlight. Ira watched the young woman covertly; her eyes were closed as she nodded and swayed with the heavy motion of the coach.

Slipping the brooch from his pocket, Ira opened the clasp and slowly leaned down as if to rub his boot. It was no trick at all to gather up the edge of her blue skirt and pin the brooch inside it where a decorative ruffle scalloped its way round the hem. Who was bold enough to search the wife of Frank McCarty?

He felt a great sense of relief as he leaned back on the leather, watching their faces, a smile gathering on his thin lips.

As the Concord stage approached town, Faith roused herself and combed her hair, repinning the braids; she straightened her clothes as best she could; Frank would be waiting. She was tired to death, but the excitement of coming home bolstered her.

The other passengers were beginning to chatter and crane their necks from the windows as the first signs of habitation appeared. All passengers were getting off at Roseberry, even the skinny Ira Brown, who'd met the stage at Epps Station. He had a coarse habit of picking his teeth with a little finger, and she thought he constantly smiled at her, or was it her imagination? He certainly did his best to engage her in conversation, but she found herself breaking it off whenever possible. She disliked him intensely and hoped it didn't show.

The horseman was right, there was a roadblock at the edge of town. Three men halted the stage, one of them Deputy Selman Wynant whom she knew very well. They were politely asked to get out and Selman smiled. "Howdy, Miz McCarty. We been expecting you-all."

"Hello, Selman." She stood aside as they searched the coach and the men, patting them down quickly, asking questions as everyone joked and chattered about which of them was the robber.

Learning that Ira Brown had met the coach at Epps Station, the deputies questioned him suspiciously and searched him and his baggage with particular care. But he had nothing at all out of line; he was carrying a bit over a hundred dollars in bills, which he said he'd earned working for wages, and Selman allowed him to put his carpetbag back on the coach.

They piled into the coach and rolled into the depot, and there was Frank, waiting with a shiny buggy.

He opened the door and she fell into his arms, laughing as he bear-hugged her with delight, saying how much he and little David had missed her. Jack pulled her portmanteau off and lugged it to the buggy, tying it on behind, then shook hands with Frank.

Politely, she said good-bye to the others and got into the buggy as Ira Brown pulled his gear off the Concord and saddled his horse. She did not notice that he followed the buggy as it rolled through the town.

Frank rattled off the latest news of home. David was

114

taking his first halting steps, falling down and laughing; he had even found the boy halfway up the stairs to the second floor once when he eluded Mrs. Steen. It was *so* good to be back! She hugged his arm and gazed at the town, waving whenever someone greeted them.

Frank asked, "You want to stop at the store?"

"No, I'll see them in the morning. All I want now is a bath and a bed."

"Good, I'll scrub you myself."

They rolled through town without stopping; the River Road narrowed as they left the buildings behind and curved westward to follow the gentle swing of the river.

He asked, "Did you get all your work done?"

She told him about the orders and her concern that she'd ordered too little; he agreed that she should wire the company. They turned in the gate and pulled up in front of the veranda. Mrs. Steen rose from a porch chair and little David toddled toward the steps, holding both her hands in his little fists.

Frank laughed, jumped down, and lifted Faith to the steps. She ran and scooped up the baby with a glad cry. Mrs. Steen said, "He's been a very good boy today, so I told him I'd let him sit with me on the porch till you came."

"Wasn't that nice?" Faith asked him, and he laughed and swung his arms jerkily as she kissed him. "Oh—how I missed you—I missed all of you."

"He's been napping," Mrs. Steen said. "Did you have a good trip?"

"Oh, just fine." She turned and opened the door as Frank came up the steps with the heavy portmanteau. With the baby in her arms she held the door aside as Frank went in, and at that moment saw Ira Brown pass by on the road, walking his horse. It was impossible to tell if he'd seen them, and she did not wave. She went inside quickly and Mrs. Steen closed the door.

115

She gave David to Mrs. Steen and ran upstairs to bathe and change clothes. Hanging the blue traveling dress in the closet alcove, she made a mental note that it should be washed and pressed as soon as she could get around to it.

Later, as she was helping with the supper things, she began to wonder why Ira Brown should be on the River Road at that time of evening. Did he know someone who lived farther on? That was unlikely, since she'd heard him say he knew no one in town.

But then Frank came downstairs and she forgot the matter entirely.

Schuyler Wood did not meet the stage, but George had not expected him to. He walked the two blocks to the livery stable and rented a buggy from Sam, slung the bag aboard and drove to Schuyler's office to find it closed up.

He drove then to the address Schuyler had given him, Mrs. Fargo's boardinghouse on the next street. Schuyler was at home, about to go into the dining room for supper. At George's arrival, he went upstairs, got a topcoat, and they went to the hotel to dine in quiet.

"Everything is finished," George said as soon as they were alone. "I have the plates in my bag."

"Excellent," Schuyler said, rubbing his hands. "I can't tell you how pleased I am, George. Do you have a proof of the drawing?"

"It's in the bag."

He took the suitcase into the hotel with him, rummaged in it and handed over the proof. It was a black-and-white print of the drawing, showing the tree-shaded town, the river front with its steamboats and sawmill, and the legend above: GLOVER, *Crossroads of the West*.

Schuyler was delighted. "It's exactly right! You've done

remarkably well, George. We'll get started on the brochures in the morning. Why don't we go together to
Cole's shop? I've got the advertising matter written out.
See what you think of it." He handed over several sheets
of foolscap.

George propped them up against a water tumbler and
studied them as he ate his soup. Schuyler had done a very
good job, even mentioning a few points he hadn't thought
of for his own copies.

"I wouldn't change a thing," he said.

Mrs. Fargo could provide him with a room, a small
squarish ex-porch that had been boarded up with two
small windows inserted. The walls were papered in two
shades of green and there was an oval rag rug on the floor
in front of the narrow bed. The room smelled of coal oil
and the bed was lumpy.

But he slept like a hibernating bear, and dreamed for a
time of raking in money across a felt table with a picture
of the nonexistent town of Glover as a centerpiece.

It never occurred to him to wonder what had happened
to T.E. Serly.

T.E. was in a rage.

He reached Ironton late in the day, stiff from the hard
coach seats, and tired to death. Recovering his carpetbag,
he went into the waiting room, expecting to see George.
There was no familiar face in the room or outside on the
platform. He sat for a time near the big-belly stove,
smoking, waiting.

But George did not show. Maybe he was sick.

Philosophically, he picked up the bag and went out to
the dark street. He had George's address and doggedly
set himself to walk the distance. It took half an hour, and
when he arrived he was more tired than ever and hungry

as a wolf. He went up the boardinghouse steps and knocked at Mrs. Pringle's door.

Emilia Pringle was a big, rangy woman with a horse-face that seemed to bear a permanently suspicious glare. She remembered him at once, but looked him over with little expression.

"I've come to see Mr. Kilburn—"

"I thought you was partners."

"Yes, we are. But—"

"Kilburn moved out a day and a half ago and he owed me ten dollars. You going to pay it?"

T.E. gaped at her. "He moved out?"

"Moved out—you say he's your partner." She opened the door wide and put hands on her ample hips. "Then you owe me, Mr. Whatever-your-name-is."

T.E. flushed red. "I don't pay his debts and he don't pay mine. You know where he went to?"

"No, I don't." She pointed at him threateningly. "I can get the law on you!"

"No you can't. I don't owe you a thing and I can prove it." He stepped back, picked up his bag and made for the front door as she yelled at him. She was all bluff. Let her go to the damned law. No judge would hold him responsible for another man's room rent. She ought to know that.

He went out to the street and turned back toward the stage depot, walking aimlessly. George had moved out! At the first corner he stopped and put the bag down, staring back at the rooming house. It didn't make sense. Where the hell was George? He glanced about as if expecting to see the big man materialize.

But he was alone.

George had been here in Ironton four days ago, because he'd answered the wire T.E. had sent from Roseberry. T.E. sat down on the bag. Why the hell had George asked him to make the long trip to stake the

118

meadow? It didn't make sense unless George was going to go through with the plan.

George was going to sell the lots without him!

It hit him with pile-driver force. George had let him do the heavy work, had made up the brochures and gone east to sell them. George would pocket all the profits and T.E. would be holding an empty bag. He began to swear.

George Kilburn was a double-crosser. T.E. sighed and shook his head, almost sick to his stomach. All that hard work gone for naught. It crossed his mind that he could board the stage and go back to the meadow and pull up all the stakes, but he put it out of his mind immediately. It would cost too much, for one thing, and now he had to hoard his meager funds.

He was eating supper in a cheap restaurant when it occurred to him that George had employed an artist in Ironton. George had showed him the sketch and talked about a printer; maybe one of them knew where George had gone.

After spending the night in the cheapest hotel in town, he started to make the rounds of printers; there were only three, and he struck gold with the second. Yes, Mr. Kilburn had contracted for a brochure, but he had picked up the copies some days ago.

"I'm his partner," T.E. said with a sudden inspiration. "I was attending to another aspect of the business and I'm just now going east to meet George, but I haven't seen the brochures."

The printer could remedy that. He took T.E. into his office, sat him down, and disappeared to return in five minutes with a handful of the printed sheets, not yet folded.

"These are extras," the man said. "Take them along with you."

T.E. thanked the printer and left as quickly as he could. In the nearest saloon he bought a beer and took a back table, spreading the sheets in front of him. He had about twenty, and he marveled at them. They were beautifully printed and showed the town of Glover in all its busy, pristine glory. Carefully folding them, T.E. smiled and began to relax. Here was his bonanza. Surely he could sell twenty lots in Ironton . . . and take the train before anyone found out! He would make himself upward of two thousand dollars!

T.E. chuckled and ordered another beer.

Chapter Eleven

With a lightness of heart he did not feel on ordinary days, Frank McCarty dressed in jeans, blue shirt, and an old canvas jacket. He buckled his revolver about slim hips, took up his Winchester and a sack of shells, and went downstairs to the kitchen.

It was exhilarating to be able to get off by himself for a day; it was like the times when he went on cattle drives with his father or Gus Kramer—or led them himself when his apprenticeship had been served.

At the office things were well regulated also, so much so that he often had little to do—too little to do. Ken Larkin had departmentalized the widespread operations of the McCarty enterprises so that it was possible to get a quick overall picture of the various businesses each morning. He was called upon to make a number of decisions that no one else could make, but he always had time to discuss and consider them.

Little David was rolling on his back on a buffalo robe placed on the dining room floor so he could be watched from the kitchen. Frank stood the rifle by the door and stooped to tickle the gurgling baby's stomach.

"Don't get him excited, Frank," Mrs. Steen said, "or he'll be crawling all over the house and I'll never get anything done."

121

Faith came to the door. "Your breakfast is ready, dear."

He got up with a last pat, and sat down at the kitchen table. Faith was ready to go to the store, wearing a green-and-white dress that had a small, pert bustle and was flowered in front. He had long ago given up trying to sort out her clothes; it seemed to him she wore something different every day, but of course she had an entire store inventory to choose from. As he ate, Faith discussed the evening's supper with Mrs. Steen, making notes of things she would bring home later in the afternoon. Faith had no fixed schedule, but usually left for the store an hour after he went to the office.

She had propped a *Harper's Weekly* up in front of him and he read several columns: Susan B. Anthony had been fined again for her extraordinary utterances on behalf of women, and there was an item about President Grant. Thomas Nast had drawn a number of cartoons on the administration. For some reason Nast was using an elephant as a symbol of the Republican party, a rather frisky and skittish animal in the drawings.

There was talk of running Rutherford Hayes against a man named Tilden in the next elections, and Russia was expanding into China.

Finished with breakfast, Frank took the rifle and sack of shells, and Faith walked with him to the yard and looked at the sky. There were clouds overhead and it smelled a little like rain. He rather hoped it would drizzle a bit to clear the air. Kissing her, he strode to the stable and threw a saddle on the bay, remembering to roll up a poncho and tie it behind the cantle.

Riding out, he waved to Faith on the back porch and rode west on the River Road; the bay was frisky and wanted to run, and he gave the animal its head.

He had mentioned to Ken Larkin the afternoon before that he'd take most of the day off. Sometimes the office stifled him so he had to escape, get his horse from the livery and ride across the river, or halfway to Webber's Station, just to get the kinks out.

He met no one and, past the last house on the road, turned north and rode across the brown, undulating prairie, filling his lungs with clean, fresh air. It was a day with almost no wind. The slopes were velvety, myriad shades of tan and brown, yellow as honey where the sun filtered through, and deep in the shadows. He came upon a barren flat area where the bay's hoofs caused a crackling and snapping as they cut through the baked and curling crust of eroded earth.

Cloud shadows moved slowly along, dappling the land, and birds scattered at his approach, lifting in unison before him then swooping down out of sight. Larkin had shown him the latest copy of the new paper, the *Advocate*. It was being printed, Larkin said, in a converted stable across the river by a newcomer to Roseberry, Cole Stedman, who described himself as a "missionary in a land of heathen."

Larkin said it was fairly certain that Stedman was being backed by Schuyler Wood. Frank had asked Larkin to look more closely into Wood's background.

The *Advocate*, from the first edition, had called for free elections to the town council, attacking McCarty interests, implying that while McCarty might have been good for the territory and town of Roseberry once, he no longer was. It was time to break the shackles, Stedman wrote, and introduce new blood. New blood like Schuyler Wood.

Frank reined in on a rise of ground and stretched in the saddle, gazing about. It was the democratic thing to hold elections, but it wasn't easy to give up what the McCartys had always had—a major say in the town's future. There had been a time, maybe ten years ago, when he'd thought his father was a tyrant, running the town and the ranch to suit himself. He'd even taken the law into his own hands

123

when he thought it necessary. Frank recalled the stories of the hanging of one of the Redding boys, who'd been caught red-handed stealing JM cattle.

That kind of thing couldn't happen now, with a county sheriff on the job. But J.M. had lived through a period when to be weak was to falter and die. To hesitate could be fatal. J.M. never hesitated, but his son was bent by the restraints of civilization and was thereby forced into uncomfortable and annoying postures by the law of the land. In his day, J.M. would have confronted Schuyler Wood, or any other opponent, and had it out on the spot. One of them would walk away and the other would be dead.

Frank McCarty could allow himself no such luxury.

Frank nudged the bay horse and went on slowly. There were no cattle in this part of the range because Gus Kramer had ordered them driven east a month or more ago for the fall roundup. They would probably be fencing this range before next summer, much as he hated the idea. The JM brand had not been plagued with rustling, but there was always a little cattle stealing, a cow here and one or two there, probably taken by smallholders who could see no other way of making it through the winter.

Frank turned a blind eye to the thefts, as a form of charity. What else could he do? A butchered cow could be hung in the woods somewhere, while snow was on the ground, and it was damned hard to prove who had put it there. It would go against him and the McCarty name if he raised a stink about it and fined or jailed some poor man who wanted only to feed hungry mouths.

Fencing the range would make it a wee bit harder to steal beef, and it would of course end all doubts about ownership, if a jury should inquire. When a man cut a fence to steal a cow, that proved intent.

But thoughts of stolen beef did not hold Frank's attention. He went on, thinking about Cole Stedman and Schuyler Wood. Schuyler was a dapper and handsome man with gray mustachios and sideburns and a mane of silver hair which always looked carefully brushed. He had shown up in Roseberry the year before, establishing himself as a lawyer, and had worked up a considerable practice settling land claims.

It was apparent that Wood wanted to be elected to the council, wanted to be on the council no matter how it came about. He was probably one of those who desired power more than anything else, an ambitious man who obviously saw himself as a leading citizen of the community, no matter that he was a newcomer.

How long could he oppose the idea of elections? Frank squinted into the distance and pulled his hat brim down. Another year, maybe; with luck, two, but unless something happened to distract the opposition, such a clamor would be raised that it would be impossible not to listen and submit. The council as it now existed comprised older citizens of Roseberry, except for Noah, and Noah was unpredictable. He might side with any plausible argument, even if he was sorry later.

Stedman's *Advocate* was largely a throwaway sheet because it was getting started, and it probably reached only a third of the people in town. But it would grow. The more it attacked the McCartys and presented different ideas, no matter how unsound, people would read it.

Schuyler was a man who would not settle for a pittance. Schuyler wanted all or nothing, and would be an enemy to be reckoned with. With any luck, Schuyler might run the town of Roseberry in the next few years, and Frank knew he distrusted the man and his motives.

In all conscience, he could not let it happen. How to go about preventing it was another matter.

When he came to a place where a dry arroyo opened out to a wash with shallow banks, he got down. He tied the bay off to one side and looked at the sky; the misty clouds were curdling slowly but it felt a little less like rain. He paced off two rods and set up a line of small round stones along the lip of a bank.

He wrapped the holster thong around his leg and tied it, then eased the pistol and adjusted the belt so that the wooden grip was just above his wrist. For several minutes he practiced getting the gun out of the leather, pointing with one finger along the barrel. This was something he practiced daily, for the very good reason that getting his weapon into action quickly and smoothly had saved his life more than once. His father had shown him how to shoot as a boy, and he had practiced then, with a gun much too heavy and clumsy for him. As the years went by, the pistol became easier and easier to handle till, at his eighteenth year, he could handle it as no one else in his father's employ.

Faith had asked him once why he went armed, since most of the men with whom he dealt did not. He had seen a number of gunfights and knew that sometimes death struck out of nowhere with sidewinder speed. He had not told her the best reason, to his mind: that he was a McCarty and there were men who would shoot him down, armed or not.

Satisfied with the smoothness of his draw, he drew and fired at the rocks, loading and reloading, occasionally replacing the line of stones. He fired off half the shells in the sack, carefully counting hits and near-misses, pleased by the high percentage, though it was a long distance for quick revolver work.

When he halved the distance, he hit the rocks nearly every time, chipping them, sending them spinning off or flipping them over. His father had taught that speed was not the most important essential. In a gunfight most men became excited, J.M. said. The man who aimed deliberately and stayed cool was the one who came out undamaged, barring extraordinary luck.

Frank had first striven for accuracy and then, when that was established, gradually improved his speed. By the time he was twenty a good number of men had been astonished at how fast he could produce a Colt and how accurately he could fire it. Damn few were any better, they declared. A well known gunman named Peaker had ridden into Roseberry one day and tangled with him and been defeated. The battle had been written up in a dozen gazettes and newspapers and since the event, Frank had practiced religiously. There was no way to tell when some hopeful who wanted a reputation would challenge him.

He often wondered if Faith knew that was possible.

In an hour he put the pistol away and concentrated on the Winchester, setting up rocks two hundred yards distant, then halving that. After the revolver, shooting with the rifle seemed child's play. He fired up the ammunition in the sack, gathered up all the brass, and headed back with the clouds beginning to dissolve, allowing a pink sun to peep through.

Instead of returning the way he had come, he went across the prairie eastward, riding along the rising slopes of the hills to the north of town. He glanced at each of the canyons as he passed, wondering in which of them J.M. had hanged the Redding boy. Gus Kramer and Quincy had been with J.M. that day, and both of them said later that Redding had been caught before and warned, so there was nothing to do but string him up.

Gus had said, with grim humor, "It was the only way to teach him a lesson."

Entering the town near Second Street, he walked the bay along the shaded side street to the corner and went around to the livery stable. He gave the bay horse to Sam and walked to the bank building, spurs jingling. A sidewalk auctioneer had gathered a crowd in front of the barber shop, shouting his wares. He had pans and buckets and other household items. "This here's Mormon whiskey, gents. Who'll give me a dollar—do I hear a dollar?"

Frank went up the steps to the bank, turning as a column of dusty cavalry came along the street, led by a lieutenant and a guidon. The men around the auctioneer yelled to the troopers who looked as if they'd come a long way. It had been a time since he'd seen troops in Roseberry.

That afternoon he received another note from Horace Gromley asking for a meeting, and Frank sent a reply agreeing. It felt like rain when he rode to the house that night.

Gromley opened the door as before, and ushered him to the same room. If Gromley was staying with friends, they were considerate enough to allow him privacy when he had a business meeting.

He had forwarded a résumé of their talk to Ironton, Gromley said, and had received a reply that his superiors were still considering the matter. If Frank had anything to add, he would be pleased to hear it and forward it.

"Would it do any good?" Frank said bluntly. He was slightly annoyed that Gromley had not written that statement in his note and saved him a long ride. Gromley was a bland sort, and the remark slid off like winter snow from a roof. He seemed surprised at Frank's manner.

"I assure you, Mr. McCarty, that we do have a vital interest in this matter. You must recognize that it's an undertaking to lay rails that distance." Gromley sipped the drink like a man tasting poison. "I would be less than candid with you if I did not admit that there are those in power who do not favor the spur line. They must be convinced."

"What's your opinion, Mr. Gromley?"

"Of what, the line or the likelihood of its being built?"

Frank stated it as clearly as he could. "Will a line be built to Roseberry?"

Gromley looked into his glass. "In my opinion—" He waved his hand. "I have no say in the matter, mind. In my opinion . . . no."

Frank leaned back regarding the other narrowly. "You don't think so?"

Gromley shrugged. "I repeat, I have no say in the matter. I must report and abide by the decisions that come down to me. Please don't quote me. It is probably impertinent or foolish, or both, for me to venture an opinion, since the decision could go the other way."

Frank shook his head, got up and found his hat. "This entire thing has been a farce, Mr. Gromley. Good night." He opened the door and walked out, not hearing Gromley's reply.

Chapter Twelve

Ira Jalder found lodgings at Erma Taber's boardinghouse a block away from the main street. The room was small and square with a half bed, one chair, and a rickety chest of drawers, atop which sat a basin and a pitcher. The room was much cheaper than the hotel, and clean enough.

Mrs. Taber, a widow, rented out five rooms and was adamant on only one thing: her boarders must not smoke. Ira lifted the window and blew the smoke out whenever he had a cigar in the room. She would sniff at him suspiciously, but he assured her in his best manner that he never broke her rules; she allowed him to smoke downstairs on the veranda.

He quickly discovered that the McCarty family in Roseberry had two houses; the old man, they called him J.M. for the most part, lived a short distance north from the center of town in a large, imposing house on a slight rise, surrounded by trees. Frank McCarty and his wife, Faith, lived in the big house on the River Road. It was Faith he was interested in, and the house he had followed her to was the one he had to get inside. He told himself he had to do it promptly because she was sure to discover the brooch when she washed the blue skirt.

Frank McCarty went to his office each morning, and

often left it during the day, occasionally going home, frequently making trips about the town or across the river. Watching him, Ira sensed that he was a restless young man, and Ira pressed his lips together hard. McCarty had a dangerous look to him. They told him in the saloons that young Frank was the best man with a pistol that anyone had seen. None of the information made Ira sleep easier.

But he had to get into the house. The blue skirt was probably hanging in Faith's closet or lying in a basket somewhere. He was sure that if the brooch had been discovered, there would have been a public announcement. Ledwidge's wife's initials were on the brooch, after all.

He had never been a cat burglar, although he had known several. Getting into a house is easy, one had told him, and the bedroom is always the best place to look for quick swag.

He made several trips a day past the McCarty house, just to get the feel of it. He found several vantage points where he could sit his horse and look at the house. Which room did the McCartys sleep in? It might be fatal to get into the house, then be trapped in the wrong room.

When he put his horse away in Sam's Livery that evening, he noticed the carpenter shop next door. There was a light inside and a lean, whipcord man was sawing a board very carefully. Ira went inside and stood watching till the man finished, examined the sawed piece and nodded to him.

"Makin' a table," he said. "Howdy."

"Howdy," Ira said pleasantly. "You the only carpenter in town?"

"I'm a cabinetmaker," the man said. "You need a chicken pen, you go to the Larson boys." He pointed vaguely east. "One of 'em's a wood-butcher and t'other one's the town drunk."

"I was thinking more of a house," Ira said, patting his

132

tie. "I understand you can make them kind of plans." He had no idea of that at all, but there were several plans that looked like houses hanging on a nail on the far wall.

The man put the saw away and fiddled with the length of wood. "I c'n plan a house, yes. You going to build one?"

"I like this town," Ira nodded, brushed off a sawhorse and sat down gingerly. "I might just do that." He got up again and put out his hand, "I'm Ira Brown."

The other took it in a steely grip. "Glad t'meet you Mr. Brown. I'm Mort Cleary. What kind of house you thinking about?"

Ira sighed and a sad smile came to his face. "Big enough for me'n the wife and three children . . . and my mother-in-law. Probably two stories. There's one or two houses that big a couple of streets over."

"Yes there is. Cost you six or eight hunnerd dollars for that kind of a buildin', though."

"That much?" Ira seemed to consider. Then he brightened. "That McCarty house was pointed out to me a day're two ago, the one out on the River Road—"

Cleary chuckled. "Hell, cost you fifteen hunnerd for that. I know because I worked on it. That's the second house young Frank built. The first one burned down a few years ago—feller burnt them out."

"Is that right!" Ira was astonished. "Who'd do a thing like that?"

"Some sumbitch. Frank gunned for him, but he got taken by the diphtheria. We had us a epidemic through here . . ."

"I swear!"

"But Frank, he built the house back just the way it was, almost." Cleary walked to a cluttered bench and riffled through a sheaf of yellowed papers held to the wall by a finish nail. He selected one and smoothed it out.

"This here's the plan. Four bedrooms upstairs, just about like you'd need."

Ira stared at the plan and smiled. It was exactly what he needed! The master or large bedchamber was in the rear on the west side. That must be the one the McCartys used. "Yes," he said softly, staring at the precisely-drawn lines. "Yes, it is."

"What kind business you in, Mr. Brown?"

"I'm a—I'm in the wholesale trade. We handle farm tools and the like." Ira put the plan down reluctantly. "That's a pretty expensive house."

"Yes, it is. What I quoted you, fifteen hunnerd, that's just for the house, framin' it and putting on the roof. Then there's panels and wallpaper and glass and all the rest of it. Frank must have five thousand dollars there."

Ira shook his head. He chatted a moment longer, then got out with an excuse. Though he left the shop apparently saddened by the realization of high costs, he was elated inside. He had not expected that kind of luck! Of course it made sense when he thought of it, that the best carpenter in town might keep the plans of the most elegant house, but he had lucked into it. That was a good sign, a damned good sign that his luck was holding.

He stood on the dark street and fished for a cheroot. He lit it and walked slowly west along the boards. Why not push his luck? Why not do it tonight? It had to be sometime. He stopped and puffed the cigar, staring at the street. It might be a good idea to do it while the family was eating supper. He glanced around and discovered he was in front of the McCarty office building. A gold leaf sign said: *McCarty Offices Upstairs*. Ira stepped back and looked at the second floor. It was dark.

He turned then and walked rapidly back to the livery and saddled his horse again, asking Sam the time. It was just a bit after five. He rode around the block to the boardinghouse, went upstairs and got his pistol from the

134

carpetbag. It was loaded. He slipped it into his pocket and went back downstairs.

There were a dozen people on the streets, and lights were beginning to come on here and there. A few dogs barked as he rode along the side street and turned south to the River Road at the end of town. He wasn't wearing the right clothes for a burglar, his best pair of pants, a good blue coat and leather shoes, but there was no time to change. He passed a well-lighted house and caught a glimpse of the family sitting down at a table. It made him nudge the horse into a lope.

He arrived in front of the McCarty house at dusk; it was not yet full dark and he could easily see his way along the high wire fence that surrounded the house. The front gate was open and the yard in front of the house shadowy. He rode around to the west side and tied the horse to the fence. Standing on the saddle, he easily grasped a stout wooden upright and swung himself over. He fell onto hard ground, slapping the bottoms of his feet but keeping his balance. It wouldn't be that easy going back.

In a moment he ran to the house, his eyes on the upstairs windows. They were all dark. There was a wooden trellis used for training vines upward that leaned against the house between the windows. Ira paused and considered it. It was almost a ladder, and he tested it with his weight. It creaked alarmingly, but held. The top reached almost to the upstairs windows; he lifted it carefully and half dragged it to the closest window of the large bed-chamber and leaned it against the house. If he needed to get down in a hurry, it would suffice.

Then he went round to the back of the house. There were lights in the kitchen and someone talking, though he could distinguish no words. He examined the yard, seeing no one. The stable was a dark blur, and he thought he heard the muffled sounds of horses. He had feared a dog

135

or two, but none was in evidence. He went back to the front of the house and up onto the wide veranda that ran around two sides.

The front door was unlocked.

Ira bit his lip, turned the knob and pushed it, listening with his head cocked. There were voices from the dining room, and when he put his head round the door he could see the lantern light, but the parlor was dark. He eased inside and closed the door. The voices were louder and he heard the clatter of knives and forks and crockery; he was exactly on time. The McCartys were at supper.

Gaining confidence, he slipped across the parlor, the house plan before his mind's eye. The stairs were to his left and he went up them pressing against the wall, as silently as he could. Halfway up he froze. Someone came into the parlor with a candle lamp. It was a thin woman in a gray-and-white maid's costume; she fiddled with something on a sideboard, muttered something to herself, and went back to the dining room.

Ira let his breath out and moved rapidly up to the landing. With luck he could get the brooch and retreat the same way he'd come in.

In another moment he was in the large bedchamber, closed the door and struck a match. The sulphur fizzed and exploded into light as he wrinkled his nose. There was a wide closet behind a dark drape. He yanked it back and stared at the clothes. Women's clothes, more than he'd ever seen outside a store! The match burned out.

He lit another and began to push through the clothes hanging on the pegs. The match burned out, then another and another. He found a candle near the bed, lit it, and continued the search. The damned skirt was not hanging on any of the pegs. It was nowhere in the room.

Shielding the candle, he catfooted out and into the next room. There was a neatly made bed, but nothing in the closet alcove. He went into the next room and half-closed the door. By the measly light he was surprised at the disorder. There were clothes here and there in piles, as if someone had been separating them—Ira smiled. Of course! Preparing to launder them!

He pawed through the piles and found the blue skirt quickly. Frantically he slapped it, then relaxed. The brooch was still there.

As he began to unpin it, he heard someone come up the stairs.

Ira blew out the candle. He slipped the brooch into his pocket and went to the open door. Faith McCarty was on the stairs. She was humming to herself, holding a small brass lantern. Without a glance in his direction she went into the large bedchamber and closed the door.

Ira opened the door wider and looked at the stairs. If the supper was over, should he attempt it? He might run directly into Frank McCarty. And someone had told him that young Frank always went armed.

As he hesitated, Faith opened the door and hurried out to the staircase. "Frank—" she called, "Frank!" She started down the steps.

Ira eased the door shut, his heart thumping. She had seen something—the closet drape had been pulled open. He ran to the window, opened it and looked down. He was directly over the back porch and the shed-like roof was only a half-dozen feet below. If he had to, he could drop onto it and jump to the ground.

He went back to the door, listening. Faith was saying that she smelled matches when she went upstairs, and the drape had been pulled back. Frank's voice said he'd look around. "You stay down here."

Ira hesitated no longer. He ran to the window, slid outside, and hung by his hands. When he let go it was only an instant till his feet hit. His ankle turned and he fell heavily to the steeply slanting roof and tumbled off onto the ground.

It almost knocked him silly.

He got up, grabbed his felt hat off the ground and limped toward the fence. His ankle shot pains up the leg, but he could walk. There were lights on in the upstairs bedchamber. Ira grabbed the fence and began to climb. It hadn't been so bad at that. He had the brooch, that was the main thing, and he was away free.

Then suddenly someone came out the back door of the house. Ira threw his leg over the fence, boosted himself by the wooden upright, and pushed out. As he dropped, someone fired at him.

He fell heavily into deep grass, hearing the bullet whack into the upright beside him. The horse whinnied and pulled at the reins. Getting to his feet, Ira picked frantically at the loose knot, freed the horse as another shot came howling over his head, then another that clipped the branch of a tree only a foot away. In another second McCarty would hit him or the horse! Thank God for the darkness!

Running with the horse, he grasped the horn, jumped, and pulled himself up. The horse pounded out to the River Road and two more shots came after him. Then someone yelled, but he was on the road now, digging his heels into the horse's side.

Galloping west, he met no one at all. The night was dark, with murky clouds hanging overhead and mists rising from the river to his left. He was going to be chased in another moment, and by a man who knew every inch of the countryside. Somehow he had to lose McCarty!

Off to his right were fields, a few scattered houses, and trees. There was no way to swim the river before McCarty would be on him, and if caught in midstream he'd be a fine target. McCarty was sure to have a rifle.

He turned the horse off the road to the right and pounded fifty yards to the shelter of a grove of pines, reining in to listen. A pursuing horse was galloping after him! Ira sat perfectly still, listening to the drumming of hoofs; McCarty was coming too fast to see his tracks turn off the road. He had a vague glimpse of a horse and rider running full tilt to the west. In another few moments the sound of the hoofbeats faded out. Ira took a deep breath, feeling the blood pounding in his throat. That had been very close.

He moved toward the north at a walk, letting the horse pick his way across the rutted field.

Chapter Thirteen

Ira Jalder reined in and got down in the midst of a clump of dark trees, cocking his head to listen. He was alone; satisfied, he hooked the stirrup on the saddlehorn and absently tested the cinch. He leaned against the animal, looking back toward the McCarty house. That had been a near thing. It made a man's skin crawl to be shot at that way.

But now he could get out. In the morning he'd take the stage for Ironton and head east. Now that he had the brooch. His hand patted the coat pocket to reassure himself—and he stiffened.

There was no brooch in the pocket!

Frantically he searched himself, looking through every pocket, but with a growing hopelessness. Vividly he recalled putting the brooch in the coat pocket, but it was not there now. Ira hung against the roan, swearing a blue streak, bitter at himself. Now he had to go back. He had lost the goddamned brooch somewhere along the way, when he fell from the upstairs window, or when he scrambled over the fence as McCarty shot at him.

Maybe it was in the weeds on the outside of the fence.

Pulling himself onto the horse, he turned the animal, heading back toward the road—and halted. Several horsemen were tearing along the road, hoofbeats hammering the still night. He swore again under his breath. He'd caused a furor all right, and there would not be a chance of returning to the house till it calmed down. Everyone would be up and moving about.

But no one had seen him. He could be certain that even McCarty had seen no more than a blur in the night, else he'd have aimed better. The roan horse had probably been nearly invisible.

He had lost the brooch, but he could also be damned sure no one had found it, because no one knew what he'd gone into the house for. They'd think they had been visited by a common burglar hoping to grab something of value.

It relieved him somewhat to rationalize. The brooch might lie under a pile of dry leaves or in the tall grass and never be found at all, unless one knew exactly where to look. But if it was in the open yard under the window— Ira swore again.

He couldn't go back along the River Road, so he went east across the prairie, letting the horse pick its way. Once he heard a distant shot and wondered what someone was aiming at. The stars were out in splendor, dulled somewhat by drifting mists that crept overhead from the south. Ira pulled his coat closer about him and slouched in the saddle. He could not take the roan horse back to Sam's livery either. Old Sam was likely to be a garrulous type, and would tell anyone who asked that Ira had come for his horse about dusk and had returned him several hours later.

That someone might be the sheriff, who would ask questions with difficult answers. Where would he say he'd been? No, it would be better not to take the horse back at all until tomorrow.

But he had to say he'd been somewhere, because, as a stranger in town, someone was sure to suspect him. There was the matter of his conversation with the cabinetmaker,

142

too. If the sheriff learned that he'd talked about the McCarty house and looked at a floor plan of it the very night an intruder was found there, it might go hard with him. His best hope on that score was that maybe the cabinetmaker would not consider it suspicious, might never give it a thought. "Why should he?" Ira said aloud to the horse's ears.

When he reached a point where he could see the dim, glimmering lights of the town, he turned toward the river again. He wound his way around houses, along fences, barked at by a dozen dogs, and finally came out a cross street that led him to the main drag. There was no particular bustle in the town, but there were lights on in the sheriff's office. He considered getting down at one of the saloons, halted the roan in contemplation of it, picking his teeth with a little finger, then thought of the line. Was there a line in Roseberry? He had never asked anyone, but how difficult could it be to find? He nudged the horse and went on.

If he could shack up in a brothel for the night, that would be an ideal cover. The law would never question him about it. Ira grinned, pushing the horse into a trot.

He found the red lights glowing in front of several houses about a half-mile from the center of town, not far past the freight and stage yard. There were a half-dozen horses standing three-legged at the hitchrack, and tinkly piano music was coming from inside. Ira got down in front of one of the houses and pushed the door open. He was in a smallish room, filled with smoke and the heady smells of perfume, coal oil, and spilled beer. At the far wall was a bar with three men slouched over it talking; to his left was the piano with a professor jabbing at a tune, a slender bald-headed man with a pasty face, and to his right a woman in a red frilled dress was bearing down upon him. The walls were pink, the windows covered with brown drapes, and the carpet was Turkey red.

143

"Hello, dearie," the woman said, "I haven't seen you b'fore."

"I just got in town." Ira smiled at her. "I'm Ira Brown. One of the boys at the saloon on Front Street told me you were here."

"Which boy, dearie?" She took his arm and led him toward the bar. She was pretty, in a full-blown way, a shapely woman with a very pale skin and large black-rimmed eyes.

"I didn't ask 'is name," Ira said. "What do I call you?"

"Gertie," she said. "You're in Gert's place, dearie, the best goddamn house in Roseberry."

"Well, can I buy you a drink, Gertie?" He put his foot on the rail. "How many girls you got?"

"Five, sweetie. The best girls in—" She laughed. "Gimme a beer, Al."

Ira turned, "Make it two." He laid a dollar on the bar. "I just came from Jackson," he said. "Nobody hiring. What kind of town is this?"

Gert came close, giving him a lungful of perfume. "It's a McCarty town, honey. McCarty owns half of it, but there's some folks talking about taking it away from him. What do you do for a living?"

The barman slid the steins in front of them and Ira sipped his. "I'm a salesman, but I been about ever'thing. You got a nice redhead for me?"

"Hell yes, honey. Hattie is a redhead. You'll see her in a minute—she's busy right now."

"Hattie, huh?"

"Loveliest gal in the territory. You'll love Hattie. You stay right here, honey. I'll go see if she's ready."

Ira nodded and watched the woman disappear into a hall. He finished the beer. Al had gone to the end of the bar and was chatting with two others. He leaned against the bar feeling very relaxed; this was the perfect place for him at the moment. Who would look for the McCarty burglar in a whorehouse? He wandered over and stood behind the professor, watching the man's nimble fingers dance over the yellow keys. The tune sounded familiar, but he couldn't put words to it.

Gert said, "Ira—"

He looked up. She was parading three girls for his inspection. One of the men at the bar gave a low whistle and several laughed. Ira paid them no attention. He went across the room, staring at the girls; one was a brunette with a thick waist and pretty face, the other two were blondes, one slender as a reed and one short and very curved. They all wore filmy wraps that covered but did not conceal, and all were pink and round in the proper places.

"Hattie's still busy," Gert said, winking at him. "This's Daisy and Sophie," she said, pointing out the blondes, "and this little beauty is Fay. Isn't she sweet?"

"She sure is," Ira agreed. "I'll take Daisy."

Daisy gave him a wan smile and they all turned away immediately. Gert pushed him toward Daisy, who took his hand and led him into a small room that contained nothing but a stubby bureau, a washstand, and a bed. She closed the door.

"How much you givin' me, honey?"

"How much for an hour?"

"Two dollars."

"How much for all night?"

The girl's brows went up. She hesitated, then shrugged. "I'll hafta ask Gert."

"All right, ask her."

Daisy went out and was back in a moment. "Twenty dollars," she said.

"Twenty! I'll give you fifteen."

Daisy shrugged and went out again. She was back in a slightly longer time. "All right, Gert says for this one time. But no rough stuff." She put out her hand.

Ira counted out the money; she took it, went out once more, and came back to lock the door behind her. She doffed the filmy wrap in a second and stood naked in front of him.

He sat on the bed and removed his boots, looking at her. She was not as young as he'd thought, a bit more dumpy, with pendulous breasts and short legs. Maybe he should have picked Sophie. Well, what the hell, all he really wanted was a place to stay. He asked, "Where you from?"

"Upper New York State." She sat on the bed beside him. "You got the makin's?"

"No, got a cheroot though. You wanna smoke?"

"Sure." She grinned for the first time and indicated the door. "Gert don't like us to smoke, 'specially out front. It ain't ladylike."

He gave her the cheroot and a match. "You a lady, honey?"

"Hell no," she said, still grinning. She lit the cigar and puffed with obvious satisfaction.

He let her finish the cigar before he laid her on the bed. Then they talked for a time, and he was surprised that she didn't tell him the usual sob story that whores were famous for, about needing money to send home. He sent her out to the bar for two bottles of beer and they talked some more. She was a little surprised when he pulled the blanket up about him, curled his arm about her, and went to sleep.

No one had ever done that before.

Frank McCarty galloped the horse along the road in the darkness, aware as soon as he reached the bridge at the Bend that he had lost his quarry. The man had turned

146

off somewhere, undoubtedly to the right, and was probably now pounding north as fast as he could go.

He went back, walking the bay horse, swearing to himself, even though there was nothing else he could have done. He met Selman and two others a mile from his house and reined in while they held a powwow. No, he hadn't got a look at the burglar or the man's horse; no, he had no idea what the intruder was after, except perhaps money.

"I don't think I hit him," Frank said. "I didn't slow him up none."

Selman said, "We'll get after him soon's it's light then, Frank. We'd just trample the prints this way."

They went back, parting at the gate. Inside the house, Faith had made a careful examination of the bedroom. "There's nothing at all missing," she said. "Someone's been looking at my clothes, because three dresses were pulled off the pegs and fell on the floor."

Frank was astonished. "Why would a man break in and paw through your clothes?"

"I can't imagine." Faith led him to the smaller bedchamber where she'd been sorting clothes for the weekly wash. "He ran through here to get out the window when you came upstairs. Some of these clothes have been moved too, but maybe he did it when he ran through in the dark."

"And nothing at all is missing—none of your jewelry—nothing?"

"Not a thing. He moved the candle and lit it. I found it here on the floor, but that's all."

"I'll be damned." Frank scratched his head, perplexed. It didn't make sense. Faith had a few pieces of valuable jewelry, but they were untouched in a drawer by the bed. What in the world had the man come after? That the intruder was a man he did not doubt; a very lithe and agile man.

Karl Welch was equally surprised, and could offer no ideas why the man had come into the house. "Unless he had the wrong house . . ."

"Unlikely," Frank said. "It's the only two-story house on the River Road. Maybe he was going to shoot one of us."

"Then why light out as soon as he heard you on the stairs?"

Frank shrugged. "That's right. He wasn't after Faith because she went upstairs and back down. Then he ran when I went up. He wasn't after Mrs. Steen because she stays downstairs. It's a damned mystery."

The front door had been unlocked, but would be carefully locked in the future. Frank shot the bolt as Karl left, positive they were locking the barn after the horse was stolen. They would probably never find out what the intruder had been after.

In the morning they discovered that only one fence wire was broken, and Billy Quinn, the stable boy, repaired it. Frank rode out with Selman and examined the edges of the road. It took them only a half hour to find the place where the unknown rider had gone north.

Selman was a good tracker and followed the trail with ease, losing it only twice on hard ground. It led them a long looping ride across the prairie and back into town. They lost it for good on the first cross street.

"He's someone who lives right here in Roseberry," Selman said, pushing his hat back and squinting at the ground. "Or he's a stranger passin' through."

"A stranger?"

Young Selman grinned, "You make any enemies lately, Frank?"

"Hell no, not that I know of. How would a stranger know how to get into my house?"

"That's a question. But let me ask around. I might scare up something."

"All right." And they left it at that. Frank could think of nothing further to do. Maybe the man was wrong in the head. But whoever he was, he probably wouldn't be back.

Chapter Fourteen

Horace Gromley packed up and left Roseberry the day after his last talk with McCarty. He had done his bit for Schuyler, and had had as good a continuing spree as he'd ever enjoyed in Chicago or New York. Gertie's girls were a wild lot. There had been no witnesses to see or hear him with McCarty and he could be accused of nothing.

Schuyler Wood saw him off with considerable satisfaction. In his office, Schuyler prepared two letters, one to Noah Applegate at the *Courier,* and one to Preacher Rossiter. The letters were mostly the same, stating simple facts and deploring them. Frank McCarty, Roseberry's leading citizen, had been detected in a less than savory assignation with a woman of the streets. It could be proved that on at least two occasions, he had visited a house owned by Gertie de Vere at night.

What other interpretation could there be?

Schuyler signed the letters, describing himself as a candidate for office, a man vitally interested in seeing that good moral government was substituted for the slipshod, morally bankrupt town council.

He wrote out another account for the *Advocate,* explaining that an unnamed honest citizen had noticed McCarty going to the house and, being curious, had turned the information over to the newspaper. Schuyler

Wood had become interested, had investigated, and had discovered to his horror that the house was owned by Gert, a notorious scarlet woman who also operated a brothel on the line.

When questioned, said Schuyler, Gert denied any knowledge of the affair, but stated that her house was often used as a secret rendezvous by her girls and their clients.

Three hundred fifty copies of the *Advocate* were published and distributed free by Cole Stedman, who was astonished by the sudden demand for more. Another edition of five hundred copies was immediately put on sale at one dime each, and sold out within the hour.

A third edition was on the press before noon.

The *Advocate* scooped the town—and shocked it.

Noah Applegate hurried to Frank's office with the letter in his hand, arriving as Luke Dobbs showed up with a copy of the *Advocate*.

Noah glanced at the rival paper as he stood on the stairs, then thrust it back to Luke and ran into Frank's office. "We've got him this time, Frank! That son of a bitch Schuyler Wood has finally gone too far!" He put the letter into Frank's hands.

Luke unfolded the newspaper and laid it in front of Frank.

Frank nodded to them and read the letter carefully. It was instantly apparent to him what had happened. Schuyler had somehow conspired with Gromley to carry this off. He looked at the *Advocate* and shook his head in disgust.

"It's a frame-up," he said.

Noah blinked at him, the pipe forgotten. "What you mean, Frank? He's lying, isn't he?"

"Only partly. He's using the house to smear me—the reputation of the house."

152

"You mean you *were* there!?" Noah was astonished.

Frank nodded and Luke chuckled, standing at the window, hands in his pockets. "Who'd you meet there, Frank?"

"A railroad man, Horace Gromley. We talked about the spur line."

Noah sat down abruptly, staring at Frank. "You didn't know whose house it was?"

"Of course not," Luke said. "How's he goin' to know that?"

Noah was silent, chewing the stem of the pipe.

Frank told them the entire story, starting with Gromley's letter, which he still had in his files. Noah grabbed at the letter, read it and sighed. "Schuyler'll say you made this up." He waved the letter. "Anyone could get a copy of the T&T letterhead and write this note on it."

"I suppose they could."

"Be a damn long trip, though," Luke said. "A man'd have to go to Ironton for it." He pulled at his chin. "Wonder where this Horace Gromley is right now."

"He said he was on vacation." Frank lit a cheroot and looked at Noah. "I deny all the allegations and innuendos. I met Mr. Gromley at that house, not knowing who owned it, and we discussed railroad business. Specifically, bringing the railroad to Roseberry." He shrugged. "But I'm afraid you won't be able to reach Gromley for confirmation."

"We ought to run them goddamn girls outa town," Luke growled.

"All right," Noah said with a sign of resignation. "I'll print it that way, but there's some folks who'd rather hear the other story and believe it too."

"Ever'body likes gossip," Luke said cheerfully.

Schuyler was delighted with the response; the town was buzzing with the story, and he saw to it that in the third and fourth printing of the *Advocate* an item was inserted calling for free elections in Roseberry. McCarty ought to be thrown off the council.

On Sunday, Preacher used the scandal as the basis of his sermon, railing against those in high places who had feet of clay. "Whoever shall exalt himself shall be abased, and he that shall humble himself shall be exalted. . . ."

Preacher thundered the words, making the very windows rattle in his zeal. "They that are after the things of the flesh do mind the things of the flesh, but they that are after the spirit, the things of the spirit. For to be carnally minded is death."

Schuyler sat in the back and smiled. When the service was over he congratulated Preacher on the inspiring words, and reminded him again to call at the *Advocate* office to dictate his sermon for the newspaper's readers.

It was one thing to sit at his desk and talk to Noah and Luke objectively about the smear, and quite another to discuss it with Faith. Frank waited until bedtime.

He began by relating the facts as he knew them, that he'd been invited to the house by Horace Gromley, a sure-enough vice-president of the railroad. He showed her the letters from Horace.

"But what could Schuyler Wood hope to gain by smearing you?"

"Not very much," Frank said, "except satisfaction. I've kept him from getting a seat on the town council. To a power-hungry man like Schuyler that's about the same as trampling his mother with my horse."

He did not tell her that Jordy Quinn had supplied him with two men, one to ride with him and another to watch the house, for fear Schuyler would use more direct methods.

Faith had changed into a soft white nightgown; she

came close and slid her arms about his neck, kissing him. "I should tell you I've already talked with Amos—"

"You went to see him?"

"No, he came to see me today. To tell me Schuyler is not to be trusted." She kissed him again. "He didn't say that you *were,* but I think he wanted me to think so."

"For the record, I saw only Gromley. No one else."

"I know that, darling. Come to bed now. . . ."

In Ironton, T.E. Serly counted his money and found he had enough for the railroad fare to Kansas. He could certainly sell more lots in Kansas City than in Ironton. He bought a train ticket and boarded the train with his carpetbag and twenty dollars in his pocket.

He slept most of the journey, sitting up in a chair car, and stepped off the train in Kansas City dusty and rumpled. It had cost him most of five dollars for food on the train and when he looked at himself in a mirror, he was astounded. His clothes were faded, worn, and even torn in places. His shoes were scuffed and marked. He looked about as prosperous as a drunk in the gutter.

Walking from the station, he turned in at the first cheap hotel and spent the night. He had to get new clothes somehow. After his nearly two-week stint in the meadow, cutting and staking, his appearance would be no help in selling lots with the brochures. He had to put up a front.

The only way to get money was to work for it—a thought that revolted him—or steal it. It crossed his mind that he might gamble for it, but he was in such dire straits now, with less than ten dollars between him and starvation, that he dared not risk it—not with luck turning her face from him as she had lately.

He found a piece of wood, took it to his room, and set

155

himself to whittle a gun. The task took most of the day and the hotel owner knocked on his door at sunset, demanding another night's rent.

As he paid the rent, T.E. complained about the belly stove. "It needs a coat of polish."

The owner, a seedy-looking man with a paunch, stared at him in genuine astonishment. "If you don't like the stove, then you move out, mister."

T.E. explained that he was used to better things, but if the owner would give him the stove blacking, he would do the job himself.

He went downstairs with the muttering hotel man, received a can with the dregs of polish in it, and ran upstairs to blacken his wooden pistol.

That night he went out seeking money.

On Collette Street he found a line of saloons, twelve in a mile, with a scattering of red-lights in between. T.E. took his time, visiting each saloon in turn, buying himself a beer in two of them and helping himself at the free-lunch counters. He was looking for the right victim. He did not find him in the first eight places, which were mostly deadfalls catering to a working-class clientele.

In the ninth saloon he felt slightly out of place. Beer was twice as expensive, and when he ventured near the lunch counters one of the bartenders walked over and pretended to be arranging the dishes. T.E. was careful not to look at the food.

The room was large, smoky, and noisy; it was decorated in red and orange, with yellow trim, and low-hanging chandeliers threw a gaudy light, reflecting from poker tables, making the many daringly-clad girls look young and vivacious. Several of them glanced at his seedy clothes and left him strictly alone. T.E. circulated slowly among the poker tables, watching the winners, and his gaze fell upon a heavy, pale-faced man with a dumpling skin and fat fingers. The man could not lose; he won pot after pot, making him affable and expansive. He gave handfuls of greenbacks to one of the girls, saying she brought him luck—and she hung about his neck, nibbling his ear.

T.E. watched the man for two hours, learning his name was Garo. Whether it was a first or last name, he did not know. Other players dropped out of the game and new ones took their places, but Garo won steadily. He cashed in his chips a number of times, stuffing greenbacks into his inside pockets. His luck was incredible.

The girl continued to hang about his neck, occasionally whispering into his ear, at which Garo would roar. The other players glared at him and growled among themselves.

When at last Garo cashed all his chips and raked the money in, he smiled round the table, wished them all luck, and rose.

He was a big man, taller and heavier than T.E. had expected. He kissed the girl, a dimpled redhead, and followed her across the room and through a doorway, with T.E. not far behind. Garo and the girl went up a stairway; T.E. could hear the man's booming voice and the tinkling laughter of the girl. T.E. ran up the steps behind them and watched as the girl unlocked the door of Number 6.

T.E. found himself a corner nook and sat in the hallway for an hour, half dozing, as he waited. When at last the knob rattled and the door opened, Garo came out alone, turning to wave to the girl inside. He went down the stairs, coughing and yawning, with T.E. following.

Garo had a nightcap at the long bar, slapped a number of men on the shoulders, exchanged a few jokes, and went out to the street, where T.E. was propped against a cold wall in the shadows, fingering the wooden pistol. It was late and the street was dark; there were a few buggies some distance away, and a half-dozen saddled horses, but

Garo started to walk with long strides, turning toward the city. T.E. had to hurry to keep up.

His victim must have five or six thousand dollars in his pockets—T.E. had counted several hundred-dollar pots at the table.

Past the last saloon, Garo turned into a dark street lined with two-story houses and tall shadowy trees. This was a good enough place. T.E. took a firmer grip on the pistol, cleared his throat, and called to Garo.

The man stopped at once and looked back. "What you want?—Do I know you?"

"We met at the bar," T.E. said, coming close. He thought Garo relaxed. Then he produced the gun and pointed it. "This is a holdup."

Garo's mouth dropped.

"Gimme the money," T.E. said thickly, beckoning.

Garo took a breath. "You holdin' me up?"

"Gimme the goddamn money!" T.E.'s voice was thin. "I d'want to shoot you!"

Garo licked his lips, then he nodded and slid his hand inside the long coat.

"Hurry up—"

T.E. heard a muffled click then, and his brain was haggling the problem when Garo's hand reappeared with a shiny pistol. The revolver spat, a flat-sounding report, followed by three more in the next second.

T.E. felt the shoving blow of the first bullet and staggered, throwing up his arm to ward off the others. Garo's luck still held.

It was his last thought.

Chapter Fifteen

Ira Jalder made himself purposely untidy, managed to spill a bit of whiskey on himself, and, when he arrived at the boardinghouse in the middle of the morning, pretended to be still slightly under the influence. He winked at several of the other male boarders, confided to one that he'd spent a marvelous night at Gertie de Vere's establishment, and tottered off to bed.

That would effectively scotch all suspicion.

He was not surprised when Sheriff Welch came round to the boardinghouse the next day, questioning all the transients, himself among them. Ira was reluctant to tell the sheriff where he'd been the night before, and let Welch drag it out of him. He knew that Welch would hear from the other boarders and would confer with Gert. He hoped that Welch would neglect to ask Gertie what time he'd first shown up at her house. He gave Welch the idea he'd been there all evening.

Two days went by and Welch did not come back for him; he had got away with it. The *Courier*, when it came out, had a story about Frank McCarty's house being mysteriously entered. The intruder had taken nothing at all, and the *Courier* speculated that assassination had been the motive, since it was known that McCarty had enemies. Ira read the story with fascination. It was incredible what the human mind could invent out of scraps.

When he decided the hue and cry had died down, Ira walked to the Silver Spur Saloon, bought a pitcher of beer, and took it to a back table. He had let it be known he was a salesman, and sooner or later someone was bound to wonder about his not working or looking for a job. Roseberry wouldn't be safe for long. He'd go to the McCarty house that night and look for the brooch. And this time he'd go on foot so no one could later question old Sam at the livery.

The saloon was a long, not-too-wide room with a heavy mahogany bar, a dozen card tables, and a faro layout. There were deer heads with wide antlers nailed up along the walls and over the bar a picture of a plump woman, barely draped, reclining in what looked like a rose garden.

When Ira sat down they were arranging a bout between two husky men, with the big derby-hatted bartender emphasizing the rules, ticking them off on fingers like yams. "There won't be no gouging, no kicking, and no sticking fingers in eyes—you unnerstand that?"

"What the hell, Jake," a bystander protested. "You going to make it too friendly!"

"You want a knife fight," Jake said, "you go somewhere else. In here you play by my rules or you don't play. Any more objections?"

There were none. No one wanted to tangle with a man as big and ready as Jake. Men moved the tables and chairs back to give the contestants enough room, and Ira rolled a Durham cigarette and scratched a match, wondering whether to risk a dollar bet on either man. They looked fairly matched; one was taller than the other, but both were tightly muscled and looked fit. They waited while the bets were offered and taken. Ira decided to hold off.

160

"You want to fight rounds?" Jake asked. "Or go till you drop?"

"Rounds," one said, and the other nodded.

"All right, how about each round is five minutes? I'll rap on a glass at the end of each one. That all fine with you-all?"

It was. The two men squared off, bare-knuckled, and Jake put a tumbler on the bar and rapped it sharply with a knife handle. Instantly they went at it, punching and ducking. The men in the saloon cheered them on, clapping and stamping at each solid blow. Ira drank his beer in gulps as he watched them. It was incredible that a man would risk broken teeth and a smashed nose to be able to pass the hat for a few dollars.

At the end of the first round, both fighters were red and breathing hard, but neither had gained an advantage. Someone had run outside, announcing the fight, and a number of men were crowding into the saloon to watch. Ira had to stand up to see clearly, and as he did so he swallowed beer and nearly spat it up.

Bull Delling had just stepped inside the door.

Bull looked exactly the same, the same glower on his full face, the same hard set of teeth. He was blinking in the dim light, and his attention was centered on the fighters, who were beginning to dance toward each other as Jake tapped the glass again.

Ira held the beer in front of his face and sidled toward the back door, his throat constricted. Bull would shoot him on sight, that was sure. There was no reason for Bull showing up in Roseberry except to look for him. Ira was at the open back door when he heard Bull's roar. Dropping the beer stein, Ira ran, slamming the door back and running down the short passageway and outside.

A shot smashed into the wall as he dived into the alley and sprawled in the dirt. He squeaked and scrambled to

161

his feet, scuttling along the fence to the street as he heard Bull's shouts behind him.

He turned right in the street, past the photographer's shop. It was still light but the sun was preparing to call it a day, flooding the western skies with fiery clouds and golden rays that made long shadows across the earth. The photographer's shop was the last store on the street; there were corrals at the next corner, and in between were fields heavy with brown weeds and brush. There were also a few broken-down wagons and a pile of trash. Ira took off across the fields.

As he skirted the wagons, he looked back to see Bull come stomping around the shop and skid to a halt to steady the pistol with both hands. Ira hunched his shoulders—but no shot came. The bulk of a wagon was between them, then he had ducked into the next street.

He ran down the middle of the dirt street, pumping his legs as hard as he could go. He was sure Bull had come into the saloon by accident; even Bull would have been smart enough to ambush him if he'd known Ira was inside. Maybe he'd just gotten into town and was asking about Ira—and one of the first places he'd ask was at the livery stable.

Ira ran between two houses, climbed a fence, and rushed past a group of children at play. They stared at him in astonishment and a small dog barked and chased him for half a block; then he was far enough away to slow to a shambling walk, wheezing and panting. Bull was a thick-bodied, lumbering man. He would probably go back to the saloon for his horse and patrol the streets.

He turned in at Mrs. Taber's boardinghouse and went up to his room to flop on the bed. Bull had gotten wise finally; he should have expected it, but it was damned annoying of Bull to show up right in the middle of his troubles.

Of course it changed nothing, maybe hurried it along

and certainly made it more difficult. He had to find the brooch again as quickly as possible, and shake the dust of Roseberry from his heels. Bull did not have a forgiving nature, and Ira was not at all sure he could be reasoned with. He certainly had no intention of trying.

He said a silent prayer, hoping the town marshal had heard the shot and come running to corral Bull. Most towns had ordinances against firing guns in the city limits. But if Bull had gotten away with it, he'd have to be damned careful when he went out; Bull wasn't the brightest, but he wasn't stupid either. And Ira had to go out.

Without his horse. Bull might just sit across the street from the stable and wait.

He slept for a time, woke up hungry and went downstairs with the revolver in his hip pocket. It was ten o'clock, too late to get served in any town restaurant, even if he dared go into one. He sweet-talked Mrs. Taber into a meal, paying her a dollar for it, complimenting her lavishly, something she was very unused to. He had been unwell, he told her, probably a recurrence of a battle fever he'd suffered at Vicksburg. He had already noticed that Mrs. Taber had a picture of her late husband in Confederate uniform in the parlor. She swallowed the story whole and remonstrated with him when he mentioned that he was going out to walk a few miles for exercise. He assured her that it was the doctor's prescription and slipped out the back door into darkness.

It was an hour before midnight, and he saw no one at all as he walked west, then south to the River Road. There were a few lights on in town but it was silent as the river itself. He walked along the road, keeping an eye out for riders. The McCarty house was dark and the gate was closed and locked with a chain.

He went around to the west side of the fence, where he'd climbed before. With his fingers, he explored the stout post and discovered the gouge made by the bullet. This was the spot all right, but it was black as the ace of spades under the trees. He couldn't see his hand touching his nose—and he dared not scratch a match. He swore under his breath, got down and began to feel over the ground with both hands, trying to be methodical about it, starting from the fencepost and working out. It was better to search this side of the fence first, but if he found nothing he'd have to get inside somehow.

When he bumped into a branch lying on the ground, it rattled dry leaves; a dog barked from inside the fence, then came along it, sniffing and growling, and was joined quickly by a second dog. Ira sat perfectly still, hoping they wouldn't scent him, but they apparently did. They stopped, growled for a few moments, then began to howl and bark. Disgusted, Ira hurled several rocks at them and they increased their yapping.

When he thought he saw a flicker of light from the house, he quickly turned and made his way back to the road, cursing the dogs. He would never get inside the yard while they were on guard.

He went back to the boardinghouse out of sorts and empty-handed.

Bull Delling searched the area on horseback, quitting when it got dark. Ira was a slippery little hombre and there was no telling where he'd got to. Ira wouldn't use his real name either, Bull figured, so there was no use asking for him.

He had a meal in the restaurant across from the photographer's shop on the side street, and over coffee counted his money. He had about a hundred dollars left. He could afford to take a room and put his horse in a stable rather than sleep on the prairie, but he was afraid that now Ira would bolt town—and he couldn't watch all the roads at the same time. Ira might easily elude him and disappear in any direction and that would be that.

What should he do? His first thought was to alert the sheriff that Ira Jalder was the Pettis murderer, and let the sheriff turn him up.

But that would be putting *his* neck in the noose too, wouldn't it? Bull mulled it over; it was Ira's word against his, because no one had seen them commit the crime. There *was* a point in his favor—Ira had gotten away with all the jewelry and probably had it in his kick right now. If the law caught him with the goods, that would be too bad for Ira. Bull smiled. Ira might even swing for it.

But then the loot would be gone too.

He frowned, biting his lip. No, it was better to search a little more. He walked his horse along the main street and got down in front of the livery and went inside.

Sure enough, there was Ira's horse!

"Who owns that there roan?" he demanded of old Sam.

Sam looked at Bull's size. "Feller named Ira Brown."

Bull backed the old man into a wall. "Where's this Ira Brown live?"

Sam shook his head. "I—I don't rightly know, mister."

"He got to be somewheres." He shoved Sam a little.

Old Sam swallowed hard. "Well sir, if he ain't at the hotel, then he's at a boardin' house or sleeping out in the sticks."

"How many boardin' houses in town?"

"Two-three. There's Miz Wagoner's and Miz Taber's and Miz Fargo's. . . ."

"Where they at?"

"The next street over. They's signs. Course he might be at the Bend—"

"How far's that?"

"Down at the bend of the river." Sam frowned. "No—he been leavin' his horse here . . ."

165

Bull went outside and climbed on his animal. He went first to the hotel and learned that no Ira Brown was registered. He described Ira and the clerk shook his head; they had no one of that description. Satisfied, Bull went up Second Street and halted at the first side street. There were a half-dozen houses to his left, shaded by elms, with shrubbery in pots here and there. He walked the horse along, looking for signs.

The first sign announced: *Room and Board*. It was a square of cardboard set in a front window with a drape behind it. Bull got down, tied the horse, and clumped up the steps. A small, skinny woman looked him over, shaking her head. She had no vacancies at present, and no one named Ira Brown. "Whyn't you try Mrs. Taber? She's three doors down."

The Taber house was large, two stories, with a neat wooden sign tacked to the front picket fence. Bull went inside and Mrs. Taber grumped at him, "Course Ira Brown lives here."

"Where's he at now?" Bull asked. "I'm his partner. Got to see him."

Mrs. Taber shrugged. "Upstairs, far's I know. First door on the left." She snapped at him as he took the stairs. "I don't allow no smokin' inside, mister. . . ."

"I ain't smokin'," Bull said.

At the top of the steps he drew his revolver and tried the knob on the first left. It was locked. Bull chewed his lip; that probably meant Ira was inside, but if he let Ira know who was in the hall, Ira might go out the window. He stepped back and crashed his heavy shoulder against the door. It gave, slamming back against the wall with a clatter that brought a yell from downstairs.

Bull grinned, pointing the revolver. Ira was on the bed, eyes round and staring, mouth hanging open. He looked at Bull, then at the muzzle, as if wondering when the shot

166

was coming. He sat up and put his legs down on the floor carefully.

"Hullo, Bull . . ."

Bull came inside and closed the door, ignoring the shouts from the stairs. "You diddled me, Ira. I'll kill you f'that." He pulled back the hammer of the pistol.

"F'God's sake, Bull! What're you talking about?"

Mrs. Taber pounded on the door, then opened it. Her face changed, seeing the pointed revolver, and grew pale. "What're you doing?"

Bull turned with a growl and pushed her back, slamming the door again.

As he did, Ira scuttled toward the open window. He got a leg over, when Bull cracked him alongside the ear with the pistol barrel. He felt the blow, but blackness enveloped him before he hit the floor. Bull caught him and laid him down, not too gently.

Then Bull searched the room. He was fully convinced that Ira had the jewels on him—or the money from their sale. But Ira had neither! He had about ninety dollars in his pants and that was all. There was nothing in his carpetbag or anywhere in the room.

Outside in the hall someone was moving about, and finally a man's fist hammered on the door, opened it, and Bull was gazing into the muzzle of the marshal's pistol.

"What's goin' on here?"

The marshal was a farmerish looking man, strong and young, with a hard face and a steady hand holding the gun. "Speak up, mister." His eyes flicked to Ira on the floor. "He dead?"

"Naw," Bull growled. "We had us an argyment, that's all." He had Ira's money in his fist, and he peeled off a bill, handing it over the marshal's shoulder to Mrs. Taber. "That's for the door, ma'am."

The marshal motioned him away, entered the room and

knelt by Ira, who was beginning to breathe audibly. With help, Ira sat up, his head in both hands, moaning lightly.

"This here's just a business quarrel, marshal," Bull said. "Nothing for the law."

"That what you say?" the marshal demanded of Ira.

Ira nodded weakly, his breath hissing.

"Better get him a cold pad," the marshal said to Mrs. Taber. He put the pistol away, looked hard at Bull and went down the steps.

"Don't you hit him agin," Mrs. Taber warned.

"Hell no," Bull said. "We're old friends. He was just about to tell me something, wasn't you, Ira?"

Ira nodded sadly.

Chapter Sixteen

Karl Welch sat Frank down in an arm chair, offered him a cigar and match. Karl was a stocky, quick-eyed man with a moustache and black hair slowly turning gray. He was the first sheriff the county had elected, and would probably keep the job as long as he wanted it.

Karl went to the small stove at one side of the room, swirled a coffeepot, poured out two cups and brought them back. "Got me a little problem, Frank. Thought I'd saddle you with it if I could."

"What's it about?"

"D'you remember that killin' over at Pettis a while back? A man named Ledwidge got himself shot over some jewels he was bringin' home."

"Yes, I remember."

"Well, there weren't no witnesses to the crime, but two-three folks in Pettis recall seeing a man in town that day, a feller they never seen before. A saddlemaker and a sign painter in particular. They were talkin' in front of their stores and they say this little hombre was readin' a newspaper outside the bank and when Ledwidge come out, this feller followed him. I got a pretty good description of him." Karl sipped the coffee. "Kinda slow police work, but Pettis ain't got but two marshals."

Frank nodded. "All right, you got a description."

"Oh, I got more'n that." Karl smiled. "Ain't this terrible coffee? Selman made it this morning. I swear that man puts in rat droppings."

"It's too damned strong, that's all."

"Yeh. What I got is the feller in jail here." Karl jerked a thumb over his shoulder. "I bet you it's the one all right, but I'll play hell proving it."

Frank put the cup aside and leaned back. "You've got a man in jail?"

"His name is Ira Brown. Been living over at the widow Taber's boardinghouse. He says he's a salesman, but he don't look for work, and yesterday another big hombre like to killed him in his room."

"What about?"

"I don't rightly know. Bill Spencer went over when the widow sent a boy for him. Both of 'em said they'd had an argument, so Bill let 'em be. When he told me about it, I went over and took a look at him and hauled him in. I think he's the man killed Ledwidge."

"But you can't prove it?"

Karl sighed. "Well, a lot of things line up. He matches the description, and he come into Roseberry just after the killing—on the same stage with Faith, as a matter of fact. He got on the stage at Epps Station sayin' he'd come from Jackson. But he could just as easy have come from Pettis."

"Did he have the jewels?"

Karl smiled. "You go right to it, Frank. No, he didn't have the goddamn jewels—or the money they'd have brung if he'd sold 'em. He had about ninety dollars in his kick, a pistol, and a roan horse over at Sam's. That's it."

Frank said, "Hmmm. What about the other man—the one he was arguing with?"

"He got out. I put a man out looking for him but we haven't turned him up yet. Why?"

"I thought maybe *he'd* have the jewels. Did this Ira Brown have a partner in the Ledwidge killing?"

Karl shook his head. "Don't know."

"What d'you want from me?"

"The problem is, what to do with him. I sure as hell hate to turn a murderer loose, but I haven't got a goddamn to hold him on. I wired the marshal at Pettis for all the information they got, and they're going to send me the vest the feller in Pettis wore."

"A vest?"

"They found a red vest in the hills outside of Pettis. The saddlemaker and the sign painter both say the man they saw in town that day wore a red vest. I'm just curious t'see if it fits Ira Brown."

Frank got up. "Can I see this prisoner?"

"Sure." Karl opened the heavy plank door to the rear and took down a ring of keys. He unlocked a second door and stood aside. Frank went in, a large square room with four cells that smelled dank, and was lit by only a single dangling lantern. The cells were two on a side of the room and only two were occupied. In the nearest a man set up a clamor immediately, yelling that he was due out, that his brother was coming for him.

Karl said, "Shut up, Charlie. You'll be let out when it's time." He shook his head at Frank. "I found 'im last night down in the river tryin' to float. The damn fool would have drowned himself."

Frank smiled. "Hello, Charlie."

"This'n's Ira Brown," Karl said, pointing out the other prisoner. He was dressed in shirt and checked trousers; a coat hung on a nail. As they entered he stood, a short, middle-aged man with a lined face and squint eyes. He looked surprised to see a visitor.

Frank thought the man's eyes widened when Karl introduced him. "Ira, this's Frank McCarty." Ira's eyes darted to the pistol under Frank's coat and there was a flash of something that might have been fear in the young-old face.

"What you want of me?" Ira asked. He moved back and perched like a bird on the edge of the bunk. He seemed ready to take flight, though there was nowhere to go.

"Where do you come from?" Frank asked.

A pause. "Kansas City."

"What're you doing here in Roseberry?"

Ira Brown sighed deeply. "Looking for work, Mr. McCarty. I got a little bit of money saved up—the sheriff got it all now—and I'm lookin'."

"You ain't lookin' very hard," Karl said. "The way I hear it you spend your time in saloons."

"What can you do?" Frank asked.

"I'm a salesman. I sold ever' damn thing from buttons to plows." He put on an earnest face. "I work hard when I work."

"His hands don't look like he been working very hard, Frank."

"I been a clerk," Ira said quickly. "I'm good at figures. A man don't get no calluses at that kinda work."

Frank nodded, though Ira didn't look like any clerk he'd seen. Ira was probably a gambler—or worse. He said, "You ever rob a man, Ira?"

Ira's eyes widened again and he stood up. "I never robbed nobody!"

"I think you did," Karl said, leaning on the bars. "I think you killed that Ledwidge feller over at Pettis. You ever been in Pettis, Ira?"

"Pettis—where's that?"

Frank turned away. They'd never get anything from this little man, he was sure. Ira had probably been in a dozen jails before this one and would lie like a horse thief. He went back to the front, with Karl locking the door behind them.

"What d'you think, Frank?"

Frank shrugged. "Hold him for a while. He's a shifty little gent all right. You could be dead right about him and Ledwidge. If that vest fits maybe you ought to take him back to Pettis and let the witnesses have a look at him."

"I was thinkin' the same thing." Karl smiled.

Bull Delling sat in the back of the room in Kelly's Saloon, glowering at the far wall, drinking beer. The law had got Ira in jail, and that wasn't doing anybody any good.

Did it mean that they suspected Ira of the Pettis job? But how could they?

He had searched Ira and the boardinghouse room and found nothing. Mrs. Taber wasn't keeping anything for Ira either. That left only two possibilities. Either Ira had never stolen the gems in the first place—or he'd hidden them somewhere. Naturally Ira swore he didn't have them. But Ira was a slippery little coot; he might have buried them alongside the boardinghouse, or anywhere. . . .

Bull finished the beer, and let out his breath. The best thing to do was get Ira out of jail. Then he could choke the truth out of the little weasel.

He went out to the street, hands in his pockets, thinking hard. How to get Ira out. He turned west and walked to the end of the next block and stood on the corner, brooding. It was out of the question to try to bust him out, so it had to be some other way. Maybe he could put up bail. He was about to turn and go back to see the sheriff when his eye was caught by a sign on the far side of the street: *Law Office.*

Quickly he crossed and stood in front of the door.

173

There were two names on it: *Schuyler Wood and Robert Heiner, Attys at Law.* Bull opened the door and went in.

The single room had been divided in two by partitions, and the nearest door was open. A man, in shirtsleeves, sat at a desk reading the top sheet of a sheaf of papers, making notes now and then. Bull cleared his throat and the man looked up, saw him, and rose.

"Can I help you, sir? I'm Schuyler Wood."

Bull took off his hat. Wood was tall and looked like a judge, which made him uneasy; Bull bobbed his head, blurting that he wanted to get Ira out of jail and that Ira hadn't done anything—

"Hold on," the lawyer said. "Let's take it slower. Start at the beginning. What's this man's name?"

"Ira Brown."

"And what relation is he to you?"

Bull told him as good a story as he could think up in the short space. That he and Ira were partners, just traveling through, and the sheriff had locked up Ira for no reason. "How much will it cost to get him out?"

"Well, I don't know . . ." Wood tapped his chin. "Suppose you give me ten dollars as a retainer and I'll go over and talk to the sheriff. If your friend's innocent, as you say, it shouldn't be any trouble at all to get him out."

Bull fished out the money and handed it over. Wood gave him a receipt and a handshake. "Where can I get in touch with you, Mr. Delling?"

"How about Jake's Saloon?" Bull fumbled with his hat. "You goin' to work on it today?"

"I'll go right now." The lawyer gathered up a coat and shrugged into it.

Bull loitered along the street, watching the tall figure of the lawyer stride down toward the sheriff's office. He went into Jake's Silver Spur, ordered beer and smoked a cigar.

The lawyer was back within the hour, and Ira with him.

174

"They had no charges," Schuyler Wood said. "They were holding him on suspicion—entirely unconstitutional, as I explained to the sheriff. I'll have a beer, Jake."

Ira was apprehensive, seeing Bull, and slightly surprised to hear that Bull had actually paid money to get him out of jail. "I'll pay you back, Bull." He fished out the money Sheriff Welch had returned to him and handed over a ten.

They took a table in the back of the room when the lawyer departed. "Thanks for getting me out, Bull."

Bull smiled, the same smile the spider smiles entangling an ant. "You couldn't tell me where you hid them jewels while you was in the can, Ira."

"But I never seen the goddamn jewels! Somebody—his wife made up the story! She's tryin' to bilk the insurance company!"

"I'll cut your heart out if you're lyin' to me, Ira."

"I'm not lying, Bull! Have I got the damn jewels? Search me. Search anything I got!"

Bull sighed. "I already did."

"Then you know all I got outa that job was the same as you got . . . and that's the truth. There wasn't no jewels . . . or if there was, I never seen 'em."

Bull scowled at him. "Then why'd you want to split up so sudden?"

Ira's eyes grew round and he leaned forward, and his voice was only a whisper. "Because we killed a man, goddammit! We're both guilty, and it was the sensible thing t'do."

Bull frowned. That made sense, all right. He stared at Ira, not entirely believing him, but forced to admit the story sounded good. Well, he'd never let the little son of a bitch out of his sight.

Then Ira smiled. "Listen, Bull, how much money you got left?"

"Why?"

"Because you probably ain't got any more'n I have. But I know where there's a lot more."

Bull leaned toward the other. "Yeh?—Where?"

"Right across the alley, in the bank. I been asking around. They never had a holdup in this here town, not once. That bank is a sitting duck. I was in there t'other day and they are ripe for a quick job. What you say?"

Bull blinked and glanced around the saloon. No one was paying them the slightest attention. "I'll have to look it over first. . . ."

"The stage brings in a bundle from Ironton every week, on Tuesdays. There's bound to be more money than you ever seen in that bank Wednesday morning." Ira patted Bull's arm. "Ten minutes' time and we'll be rich."

Bull was easily convinced. The Roseberry Bank did look easy. He sauntered in, changed a ten-dollar bill, and gazed around, noting the positions of cages and doors. They had arranged the partitions well, but he could see no evidence of real security.

But how to get away afterward? He met Ira outside and Ira had an idea. "We'll go straight north and lose any pursuit in the hills."

"You know them hills?"

Ira shrugged. "No . . ."

"Then let's go look at 'em first. It don't pay to get rich inside the bank then lose it all in the next hour."

They headed north from the bank, found they had to veer east to get around a number of fences and gardens, then, as they left the houses behind and rode over the open fields, came to a barbed wire fence.

Ira got down, produced a pair of clippers, and cut it. He put them back in the saddlebag with a flourish. "Easy as that, partner."

"We better make sure that fence is still cut 'fore we do the job," Bull said, riding through.

They continued over the fields, heading straight for a notch in the hills. The notch widened to a narrow valley; they rode through it to the desert on the far side, and halted. It was as good a getaway route as any, Bull admitted. They went back to town, deciding en route to do the job the next morning.

There were only six employees in the bank, including the manager, and if they were frightened enough they'd give the sheriff a half-dozen different descriptions.

And to help their cause, they strolled along the main street of town well after dark and managed to steal two linen dusters that were tied onto waiting horses' saddles. With these over their clothes and masks on their faces no one would know them.

Before they went to bed, Bull rode out and made sure the fence was still cut.

Chapter Seventeen

Late on Saturday night there was a ruckus at the Miller Dance Hall and two soldiers were shot dead. Marshal Bill Spencer was slightly wounded by a drunken cowhand, but subdued the man and dragged him off to the pokey. The dead soldiers were laid out on the sidewalk till morning when Doc Litchfield's wagon picked them up.

One of Gertie de Vere's girls, black-haired Camille Zimmer, had been in the hall getting two buckets of beer to take across the street when the shooting started. She came running back, leaving the beer, wide-eyed because one of the flying bullets had smashed a picture frame only two feet from her head.

"It coulda killed me!" she said to Gertie, who came from her office room, tying a wrapper about her.

Another one of the girls said, "She forgot the goddamn beer."

"You would too!" Camille flared. "Bullets were flyin' everywhere. I heard they killed three men in all, maybe four."

"Go back and get the beer, honey," Gert said. "Did you pay for it?"

But Camille would not return and finally Gloria Smith went, with appropriate remarks out of the side of her mouth. Gertie went into her room and flopped on the bed, thinking about Natchez. This town was getting just as wild. For two shin-plasters she'd pick up and get out.

Bill Spencer rode to Doc Nichols's office and had his arm sewed up and bandaged. Doc clucked over it but Bill only chuckled. "Hell, it ain't bad t'night, Doc. Too damn cold for real trouble. Just you wait till spring."

Karl Welch was waiting for Frank at Sam's livery on Wednesday morning. Frank smiled and got down, "Howdy, Sheriff."

"G'morning, Frank." Karl walked with him to the door and paused to scratch a match on the frame. "You r'member that little hombre, Ira Brown?" He lit a cigarette.

"Of course."

"Well, your friend, Mr. Schuyler Wood, come and got him out."

"Schuyler!? How the hell did Schuyler know Ira was there?"

"I dunno, but he did. There wasn't a thing I could hold him on, 'cept suspicion, and I didn't have no real evidence to back that up. Mr. Wood, he threatened to go to the governor and make trouble for all of us. I finally just turned him loose."

Frank sighed. "Well, there was nothing else you could have done, Karl."

Karl nodded. "Selman's been snoopin' around, asking questions. There don't seem to be anyone in town who's trying to get even with you for anything. I expect we'll just hafta write off that robbery attempt as nothing."

"Yes, I expect so."

Frank walked to the office, wondering again why anyone would break into the house and paw through Faith's clothes. He had never gotten a look at the intruder; it

180

could have been a boy from town on a prank or a dare. It seemed the most likely explanation.

In front of the barber shop he met Alvin Titus and his wife, Flavia. Alvin was a stringbean, with clothes hanging on him, a wiry little man who made a living as a saddlemaker, working out of his barn at home across the river. Flavia was plump and short, wearing a pale green dress and a small bonnet. The Titus couple had just climbed down from their buggy when he greeted them. Alvin said they were going into the bank to see Mr. Donaldson.

"Maybe you'll put in a word for me, Frank."

"What about?" Frank lifted his hat to Mrs. Titus, glancing along the street as two men in linen dusters came from the opposite direction and reined in near the steps of the bank.

"I've got me a chance to open a store in town. They's an empty one over north of Doc Litchfield's parlor. I'm doin' 'bout all I can outa the barn, but if I was to come into town there'd be more business."

"He could put up a sign," Flavia said.

Frank nodded, watching the two men in dusters enter the bank. Alvin Titus was the only saddlemaker in town and there was no reason why his affairs would not prosper. "I certainly will talk to Cliff for you," he promised. "I know the store you have in mind." He nodded toward the bank. "Why don't we go talk to him now?"

The Titus couple beamed. A loan advocated by Frank McCarty would hardly be refused by the bank manager.

Titus led the way up the steps and opened the bank door. He paused, waiting for them; Flavia was telling Frank about her garden—she had enlarged it and was growing potatoes enough to sell to her neighbors. Suddenly someone pulled Titus inside.

Flavia gave a gasp and rushed into the bank. For a few seconds Frank stood in the open doorway, staring at the scene. The two men in dusters were holding up the bank!

Each man had a pistol—the bigger of the two had two pistols pointed—and there were four heavy sacks filled with money sitting on the counter. The big man had yanked Alvin Titus inside and pushed him against the wall. He came toward the door with the obvious intention of shutting it, when Flavia appeared and ran into him.

He swore, pushing her aside, and motioned to Frank with one of the pistols. "Come inside, dammit, and shut the door!"

The shorter bandit yelled suddenly, "That's McCarty! Watch him, Bull—that's Frank McCarty!"

Bull turned instantly, cocking the gun. His eyes, blazing through the holes in the black mask, seemed unnaturally large and Frank thought he was about to pull the trigger. He put his hands up shoulder high and remained motionless.

For half a moment Bull stared at him, then growled, "I told you t'shut the goddamn door."

Moving slowly, Frank closed the door and put his hands up again. It might be possible to draw and fire, but it would be better to wait till the bandits left the building so no one would be caught in the firing. He moved toward the counter as Bull motioned. The shorter man tossed the filled sacks to the floor in front of the door.

Two women clerks and two of the tellers had been put into one of the rooms, Frank guessed. He could hear one teller rifling drawers and filling a canvas sack under the supervision of the short man. Bull paced up and down, his pistols constantly moving; he was extremely nervous and edgy, growling at the teller to hurry up.

Cliff Donaldson, the bank manager, was standing on the far side of the counter, with both hands up, peering at Frank with frustration in his face. He was a short, dumpy man with bags under his eyes, and looked harmless as a rabbit.

"That's enough," Bull said. "Let's get going!"

The short man ordered the teller into one of the rooms and turned a key in the lock. He was coming back through the counter gate when the front door opened and two men came in.

The newcomers halted abruptly on seeing the waving pistols, and one of them yelped and jumped down the steps outside, yelling that "robbers were in the bank!" The second man ducked as Bull swung at his head. He fell to the floor and scuttled out of the way, eyes like saucers. One of Bull's pistols went off and the bullet slammed into the wall.

"Down on the floor," Frank yelled at the Titus couple.

Bull turned, and a second shot smashed a glass-covered picture. The smaller man was shouting at Bull to get out; his gun turned toward Frank, who dived for the floor and rolled. In the next instant Cliff Donaldson had snatched up a shotgun and fired both barrels, Boom, Boom, as fast as he could pull the triggers. The loads smashed into the heavy double doors, reverberating in the small foyer.

Frank sat up, the Colt in his hand, but the two robbers were already through the door and bullets were whistling back, rapping into the walls. He glanced at Donaldson, still standing with the smoking shotgun in his hands, white-faced and obviously scared.

He heard horses outside, then Flavia screamed. Frank scrambled up, ran through the door, and snapped five shots at the retreating pair. He thought he saw a horse stumble, but could not be sure. In the next moment they were out of sight, flying like the wind up the alley.

When he went back inside, Alvin Titus was dead, stretched out on the floor with Flavia sobbing over him. Frank leaned against the door and bit his lip; a stray bullet had drilled through the skinny man's chest.

The bandits had left the money sacks behind, and Frank kicked them against the counter. Donaldson, hand shaking, was unlocking the doors, letting the clerks and tellers out. Frank sent one of them for the sheriff and Dr. Nichols, though he knew there was nothing to be done for Alvin. The women came to console Flavia, and Frank stepped outside, fishing for a cigar.

The shorter of the two men had looked somehow familiar, though mostly because of his size, perhaps because of his voice. An excited crowd was gathering, and he heard voices from the windows above. When he glanced up, they stopped and faces stared at him. The bank's money was safe, he told the crowd, the bandits had escaped without it and Sheriff Welch was on his way. He gave a boy a dime to go get his horse from the livery, and in a few moments Karl Welch galloped up with a deputy following.

Karl shook his head on seeing Alvin Titus. They went through the gate into Cliff Donaldson's office. Donaldson said, "They didn't get a thing, Frank, not a blasted nickel."

Karl asked, "Who were they?"

"Two men, one big and one small," Frank said. "I got a hunch the small one was Ira Brown. They wore dusters and masks, and the big one was called Bull."

Karl regarded him. "Ira Brown, huh? If we catch him, this time he'll stay in the calaboose. You see which way they took?"

"Up the alley, north."

"Then let's go see if we can run 'em down." Karl led the way out to the street. Tim Oxford, his deputy, had rounded up four men with horses and rifles; Frank's horse was tied at the hitchrack. They mounted and loped up the alley.

The bandits had been seen by a number of people cutting across the fields toward the hills. Their tracks were easy to follow, heading for one of the narrow valleys and through it. It was an overcast day and, past the jumble of hills, the desert wind was biting cold.

184

They followed the thin tracks for several hours, with dust and twigs hurrying away on the wind. When they came to a hardpan area, the tracks disappeared and Karl reined in. He looked round at them, up at the sky, and shook his head.

"Let's scatter out there and see if we can pick up anything, boys." He waited for them to move away and spat. "No tellin', Frank. I think they'll head for El Paso or Kansas City, one."

Frank agreed. The two would certainly not hang around Roseberry after their fiasco.

Noah Applegate's *Courier* described the attempted robbery and the murder of Titus in factual and sympathetic terms. Alvin Titus had been a hard-working and well-liked man, and it was an outrage that two saddle tramps should take his life in such an offhand manner. The bank was offering five hundred dollars, dead or alive, for either of the two men, one thought to be Ira Brown, who had lived for a time at Mrs. Taber's boardinghouse. Mrs. Titus had put her land up for sale and would return to the East.

The *Advocate,* on the other hand, accused Sheriff Welch and the town marshal, Bill Spencer, of providing less-than-adequate protection for innocent citizens on the streets of Roseberry. Something should be done, Cole Stedman wrote, to replace both lawmen at the next election. It was well known that Karl Welch was practically a part of the McCarty clan and only kept his office because of that fact. And everyone now knew what McCarty was.

A Citizens' Committee, represented by Thomas Sawyer, also deplored in print the death of an honest, worthy man and asked, "What is being done to avenge his death?"

Preacher Rossiter led his congregation in prayer for Alvin Titus's soul on the next Sunday and took up a collection for his widow which Preacher delivered himself following the services.

Chapter Eighteen

Ira and Bull split up to mislead any pursuers, then each gradually made his way back to the river and along it to the Bend. They met two days after they'd split and moved south to find a haven among the hundreds of limestone caves of the area.

Bull was all for moving farther south. "Godammit, Ira, maybe we're a jinx team. We ain't made more'n a handful of dimes since we been together."

"Don't say that, Bull. It's just damn poor luck, that's all."

"I don't see no sign of it goin' away."

Ira had a small fire going; Bull had shot a deer and they had butchered it and hung it in the cave, with steaks sputtering over the coals. "Luck don't last forever, you know that, Bull, good or bad. We had some bad luck, but it's gonna change."

"Change how?"

"I got me an idea."

"Damn you!" Bull almost shouted. "Ever' goddamn idea you has pays off in pennies."

Ira bristled. "Is it my fault that goddamn Ledwidge didn't have no money on 'im? Is it my fault McCarty come into the bank just when we got four-five sacks full of cash sitting at the door? Hell no, it ain't!"

"It's a jinx," Bull muttered.

"Don't get yourself thinkin' that way," Ira protested. "It ain't no jinx at all. It's just plain cussed luck, nothin' else. It could just as easy go the other way."

Bull chewed on half-raw meat. "What's your idea?"

Ira leaned closer. "There's one man in this here territory with all the money—that's McCarty, ain't it?"

"He's that hombre in the bank? I should have plugged 'im."

"Maybe so. But I know where he lives."

Bull shrugged. "What does it pay us to ambush 'im?"

"Sometimes I wonder at you, Bull. You ever read the papers?"

"What's your damn idea, Ira?"

"There's been two-three things in the papers the last month or so should interest you'n me. Made to order for McCarty." Ira grinned and Bull glowered at him.

"What, for crissakes?"

"Did you read about the Indians kidnappin' that woman last month? The government paid 'em five thousand dollars to return 'er."

Bull grunted. "You want to kidnap McCarty? Ira, you're out of your head." He made a twirling motion with his finger at Ira's ear.

"Not him—I want to kidnap *Mrs.* McCarty."

Bull stared.

Ira grinned across the fire, the red-hot coals lighting his face diabolically. "I know where they live, and I also know she goes into town ever' day. Alls we have to do is intercept 'er and cart her across the river then send McCarty a note tellin' him where to put the fifty thousand dollars."

Bull's lips moved but no sound came out.

"Fifty thousand dollars," Ira repeated. "And almost no risk."

Bull took a breath and found his voice. "How you fig-er that?"

"McCarty ain't goin' to run us down for fear of shoot-ng his wife. Hell, that ain't no money to him. All he vants is her back. They got a kid—"

"What about afterward?"

"Alls we got to do is be smart about picking a spot for he payoff. We pick a place where we can go a couple ways. If we can get a day on him, we'll get away clean, either to a stage line or a railroad."

Bull scratched his chin.

"And best thing of all," Ira said, "is gettin' even with McCarty. If it wasn't for him walkin' in the bank we'd have ourselves all that loot right now, dividing it."

"Yeah," Bull nodded. "What's she look like, this McCarty woman?"

"Pretty as a picture," Ira said, and Bull smiled.

Ken Larkin received two wires, read them with a grunt, and went in to lay them in front of Frank. "Schuyler Wood was a judge, all right, and served one term in the state legislature, but they told him not to run again or they'd file charges."

"What kind of charges?" Frank frowned at the second wire.

"Taking bribes."

Frank sighed and handed the papers back. "So he real-ly came here to get another start."

"He had to," Ken said.

Cole Stedman had a limited supply of type and almost no display fonts, but he set up the copy that Schuyler gave him, pulled proofs and made changes to Schuyler's satisfaction. The black run on the brochures was excellent, but the colors were poor; the reds looked rusty and the yellows had too much of an ochre cast, and the paper stock was poor. To George Kilburn, fingering one of the proofs, it was cheap and unimpressive.

Schuyler's brochures could not hold a candle to the excellently printed ones he had locked up in Ironton. So far he had not been able to get Schuyler to discuss money. If he could talk Schuyler out of five hundred dollars for selling expenses he would be on his way. But the lawyer was busy with some "important business" he would not talk about, so George bided his time. Whatever money he got from Schuyler would be gravy.

Cole Stedman made a number of attempts to improve his work and George, at Schuyler's insistence, stood by making suggestions. Stedman finally solved his registration problems to the point that his color runs did not overlap so much; the brochures could be used, but he could not improve the paper. He delivered several hundred to Schuyler's office, and later in the day Schuyler asked George to look at them.

"Excellent," George said, pretending to examine the unfolded brochure. "It's as good as you could get in the East." He could see that Schuyler was pleased; of course the lawyer was eager to get on with the selling, so money would roll in. He had already contracted for a number of buildings at the townsite. A builder had agreed to come out from Ironton, draw plans and survey the site.

Cole worked long hours to finish his three runs, and when the ink was dry, he packaged one thousand brochures and turned them over to George. George had them carted off to the stage depot and consigned to Ironton. When he got to Ironton he would hire a wagon, load them on and take them out in the hills and bury the entire shipment.

That evening he insisted on a meeting with Schuyler, and to his surprise the lawyer quickly agreed, putting aside whatever other business he was engaged in. They went to the hotel for supper, sitting at a quiet table in the rear of the room. Schuyler had one of the brochures with him and propped it up on the table, gazing at the drawing of the town.

He also had a name and an address for George. "I want you to send the brochures to this man." He handed over the slip of paper, and George read the Chicago address. The name meant nothing to him.

"Chicago?"

"I haven't been idle," Schuyler said. "I have a few friends in Chicago." He tapped the paper in George's hand. "They'll help you to get the brochures into the right hands."

George looked hurt. "Don't you trust me, Schuyler?"

"It's not a question of trust, old fellow. Our arrangement remains the same, but we can use all the help we can get to see the project underway as quickly as possible. Don't you agree?"

"Yes, of course I do."

"Very well. Send the brochures there, and go there yourself as quickly as you can. You'll find a great deal of spadework has already been done to make your task easier, and naturally you'll receive more money the more you sell. I don't see that you can object."

"I don't," George protested. "I admire your organization, Schuyler. I hadn't expected it, that's all."

Schuyler smiled. "I selected you in the first place because of your salesmanship, George. I hope you'll train a few others to help us."

"I certainly shall." He made his voice hearty.

"Good."

Schuyler produced a carefully drawn plat map of the proposed town, showing each numbered lot. He had set

down the prices; the lots in the center of town would ▮
sold for one hundred dollars each, those on the outskir
for less.

"I want to attract buyers with low prices—is that
good idea?"

"Very good," George said. He would have agreed ▮
anything. "Let's talk about expenses."

Schuyler sighed, nodding. "I had rather hoped you'
hold up your end, George. Are you entirely broke?"

George put on a face, slight embarrassment mixed wit
reluctance, and spoke very slowly, glancing about as ▮
afraid of being overheard. "I have to confess, Schuyle▮
that I have less than twenty dollars to my name. I didn'
want to admit it . . ."

Schuyler grunted. "I suppose I can advance tw▮
hundred—"

"Two hundred dollars?" George looked startled. "Bu▮
Schuyler, I have to go all the way to Chicago, pay for th▮
brochures, a hotel, and food—it won't do!"

"It seems a great deal of money to me," Schuyler said
stiffly.

"But I have to put up a front! I'll be meeting importan▮
people, selling our proposition! I can't drag in like a bum
half fed, clothes rumpled—no one would listen to me fo▮
a second!"

Schuyler's voice grew edgy. "How much do you want,
George?"

"I think six hundred would nearly cover it."

"Out of the question! I have only limited funds, after
all. I don't expect you to purchase a new wardrobe! I'll
advance three hundred."

George shook his head moodily. But in the next half-
hour he squeezed another hundred dollars from Schuyler,
and signed a chit for Schuyler's files. The four hundred,
Schuyler said, would be deducted from his earnings.

That was fine with George Kilburn.

He got up early next morning, had breakfast in the restaurant near the stage station, boarded the stagecoach when they brought it around, and settled himself with a long sigh. It was a drizzly day, promising rain, and he steeled himself for a cold, miserable journey.

But he would never see Roseberry again. He would never see Chicago either, for that matter. He allowed himself a smile, wondering how long Schuyler's friend would pace the railroad station waiting for him.

Five minutes before the stage left, a young woman clambered aboard and arranged herself on the seat beside him, giving him a dazzling smile. She was followed by an older couple, a man with thick-rimmed glasses, hardly able to bend stiffened knees to fight his way into the coach, and a stout woman, bundled in a heavy cloth coat, with a blanket over her arm.

Then the horn blew and they were off, the stage jerking, swaying and rattling over the rutted street.

When everyone was settling down, George introduced himself, "I'm George Wilson," he said, smiling at the woman. "We'll be a long time together—"

"Yes, indeed," she said. "I'm Rowena Preville . . . going home to see my . . . mother."

"Happy to know you, Rowena." She was dressed conservatively, except that under her dark pelisse, which gaped open slightly, he was able to see the neckline of her dress, scooping very low to exhibit generous cleavage. She noted his look and drew the pelisse together, buttoning it, giving him a small intimate smile at the same time.

She called him George after the first mile, and it was obvious Mrs. Martha Blair did not approve. George had taken the precaution to bring along a bottle of medicinal whiskey in his bag, which he was willing to pass around. Old Mr. Blair had a nip, but Martha turned up her nose and glared into her lap when Rowena tossed back a generous dollop and laughed at George's jokes.

193

By the time they arrived late in the evening at Epps Station, neither George nor Rowena noticed the inclement weather, being well fortified. The bottle was finished and had been tossed out, and Martha Blair registered a strong complaint and objection with F. L. Epps when they arrived.

"That woman is a hussy and I've no intention at all of riding in that coach tomorrow! You must put them off!" She pounded the table. "I demand you put them both off!"

F. L. did his best to calm her, explaining that Miss Preville had paid for her passage, as had Mr. Wilson. He talked to the driver, who said nothing untoward had happened during the trip, except that the stage had been held up at every comfort stop because of the time it took Mr. Blair to get in and out.

After supper, F. L. attempted to talk to Mr. Wilson also, but Wilson was nowhere to be found, not in his room and not anywhere on the station. F. L., having been a station master for some years, then listened outside Miss Preville's room. It was true, as Martha Blair said, that Wilson and Preville were very close.

The Blair couple stayed behind when the stage left the next morning. Martha Blair would not ride an inch farther with the hussy, preferring to stay over and wait for the next coach. Jacob Blair did not agree, but he had no say in the matter.

George and Rowena went on alone; the stagecoach picked up two passengers at Somers Station, two cattle buyers who stared at Rowena most of the day and talked among themselves, eyeing her.

In Ironton, George signed for a package, loaded it and Rowena into a rented buggy, and they drove to the Culver Hotel and registered as man and wife. He shoved the package into a corner of the room and called for bath water. They soaped and scrubbed each other of the trail

194

dust, went downstairs and celebrated the trip, and fell into bed at midnight.

The next morning, while Rowena was still in bed, George went downstairs, rented a light spring wagon from a man pointed out to him, got the man to lend him a shovel, and drove to the stage station. He signed for the large package of brochures printed by Cole Stedman and drove out of town. In an hour he reined in under a stand of elms, far out of sight of town. There were low sand hills behind him and an arroyo not far off; there was nothing but low brush and grass where he stood, and the digging was easy.

He dug for a half hour, smoked a cigar and dug some more, then shoved the package of Schuyler's printed matter off the wagon and dropped it into the hole. Shoveling in the dirt, he tossed the shovel in the wagon and went back to town. Rowena was just getting up.

In four days, half the money Schuyler had given him was gone. He began to sign for meals and drinks in the hotel, and at the end of the week a soft-voiced manager called him into the office and requested payment. George stalled him.

Upstairs he said to Rowena, "I'm broke, honey. You got any money?"

She looked at him as if seeing him for the first time. "Hardly any, George. Just my ticket east and a bit of food money."

"We've got to pay the damned rent. D'you suppose you could go down to the bar and pick up a—"

"No, I couldn't," Rowena said shortly. "I'm not doing that anymore."

"You must have ten dollars," George said in a desperate voice. "He'll lock us out of the room and grab the suitcases!"

Rowena sighed and dug into her traveling money, showing him how little it left her. She said nothing about the several hundred dollars she had tucked into her reticule. When he went downstairs to turn over the money, she packed her bag, draped a coat over her arm and hurried down the back stairs.

She was in time to catch the train leaving for the East.

George paid down the ten dollars at the hotel desk, saying that one of three payments he was expecting had arrived. More money was due in two or three days. He went into the barroom, signed a chit for several drinks and idled over them, wondering what to do about Rowena. The affair was over, of course, but she might not understand that; he hoped she wouldn't cry and protest when he told her he had to move on.

He was astonished, when he finally went back upstairs, to see that she had dusted already.

He paid his hotel bill, packed his bag, and had bag and package carted to the depot, where he consigned the package to himself in New York City under the new name he would be using in the future, Alexander Wilson.

Chapter Nineteen

It was a rainy morning when Ira and Bull left the limestone caves and rode slowly down to the Bend bridge. The rain let up as they sat the horses under the trees, waiting as a single buckboard rattled across the bridge and disappeared in the trees on the far side.

They must make sure nothing went wrong, Ira said. They would capture the woman and take her across the prairie to Sunray, a burg about a hundred miles northwest where there was a railroad and a telegraph line. McCarthy would be instructed to bring the ransom money with him; he would leave it with the proprietor of Wright's Store, the only building at Wright's Crossing on the Crowfoot River. McCarty would then retreat five or ten miles, remain for a day, and go back to Wright's and pick up a message telling him where to find Faith.

"Will he do all that?" Bull asked, frowning at the sketch Ira had drawn.

"He will if he wants his wife back."

Ira prepared the letter for McCarty using a stub of pencil, wetting it frequently so the writing would show. Then he read it over, picking his teeth with a little finger and studying Bull covertly. To his mind, the plan had a number of variables, though Bull probably didn't see them. The main thing was to get their hands on the money and not get caught.

They crossed the bridge and walked the horses down the River Road toward the McCarty house. It was still early, too early; they got down and walked the last hundred yards to a clump of brushy trees, leading the horses, and sat down to wait. A light drizzle was feathering down and wraiths of mist rose from the river. Bull hunched over, swearing under his breath.

Ira looked longingly toward the fence; somewhere in those dry leaves and grass was the lost brooch—so near and yet so far. But one day he would return and search for it.

They waited more than an hour before McCarty came trotting a sorrel horse from around the far side of the big house. They watched him unlock the gate, move through, and merely loop the chain over the hasp. The gate was left unlocked during the day, a fact which Ira had already ascertained. McCarty then disappeared along the road to town.

Bull got up and swung aboard his horse. "C'mon, dammit, Ira."

Ira got up stiffly, stretching. There was plenty of time now. Jesus, he was getting too old to be squatting in the wet and cold trying to make a dollar. This affair had better be his last fling; he would take the money and go east and never come back. He hadn't thought ahead to how he would deal Bull out of the pot, but somehow it would happen. Even if he had to use his pistol. He needed that fifty thousand.

Mounting his horse, he followed Bull to the gate.

The house was gray and quiet as they rode toward it, the horses snuffling, blowing steam. There was a buggy in front of the stable and a buck-toothed boy was pushing a black horse into the traces. He saw them and stopped what he was doing to stare. Ira waved and smiled at him and he continued to hook up the black, still staring.

Ira said, "When'll Miz McCarty be out?"

"D'rectly," the boy replied. He glanced toward the back door of the house. "What you want?"

"Want to see her," Bull growled.

"Now, now," Ira said quickly. "We're from the store, that's all. Got a message for her."

The boy looked them over. "From the store? I never seen you b'fore."

"Well, we don't *work* at the store, sonny. Like I say, we got a message for—"

The back door slammed and Ira jerked his head around. A woman in an olive-green dress stood there, hands on her hips. "What message?"

"You Miz McCarty?" Bull asked, moving toward her.

She saw Ira then and her brows climbed. "Mr. Brown! What is it you want?"

Bull drew his pistol. "We wants you." He cocked the pistol suddenly as she seemed about to grab at the door. "Don't you do nothing foolish, Miz McCarty." He got down and approached her.

Ira slid his pistol out and pointed it at the boy. "You—go in the stable there and saddle up a ridin' horse for Miz McCarty."

The boy closed his mouth, nodded, and jogged for the stable. Ira followed, walking the horse.

"I'm not riding a horse anywhere!" Faith said.

Bull climbed the steps and opened the door. He pushed her inside. "Go get a coat."

"What are you doing?" Faith cried. "What do you want?"

There was an older woman in the kitchen, warming a pan of milk on the stove. Her eyes were like saucers and she was stammering. Bull demanded, "You the cook?"

The woman nodded. She was pale and seemed about to faint.

Bull said, "Get us some grub together. Bread, meat, cheese—put it in a sack." He waved the pistol toward her as she hesitated. "G'wan—move, woman!"

He shoved Faith again. "I tole you, go get a coat. You going with us."

There was a coat on a chair back and Faith picked it up. Bull looked at her dress and at the coat; he shook his head. "Them ain't no clothes. Go put something on. You going out on the prairie. Put some pants on if you got 'em." He pushed her again, "Do like I say!"

Faith went into the hall, dropped the coat on a chair and stumbled upstairs with Bull following. He stood in the bedroom, grinning at her as she pulled off the olive dress and donned a worn flannel shirt. She was a mighty good looking woman, all smooth and silky under the chemise. She rummaged in an alcove and came out with a pair of jeans, stepping into them. Bull had never seen a woman in pants before. He had seen girls in divided skirts in a Bill Show once, but he was astounded at the change it made in this one. The jeans were a little too big for her and now she looked dumpy and rumpled instead of stylish.

"Put on something warm," he told her. "It's raining out there."

She put on a heavy coat. "There's a poncho downstairs. When my husband hears about this—"

"Shuddup." Bull growled and grabbed her arm, yanking her through the door.

The cook had a sack ready and cowered back as he snatched it up. They'd wasted enough time here. "Get the goddamn poncho," he said. She took it from a hall shelf and he pushed her ahead of him to the back door. Then he went back and tied the woman cook to a kitchen chair.

Ira had a roan horse saddled. "Come on," he yelled.

"What you taking so much time for?" His face changed when he saw the woman, and he nodded. "That's a good idea. Get on that horse, ma'am."

Bull showed him the sack of food and Ira grinned. Bull was using his head for once. He watched the woman awkwardly mount the roan and settle herself. Her face was strained and white, though from fear or anger, he could not tell. He leaned out and slapped the roan's rump and the horse pranced. "Let's get a-going."

Ira led the way down the drive and out through the gate, glancing along the road toward town. Nothing moved there and he smiled. It had gone like goose grease, not a ripple to disturb the surface. He leaned down to put his letter in the McCarty mailbox.

"Now let's make tracks."

They went west, past the bridge, following the river where there was a trace of path. They made no effort to hide tracks because it would take too much time; besides, no posse would close in while they had the McCarty woman. She was their ticket to both freedom and wealth.

They rode steadily, not stopping at all for several hours. The drizzle persisted and a few times rain lashed them, then let up. When at last Ira called a halt and got down to breathe the horses, the drizzle stopped, and for a moment the yellow sun broke through the smother of clouds. It was like an omen of good luck, Ira decided, gazing at the slanting rays. They were going to pull this off all right.

They chewed cold meat and Bull said to the woman, "What's your name anyway?"

"Faith."

Bull made a face. "Knew a gal named Faith once. She was workin' a boat along the Missouri, her'n four others. Damn if she—"

"That ain't no way to talk to a lady," Ira said. "You

201

ain't got no goddamn manners or bringin'-up, Bull. You want some meat, ma'am?"

She shook her head.

They got on the horses again and went on. Late in the day Ira led them into a wide meadow and, crossing it, called a halt. "What the hell is that?" He sat, astonished at the vast number of stakes set out in the flats.

Bull rode forward and pulled up a stake. "They's stakes," he said, turning it over and over in his hands.

"Who the hell is setting out stakes in the middle of nowhere?"

Bull shook his head and dropped the piece of wood. Ira led them at a walk, staring at the neat rows of cut saplings. Some fool had been hard at work all right, and he blew out his breath in wonderment. It didn't make sense.

Past the meadow they turned northwest and, near dusk, came to an abandoned adobe hut set against a shelving sandstone hill. Bull got down with his rifle and investigated. He poked through the hut and came out shrugging. "Nothing inside."

The hut was filthy, filled with weeds and animal smell, but they cleaned it out and built a fire in the center, under a blackened ceiling hole, and the room seemed more cheerful, though the woman did not. There was plenty of firewood, mostly wet, and the drizzle came again as it got full dark. The hut had a plank door that Bull propped over the opening; the leather hinges had rotted away long ago, but the heavy wooden supports were in place and he slid a length of thick tree branch through them to effectively bar the door closed.

Then he turned and grinned at Faith.

Billy Quinn struggled with the rope binding him to the post. The smaller man, the one Faith had called "Mr.

Brown," had got down from his horse and tied him to the ceiling post—tied his hands behind him around the post. His feet were free, but that did no good.

Mrs. Steen had not been tied tightly, and after a period of tugging and twisting she got one hand free. There was a kitchen knife handy and she slit the ropes and tottered out to the stable and cut Billy free. Then he jumped on the black, hammered with his heels, and galloped bareback all the way into town. He pulled up in front of the bank and threw himself off the horse and ran upstairs, shouting for "Mr. Frank."

Frank hurried out of his office. "What is it?"

Billy was wild-eyed and panting. It took a minute to get the story out of him. Two men had come to the house and ridden off with Faith!

"Send somebody for the sheriff," he said to Ken Larkin. To Billy, "Who were they—did you get a good look at them?"

"Miz Faith knew 'em—or she knew one of 'em. She called him Mr. Brown. He was a little—"

"Ira Brown!"

"He was a little hombre, the other one was big as a house and mean lookin'. They made Miz Faith change into man's clothes, then they put her on a horse and took off west."

Frank yelled for someone to go for his horse and continued to question Billy. The men had taken food from the house too, but they had not harmed Mrs. Steen or the child. When his horse was brought, Frank ran downstairs, shouted to them to tell the sheriff where he'd gone, and galloped home.

Mrs. Steen was scared to death but unhurt. They had not tumbled her about, she said, and the outlaws had not even looked into little David's crib.

Frank felt a measure of relief. The men had forced Faith to change into male attire so that riding would be easier for her and for them. It was an indication, he thought, that they meant her no harm. It was obvious the two had come for her alone—they hadn't ransacked the house for money or valuables—and intended to ransom her. He questioned Mrs. Steen about a note or other instructions from the men, but they had given her nothing.

He was upstairs changing into jeans and woolen shirt when he heard Sheriff Welch and several men ride into the yard. Buckling his revolver about his hips, he went downstairs pushing arms into a blue jacket. Mrs. Steen had made up another sack of food for him to take along and was talking to Karl in the kitchen. Frank draped a heavy poncho over his shoulder, took up his Winchester and said, "Howdy," to Karl.

Karl handed him a sheet of paper. "Found this in your mailbox."

Frank read it with mounting anger. He was to bring fifty thousand dollars with him in cash and go at once to Wright's at the Crowfoot Crossing. He looked at Karl. "You read this, of course."

"Yes."

Frank swore under his breath and ground his teeth. It meant a delay. He'd have to go back to the bank for the money. "Who've you got with you?"

"Tim Oxford and Joel. Joel was in town this morning."

That was good news. Frank folded the paper. "I'll go back to the bank for money and take Joel with me. All right?"

"Sure, Frank." Karl went to the back door. "See you at Wright's." He went out.

Frank said, "Are you all right, Miz Steen? Send Billy for someone to stay with you, if you like. I've no idea how long we'll be gone."

"I'll pray you get them, Mr. Frank!"

"Oh, we'll get 'em," Frank said with confidence. "Don't

you worry your head about that. But I'd feel better if you'd get someone—"

"I can ask Miz Matthews to come in. She's good company."

"Good." Frank took up the rifle and hurried out.

Joel Beale was sitting a bay horse, his hat pushed back. He was a big man, round-shouldered as a black bear, with a wide grin. Billy was holding the sorrel horse; he had tied on a rifle scabbard and hooked a pair of saddlebags behind the cantle.

Frank reached up, shaking hands with Joel. "Glad you're here, Joel."

"Karl says you going into town for money. You're not goin' to pay that ransom are you?"

"I will if I have to." He shoved the Winchester into the boot and tied on the grubsack. He mounted. "Thanks, Billy. You stay here and see to Miz Steen."

The boy nodded glumly, wanting to go along.

They loped back along the River Road and Frank went into the bank with the saddlebags over his arm. It was obvious that everyone knew of the kidnapping, the way they stared at him. He went through to Cliff Donaldson's office, telling the bank manager briefly what he needed and why.

It took Donaldson only ten minutes to get the money together. They crammed it into the saddlebags; Frank signed for it and hurried out with Donaldson's blessings. And as they returned along the river, his anger at Ira Brown burst.

If he'd been able to reach Ira at that moment—God help the little bastard!

Chapter Twenty

Preacher made his rounds every day, calling on members of his flock, those who were sick and those who were mending, and those who needed someone to listen. In the course of a few weeks he picked up an enormous amount of gossip and information—none of which he passed on.

Only a few days after Rowena Preville left town Preacher heard about it, but the fact made little impression on him at the time; he noted it, said a silent prayer that she would ultimately see the error of her ways, and went on about his business.

At every opportunity, including every Sunday from the pulpit, Preacher talked against the saloons and dance halls that were beginning to crowd the east end of town. He made trouble, of course, and was often threatened because of his view that all of them were enemies of the Lord, the pimps and whiskey sellers and the girls. He ranted against wholesale sin in his newspaper column and his church was filled to overflowing every Sunday.

He thought of Gertie often and, after he heard there had been a fight and a shooting at her house, he went to see her. As before, he rapped on the back door and a Negro woman came to let him in.

The woman led him to the same small bedroom and he sat on a chair, waiting, the sounds of the house strange to his ears. Someone was singing in the front where the bar was, now and then joined by several others; a piano was tinkling, and in a nearby room a man shouted in laughter. Footsteps came and went by the door, a girl's voice said distinctly, "Dammit, he tore my lace off—"

Then Gertie came in and closed the door behind her. "Hello, Preacher, what you want?"

"Just wanted t'see if you was all right. Heard there was a shootin' in here."

She seemed surprised. "You came t'see if I was all right?"

He nodded, then smiled. "Course I want t'start that Bible readin' class we was talking about too."

Gert sat down on the bed and crossed her legs. "You're a good, lovin' man, Preacher. I'm fine, thank you." She was wearing a bit too much rouge, he thought, a shiny black dress, and a glittering necklace about her throat. Its dangling pendants twinkled in the dim light. "I dunno about the Bible class, though . . ."

"Why not?"

She smiled ruefully. "You're not very popular on this street, Logan, now that you're preachin' regular against us girls."

"I never mentioned nobody by name."

"That's what I hear, but I'm telling you what folks say."

"I'm mighty sorry to hear that, Gert. You know I preach again others too—"

"You're doing a wrong there, too, Preacher." Gert bit her lip and stopped short.

"What you mean?"

"Nothing." She shook her head. "I talk too much."

"What'd I do wrong, Gert? You mean I said a wrong thing about somebody?"

She took a breath. "I got no business mixing in—"

"Gert! You know something I don't." He grabbed her hand. "What is it?"

She pulled away. "I know you don't want to hurt nobody, Logan. But if it got back that I told you—"

"It won't. I swear, Gertie, I'll never tell a soul."

For a moment she was silent. "Frank McCarty never met any woman at that house like they say. He went there for a business meeting and nothing else."

Preacher's eyes widened. His voice was hushed. "That's the truth? How d'you know it?"

She sighed. "Because it's my house. I let Schuyler use it."

He stared at her. "Are you tellin' me it was a frame-up?"

"Yes, it was."

"Schuyler Wood did it?"

"That's all I tell you, Logan. Don't ask any more."

He took her hand again, patting it. "Gert, d'you swear to me by the Lord's name that you're telling the truth?"

"Yes, I swear it, but only to you in private."

Preacher got up slowly. "All right, Gert. I thank you deeply for tellin' me." He went to the door. "Take care of yourself. . . ." He went out and closed the door gently.

It was a terrible thing he'd done, preaching against McCarty, and preaching a lie. He had probably caused McCarty's family a great deal of suffering. And all because he was so quick to rail against what he thought was degradation. Preacher got down on his knees in the dark behind Gertie's house. With the tinny piano and the raucous voices bruising the night airs, he bowed his head and begged forgiveness for the thoughtless things he'd said.

Ira and Bull gathered sticks of wood and Ira set to work with a knife to curl off shavings and splinters, which he fashioned into a tiny tent in the blackened space ringed by field stones that was the fireplace. He struck a lucifer, wrinkled his nose at the smell, and fired the tent. As the flames took hold, feeding on the shavings, he gently laid on thicker slivers, and light crept outward as the fire crackled and smoke rose in gray puffs, flowing into the room and making their eyes water.

Bull got out the food sacks and emptied one, pawing through it. Faith crossed her arms and stood against the wall, so far from them as she could get. How long would it take Frank to rescue her from these two grinning outlaws? It never once occurred to her that he would not.

They had kidnapped her for money, fifty thousand dollars, Ira said. "That's all we want from you, missy. Then you can go free and that's all of it. Bull'n me, we'll go to South America and you'll never hear o' us again."

She had noticed that Bull looked startled at Ira's words, so she assumed the two had not really talked about what they'd do when they got their hands on the money.

But before either of them got very far, Frank would appear and shoot them down; there was no other way they would be taken, and she knew he would do it. There had been a time when she was afraid of guns and hated to see Frank strap his pistol on. But one day, in Leah and J.M.'s house, she had been forced to fire a revolver in self-defense. She had killed a man who was trying to kill her, and afterwards her opinions had undergone a subtle change. There were times when a gun was a very handy tool.

The two men made coffee and gave her a tin cup full; Bull toasted bits of meat on sticks and gave them to her half raw. They were stringy and saltless, but she chewed them all and drank the coffee. Frank would be on their trail by now; she could imagine his consternation at the news that she'd been kidnapped. Such a crime was almost unheard of.

She had no idea where the two were heading; they didn't talk about it in front of her, but they did not seem unduly concerned about their safety. They had not hesitated to light a fire, for instance. Perhaps it was because she was there and they knew Frank would not come bursting in, a pistol in each hand.

That subdued her somewhat. Frank might follow, but he could not overtake them and force a fight. It put a rather different complexion on the situation.

She stared at the two, memorizing their features. Had Ira Brown boarded the stage that day at Epps Station with the idea then to kidnap her? Or had it developed because he had met her and learned of the McCarty family? She barely spoke to him in her disgust, but he was more affable than the big one. Bull was hardly more than an animal, with no redeeming qualities at all that she could see. He growled and snarled every word, tore at his food like a vulture, and scowled at her constantly; God only knew what monstrous thoughts were churning through his head. She was positive it was only Ira's presence that saved her from a horrible fate.

Bull tossed her a blanket and indicated she was to lie down against the far wall. He piled wood on the fire, keeping the chill off, but it would not last. She wrapped herself in the smelly blanket and lay on her poncho, thoughts turning homeward. Little David would cry for her, and Mrs. Steen would do her best to console him. . . .

She woke slowly, realizing she had dozed. The room was silent except for the deep breathing of the two men. She was cold—probably the reason she had awakened—and there was no sound from outside. It was dark, the fire had long since died out, and she was stiff. Pulling the blanket more tightly about her, she closed her eyes and tried to sleep. She would need all her strength.

But sleep would not come. She was too cold. Perhaps she could unfold the poncho and pull half of it over her. She sat up slowly, turning and twisting to get the kinks out, hugging herself. The room was not black. She could make out the unmoving forms of Bull and Ira in the grayness—it was close to dawn.

For long moments she sat there, listening to their breathing, blinking sleep from her eyes. She could make out the door, with the branch that barred it.

Pulling the blanket off, she stood up slowly, biting her lip. If she could get outside, she could get on one of the horses and gallop away—maybe even take the other horses with her!

She took a step toward the door, planting her booted foot softly, watching the two. They were sprawled on the hard dirt, Bull snoring gently, Ira curled up, his head on a saddle. She took another step—and another, gaining confidence when they did not stir.

Touching the heavy branch, she grit her teeth and curled both hands under it. It weighed a ton, but she strained, patiently lifting it an inch at a time, praying it would not suddenly tip sideways and thump to the floor. Her heart was pounding, but the branch came free of the supports and she knelt on one knee to carefully set it on the floor.

There had not been a sound. She opened her mouth to breathe silently and looked at her captors. Neither of them had moved. Relieved, she stood again and put both hands on the plank door. It was going to be very heavy indeed, but if she could open one end of it she should be able to slide through.

She put her weight on the door, swinging it sideways—and it scratched along the earth. She halted it instantly, waiting, unable to see behind her. Taking a deep

212

breath, she moved the door once more, as slowly as possible.

Then, from the far side of the room, she heard the unmistakable sound of a revolver hammer being pulled back, click clack. Ira's voice said, "Get away from the goddamn door, girl."

She nearly cried.

Ira was angry. "Get the hell over there on your blanket."

Bull came abruptly awake, snorting and coughing, wanting to know what the matter was, and when he learned, glared at her, shaking his huge fist. "We got to tie you up, dammit?"

Ira went outside as Bull made a fire. The horses were all right, he said on returning. There was no sign of anyone around. He said it with a sneer, ordering Faith to make coffee.

They cooked more meat for breakfast, drank the coffee, and went on. It was barely light, cold, with no wind at all but no rain either. Faith huddled under the thick poncho, content to let the horse take her, her mind flooded by hopelessness and exasperation.

It was impossible to tell in which direction they rode, but she thought it was north, with Ira constantly riding ahead looking for landmarks. The prairie was formless and vast, hardly broken at all except for an occasional wash, sometimes with a swiftly flowing stream, sometimes puddled. The skies were overcast, drifting mists swirled by them, smelling clammy, and she had never felt so alone in her life.

Looking back, she could see no pursuit . . . nothing.

Toward evening a light rain began to drizzle about them. Ira and Bull dug out ponchos and shrugged into them. Faith had no hat, bowed her head and did her best to pull the poncho up for relief, but she was thoroughly miserable.

But the two men were in a good mood. Even Bull joked and laughed in a harsh chuckle. She could not hear their words, but the tone of Bull's voice grated on her nerves. Why didn't Frank come riding out of the mists and scatter them?

Ira told her, after a bit, that their journey was almost at an end for the time being. They would reach their objective in a few more miles.

She expected a habitation and was disappointed. They came to a broad wash, crossed it and halted at the foot of a low ridge where willows and shadowy cottonwoods were growing in clumps. Everything was wet and dripping, the horses stood with heads down, and she waited while Ira and Bull conferred out of earshot. Finally Bull came back toward her and Ira went off over the prairie, heading north.

"Get down," Bull said. "I'll make a fire back in them trees."

She slid off the horse and swayed, grasping the saddle as Bull leered at her. She was sore and tired; it had been years since she'd been astride a horse, and she'd never ridden all day long before. Bull led the two horses under the trees where it was slightly dryer and stripped off saddles and bridles. He picketed them in deep grass then gathered up an armful of twigs and branches and produced flint and steel. She sat dully and watched as he got a fire going. When she asked where Ira had gone he only growled at her.

Ira went along the wash, another mile or two he figured, and halted in sight of Wright's place. It was one single adobe-and-board building with several shacks attached and a privy behind them near a corral. There were four horses in the corral, huddled under the partial shelter of a board awning; he could see no one at all and, as he circled the place, could find no tracks.

They had gotten here well ahead of McCarty.

Down along the river he saw smoke and, riding that way, glimpsed a grouping of brown tepees. Indians coming to trade at the store, probably. He grunted and spat.

There were no horses at the hitchrack in front of the store, so he went in and got down, looping the reins over the pole. The store was battered, whitewashed years ago and neglected since, with heavy round logs sticking through the plaster in the Spanish fashion. The name, *Wright's Store,* was printed in fading letters across the front above the door.

A man came to the door, opening it as Ira went through into the large square store. "Howdy," the man said. "You must be lost."

Ira grinned and pulled off his sopping hat. He shook his head. "I had a map. You Wright?"

"I'm Jamie Wright." He put out his hand and Ira took it. Jamie was a tall, stooped man with a black beard and weak eyes behind steel-rimmed specs. "My old man, he started this store. I guess I'm stuck with it. Nobody t'sell to and not 'nough business to stick in your ear."

"You got a drink?" Ira looked around. The store smelled of oil and grease and ashes, some of it from the huge black stove in the center of the room. There was fire going and the room was warm, not at all hot, but enough to drive away the chill.

Jamie produced a bottle behind the counter and poured out a half glassful. "There you go."

Ira laid down a dollar for the drink and a sack of Blackwell's. He drank off the whiskey and coughed, thumping his chest. "Damn me, that's good. Give us another." He held the glass while Jamie poured.

Behind the counter to the left was a long section of pigeonholes, some with letters or papers stuck in them.

"Like to leave a letter for a feller."

Jamie nodded. "Cost you a quarter. But I'll supply a envelope."

"Fair enough." Ira leaned on the counter and printed out his letter to McCarty.

Leave the fifty thousand dollars here in a sack. Then you go off five miles east and wait. Come back the next day and get your wife. No tricks.

Ira did not sign the note. He folded it into the envelope and sealed it, writing McCarty on the front. Jamie looked at it. His eyebrows rose, he glanced at Ira, but put the envelope in one of the slots.

"McCarty's comin' here?"

"He better," Ira said.

Chapter Twenty-one

The trail left by the pair and Faith was plain to see on the muddy ground and Frank, Karl, and the others followed it at a near gallop. It went along the river where, hours later, they came to a wide meadow and stopped to stare at the rows of stakes.

It was dark but the fresh-cut tops of the stakes reflected slivers of light, rows and rows, marching into the darkness.

"What the hell is that?" Karl said, walking his horse past them. "Somebody's staked out fields."

"Not fields, garden plots maybe," Joel said. "Hell of a lot of 'em."

Frank was not interested. He left the others behind and went on, leaning from the horse to determine that the tracks had passed by, crossing the meadow and the small stream that bordered it. He reined in on the far side of the stream and got down. There wasn't enough light.

They made camp near the stream, under a grove of trees. Frank ate a few mouthfuls of supper and walked upstream, away from the others, to stare across the shadowy meadow. It would be dangerous for Faith's sake for them to catch up to the kidnappers, and yet it was a terrible strain not to make every attempt. Mrs. Steen's impression of the men had not been favorable. She had described them both as desperate looking characters. He recalled Ira Brown in Karl's jail. The man had a shifty attitude, and would probably do anything he thought necessary to protect himself, even to destroying Faith.

So, for the time being, it would be best to follow the instructions given him. Ira Brown had not looked stupid. If he got the ransom money, he would probably figure it was best to leave Faith and get out fast.

That was a comforting thought. The money was a hell of a lot less important than Faith.

Faith was not a weakling, of course; she had been reared on a farm and was strong and wiry despite her looks. She would be able to keep up, no matter what their pace, if they didn't abuse her.

And if they abused her, he would track them to the ends of the earth and get rid of them both, one way or another.

In the morning they came upon the adobe hut in the first few hours, and it was obvious their quarry had slept here. Caught on a sliver of wood inside was a shred of white cloth that was so sheer and silken it had to be Faith's. Frank picked it up, staring at it in his palm. Had she left it for him to find?

The rain caught them soon after and by noon the trail was impossible to follow, but by then the kidnappers could hardly be making for anyplace but Wright's.

They got down and made coffee, shielding a tiny fire from the drizzle with ponchos and their bodies, chewed cold meat, and debated.

"It could be a goddamn trick," Tim Oxford suggested. "They could swing south to Santa Fe . . ."

"What for?" Karl said. "They after the money."

Joel said, "They're asking Frank to leave the money at Wright's, but they could take Faith with them as insurance."

"She'd slow 'em down some," Tim thought.

218

"Or they could go on to Killrain," Karl said. "That's a couple hundred miles past Wright's, and there's a railroad there."

"What about Sunray?" Frank asked. "There's a railroad there too."

Karl sighed. "Too damn many things them sonsabitches could do. And we got to stay two jumps behind 'em."

"Until they turn over Faith," Joel said.

"Sunray's the closest town to Wright's with a railroad," Frank persisted. "If they get on a train we might never catch up."

"It ain't rightly a town," Tim Oxford said. "I was there once, five years ago. It's a wide place in the road, not as wide as the path to the privy. Trains stop there for water."

Karl looked at Frank. "What you thinkin', Frank?"

"I'm trying to put myself in the place of a couple of goddamn kidnappers. What would I do?" He sighed. "Besides hold my hat and hope."

Faith was asleep, rolled in the smelly blanket, when Ira returned from Wright's. She woke, despite her tiredness, when she heard the horse. Ira rode in, pulled off the saddle and picketed the animal, then he and Bull talked by the fire. She could hear their voices in a low murmur, but could make out no words.

Ira had brought back a bottle and they shared it, becoming slightly noisier, laughing and making jokes.

But she slid off into sleep again, and woke at dawn, blinking and gazing at the leaden sky. There was no rain, but it was cold. She heard the two stir, then roll out and grump, lighting a fire and swearing, with Ira complaining and Bull growling.

She got up slowly, feeling itchy, combing her hair with

clawed fingers. Ira gave her a cup of steaming coffee and she sipped it gratefully, wondering what the day would bring. Any minute Frank would show up with Karl and a dozen riders, surround them and rescue her . . .

If only he would!

Ira and Bull saddled the three horses and they rode, with Ira in the lead, for a half-hour and halted. The two talked out of earshot, arguing and gesturing, and finally Ira beckoned to her. When she joined them Ira said, "You go on with Bull, missy."

"Where to?"

"Just you come," Bull snarled. "You ain't askin' the questions." He motioned and she nudged the horse, pulling the poncho about her.

They went on at a walk for hours. Now and then a brief drizzle feathered down; the horizon changed from deep blue-gray to light, seeming like smoke in the sunlight, then fading. A cold wind pushed her from behind, tearing up bits of grass and flinging them ahead of her like a petulant child; nothing else moved on their circle of prairie.

Bull was looking for landmarks, she realized; now and then he changed direction, but by nightfall they had seen nothing but the eternal prairie. Bull halted in the midst of some low, grassy hills and told her to get down. It was a cold camp, with cold food and no trees for shelter. Faith slept huddled in the blanket and the clammy poncho, waking fitfully a dozen times at night, dreaming terrible things. She woke, feeling more tired than when she'd dropped off. The air was chill and she was surprised to see a thin scattering of snow on the ground.

Bull swore when he saw it and got her up and mounted as quickly as possible. But the snow disappeared in the first hours after dawn, and Bull's mood became more cheerful. She realized that the snow had showed their path very clearly, but when it was gone there were no tracks to be seen.

Toward dusk, they came to the railroad.

Bull climbed the embankment and stared each way, frowning and muttering to himself. He looked at the sky, at her, and finally decided on a direction; they went to the right, following the curving rails and the lonely posts that held up the telegraph wires.

It was full dark when they saw the flickering lights of Sunray in the distance.

The weather was miserable and it grew colder; the wind bit into a man's bones, and Frank hunched over the horn feeling useless. It was anyone's guess what they'd find at Wright's—if anything at all. Karl said he'd never known a thief who wouldn't lie when it suited him. He had a low opinion of Ira Brown, but they had no option but to go to Wright's place.

Karl had no great opinion of Wright either. Jamie Wright had been accused of illegal trading with the Indians—liquor and guns—though no one had been able to prove it because he was so far out in the sticks. How the man stayed alive selling beans and bacon to passing pilgrims was a mystery, in Karl's opinion. If Jamie was indeed peddling illicit goods and trading with Indians and men two jumps ahead of the law, as some said, then the location of his store made better sense. But Wright's was not in Roseberry County, and therefore not Karl's concern.

They came across the Crowfoot River a bit past midday and followed it for several miles; it was running full, muddy and laden with brush and twigs, tearing out banks and, as Tim said, having itself a hell of a time.

Wright's was built on high ground where the river bent

north in a slow sweep, wide and shallow; in summer it was no more than a trickle and a man could walk across anywhere. In winter it was still fordable, but dangerous—and icy.

Frank halted a half-mile away and used his field glasses. There were no horses tied in front of the single building, a bleak, uninviting picture. Far off to the left he could make out the peak of a tepee where a smudge of smoke blended with the gray skies. He handed the glasses to Karl, who swung them at once to the tepee and grunted.

Joel said, "C'mon, let's get a wiggle on. Wright's got a fire going."

"Ain't nobody around," Karl agreed. He moved ahead slowly.

They saw no one at all as they walked the horses to the store and got down to loop reins over the hitchpole. Someone was shouting inside as Frank opened the door. The shouting ceased like magic, and then a man stuck his head up from behind a low partition and his scowl turned into a smile.

"Howdy, gents, come right on in, come in." He was tall and bearded, polishing his specs and blinking at them. "Just talkin' to my ol' lady . . ." He caught sight of Karl's star and swallowed hard. "Something I can do for you gents?"

Frank noticed the Indian woman behind the partition as she ducked out of sight; so Wright was married to a squaw. It might explain a lot. He saw that Karl had noted the woman also.

Karl said, "I reckon you're Jamie Wright." At Wright's nod he introduced them, and Jamie's eyes stayed on Frank.

"You McCarty? Then I got a letter f'you." He pulled the envelope from the slot and handed it over.

"How'd you get this?"

"Little short hombre brung it in. Never saw 'im before. Said you'd be along to get it and took off. That's all."

Frank tore open the envelope, read the note and passed it on to Karl. "You know what this says?"

Jamie shook his head violently. "Hell no. He never told me."

Frank looked at Joel and Tim. "Search the place, everywhere you can think of—store, corrals, sheds, everything."

Tim asked, "What you looking for?"

"Ira Brown," Frank said.

Frank went outside and looked at the sky, turning as Karl followed.

"What you going to do, Frank?"

"I'm thinking on it." He glanced around the undulating horizon. "I expect Ira Brown is watching us this minute. . . ."

Karl lowered his voice. "You ain't going to leave that money here—?"

"The main thing is to get Faith back." Frank fished for a cheroot and rolled it in his fingers. "If I leave it here, when'll he come for it—at night?"

"Of course he will." Karl frowned at the door of the store. "There ain't any telling what kind of a plan he's hatched with Jamie Wright either."

"I doubt it. He wouldn't want Wright to know what's in the package."

Karl sighed. "Maybe not."

Frank walked away from the store, gazing at the fast-moving river. He smelled the cheroot again, put it in his mouth and felt for a match. He had to leave the money for Ira Brown; there was really no choice, not with Brown holding Faith. He could not bring himself to take a chance with her life, because there was no way to know how unstable Ira or his partner was. If he tried to trick them and failed, they might kill her in a rage.

He lit the cheroot and puffed, blowing smoke that was whipped away instantly in the chill wind. He watched the gray-brown river, flowing with roily whitecaps like fluttering lace. A short distance away, near the river bank, was the Indian camp. There were three tepees and he could make out several blanketed figures moving about. Tepees were common on the prairie these days; many Indians waited for the return of the buffalo, unable to believe they would never come back. In the meantime they hunted deer and smaller animals and begged food or stole it. These had obviously come here to trade with Wright.

He went back. Joel and Karl were talking, walking up and down in front of the hitchrack, with Karl shaking his head. Joel probably was advancing some scheme or other.

Coming up to them, Frank said, "I'm going to leave the money."

"Thought you would," Karl said with a heaviness in his voice. "You'd best wrap it good." He spat in the grass. "Nobody hidin' anywhere."

Joel said, "Let me stay here in the store. I can——"

"No," Frank shook his head.

"But, dammit, Frank——"

"Dammit yourself," Frank said with heat. "Those crooks can count. Four of us ride in and three out, what the hell! They'll know you're inside."

Joel frowned, and was silent. Karl chuckled. "That's what I told him. He's still damp behind the ears."

Joel let out his breath in annoyance. "It's a chance worth taking. You can't be positive they're watching us."

"You're not staying," Frank said, "and that's that." He unhooked the saddlebags, tossed them over his shoulder and went inside.

He bought a pasteboard box and wrapping paper from Jamie Wright and took it to the far end of the store. With Karl, Tim, and Joel keeping Jamie's attention, Frank wrapped the money, put it in the box and wrapped the

224

box, tying it with heavy twine. He wrote his name on the outside: *McCarty*.

Jamie's curiosity was enormous, but he asked no questions and set the wrapped box on a shelf behind the counter, nodding as Frank told him to give the box to the same man who had left the letter.

He went out to the horse, stamped the butt of the cheroot into the ground and mounted. Well, *that* was done, and now they would see how well Ira and his partner kept bargains. He did not wait for the others, but rode slowly along the river, his eyes searching the misty horizons for some sign of Ira Brown. If only he could get his hands on the shifty little man! Brown seemed to epitomize all the factions pressuring him; his domination of the town and country, and the general seediness of the town itself. It was his fault these things had happened, because he had been too lax, too willing to accept men like Ira Brown into the community. He was guilty of accepting change for change's sake. Ira Brown and others were taking advantage of him.

When Joel called, asking him where he was going, Frank turned, scowling, then reined in, seeing the surprise on their faces. He sighed and shook his head.

Chapter Twenty-two

Edgar Tyffe and his partner, John Porter, arrived in Roseberry late in the day, took rooms at the hotel, and asked directions to Glover.

"To where?" said the hotel clerk. He stared at the two well-dressed men and shook his head. "Glover?"

"It's a town only a couple dozen miles down the river," Ed said with surprise in his voice.

"No it ain't," the clerk said. "There's no town down the river. Nothing at all for a hunnerd miles."

The men blinked at him. "No town," Porter repeated. "Hell yes, there's a town!" He pulled out a brochure and unfolded it, spreading it on the desk in front of the startled clerk's eyes. "What you call that?"

The clerk moved his lips, reading the printed words. "Approximately twenty-five miles west of the booming town of Roseberry . . ." He looked at them in astonishment. "I been in this town for two years and I never heard of it!" He turned the brochure over and stared at the name on the back. "Schuyler Wood! Hell, he's a lawyer here . . ."

"He is?"

"His office is a couple blocks down." The clerk pointed.

Porter grabbed up the brochure and the two men almost ran out to the street.

The office was closed when they arrived, and they went around the corner to the Silver Spur to talk it over. The clerk's reaction had shaken them, but there was a chance he was mistaken. Ed argued that no one could be mistaken about a town the size of the one depicted on the colored brochure, and Porter advocated going there to make sure.

"It's the only way we'll know." And after several more beers they agreed. They would get a pair of horses from the livery and make the trip.

Old Sam, at the stable, had never heard of the town either, when they asked him the next morning. The road ended at the Bend bridge, Sam told them; there was nothing at all beyond.

And so it proved. The road ended, but there was a trail of sorts, barely discernable, and they followed it with the river on their left.

At the end of the day they reached the meadow and stopped short, staring at the rows of stakes. It was apparent to both at the same instant that this was the townsite. There was even the stream described in the brochure. Ed Tyffe slid off his horse like a man in a trance; he pulled up one of the stakes and turned it over and over in his hands as if unable to believe what he saw. He gazed out over the darkening meadow as the sun's last dying light glinted on the pounded-in saplings.

"Johnny, we been suckered." His voice sounded tired all at once. He dropped the stake and leaned on the horse, both hands clutching the pommel, head down. He didn't move as Porter rode out into the meadow and halted, looking at the neat rows.

They made a camp near the stream, cooked meat and beans and drank coffee as their anger surfaced. Schuyler

Wood had tricked them, taken their money under false pretenses, and they would have something to say to that.

They were on the trail back to Roseberry before it was light, and arrived in the middle of the afternoon, halting in front of the lawyer's office.

Schuyler Wood was in. He looked up, startled, when the two men burst inside and made for him. "You Schuyler Wood?"

Schuyler nodded and put his pen down. "What is it?"

Ed Tyffe thrust the much-folded brochure under the lawyer's nose. "We bought five of your city lots, you tinhorn! There ain't even a shack on that property!"

Schuyler stared at the brochure—it was not one of his, but looked very much like it. "May I?" he said. He took the paper, folded it out and examined it with mounting surprise. It was exactly the same as the ones printed by Cole Stedman, except that the descriptive copy was different and the colors and paper were better. His name, as founder, was even on the back! His mouth opened and closed as he gazed at it, completely taken aback.

"You'll give us our money back," Ed said with a growl, "or we'll take it out'n your hide."

"Where—where did you get this!?"

Ed pounded his fist on the desk. "We want our money!"

Schuyler passed a hand across his forehead. "Wait a moment, gentlemen—I don't understand. Where did you get this?" He shook the brochure.

"In Kansas City, of course. Week or so ago."

Schuyler leaned back in the chair and stared at them. "I never had this printed. Someone else . . ." His voice trailed off and he licked his lips, thinking about George Kilburn. So George had double-crossed him after all. George had no business selling lots in Kansas City. He'd printed these brochures after he'd had the plates made for the drawing! It had to be that way!

229

"What about it, lawyer?" Ed demanded.

Schuyler jerked his head up. He tossed the brochure back to them. "Well, the way I see it, my loss is your gain. How much did you pay for the lots?"

"One hundred dollars each. Five hundred between me and Johnny here."

"Then you got them cheap, gentlemen. When the railroad reaches Glover they'll be worth triple that. I suggest you—"

Ed's face was red. "You ain't going to pay us back?"

"There's nothing there," Porter said. "Not a damned thing." He caught up the brochure and pointed to the drawing of the town. "Lookit that—warehouses, boats, schools—you're a goddam fake, lawyer."

"Calm yourselves," Schuyler said. *"There will* be a town there, and soon. A town can be built almost overnight!"

Ed said, "We want our money."

Schuyler shook his head. "I haven't got—"

"You're a goddam cheat!"

Porter pulled Ed's arm. "C'mon—we'll go to the law."

"There's nothing to go to law about," Schuyler said earnestly. "You've bought your lots, and there *will* be a town at Glover, I promise you."

Ed stormed to the door and flung it open; he paused to shake his fist at Schuyler, then he and Porter slammed the door.

Schuyler sat staring at the opposite wall, a sinking feeling inside him. George would sell the lots—but George would not share a dollar of the money; and that money was needed to build the town. He cursed the day he'd sent for George Kilburn.

That afternoon he saw Fred Ainger, the Justice of the Peace. Fred was a studious-looking man of perhaps forty, slightly stooped and hard of hearing in one ear; he habitually carried his head on one side as if perpetually listening. They met in the street near the livery and Fred told him two men, Tyffe and Porter, had filed charges against him, declaring Schuyler had bilked them of money.

Schuyler explained the circumstances, not mentioning that George was double-crossing him. The entire transaction was legal and the two men had no case, he argued, offering to show Fred the Townsite Act and his papers.

When he left Fred he went to the telegraph office and wired his friend in Chicago. The return wire was not a surprise. George had not showed up in Chicago at all.

It would be necessary to print new brochures—Cole Stedman had the plates—and start all over again.

Cole had finished the first two runs for the new brochures when another group of five men showed up in Roseberry, all of whom had bought lots in the new town of Glover. These people were followed by several more, and a wagon train was made up at the edge of town, led by a huge ex-farmer named Barky Reutzel.

Ed Tyffe and John Porter, when they heard about the train, rode out to sit by the fires and discuss their findings. Reutzel and the others were astounded to hear there was no town, and a delegation was elected and sent to town to interview Schuyler. Schuyler met them in his office, protested that they had no patience, swore the town was on the verge of being built—but refused to return any money.

The upshot was that they bundled Schuyler into his coat and brought him along with them—under violent protest—and put him on a horse.

It took an entire day for the wagons to rumble and bounce to the meadow; the first time Schuyler had seen it staked. He did his best to make a speech to the assembled group, "You can see the stakes for yourselves. Do you imagine we'd go to the trouble of complying with the law if we were going to cheat you?"

Barky waved one of George Kilburn's brochures. "This paper has got a picture of a town and dammit, lawyer, there ain't a thing here!"

His yell brought more shouts and questions, too many to answer—and the crowd was in little mood for answers anyway. There were a number of bottles being passed around and angry words were increasing. Obviously a number of people had expected to see buildings and homes despite what Ed Tyffe and Porter said. To find only a staked meadow was a terrible disappointment, and Schuyler could see they were about to hold him accountable.

As he attempted to edge out of the crowd, someone pushed him, then another, shouting venom at him. Schuyler fell to his knees, got up and ran blindly. In an instant the crowd came alive, howling like a maddened beast, and surged after him. Someone fired a revolver, and in the next second others fired and Schuyler screamed out.

They brought him down in the near-darkness; he fell, taking several stakes with him, and lay in the wet grass as a dozen men grouped around him, shouting and talking.

Chapter Twenty-three

Ira picked his vantage point with care, first crossing the river. He picketed his horse a half-mile from the store and slogged back on foot to find a spot on a weedy ridge where he could observe the store and the area around it. He had no field glasses, but he was close enough to make out details when the four men rode in.

He was surprised that there were only four; the big one was McCarty; he smiled. McCarty would be smart enough to carry out instructions.

The four stayed about an hour, then slowly rode away south along the river. McCarty had carried saddlebags into the store and out; it was all Ira could do to keep from crossing the river at once to claim the money. McCarty wasn't fool enough not to leave it. . . .

But he had to anticipate that McCarty would keep a watch on the store, just as he was doing. Ira picked at his teeth with a little finger. You had to respect an enemy, assume he was as smart as you.

The only way to be sure was to wiggle in after dark. He settled down to wait.

Sunray was a collection of blistered and weather-beaten buildings and shacks along one side of the railroad tracks, opposite the siding. There was a bulky tower—Faith could see it against the lighter sky—probably the water tower Ira had mentioned. There were two dark shapes on the siding, boxcars, and lights in only a few of the other buildings.

Bull got down at the hitchrack, telling her to stay put. She sat the horse and watched him go inside a saloon and reappear immediately. He went into the next building, stayed a few moments and came out, telling her to get down. "We going to sleep here."

She slid off the horse, her knees almost buckling, and leaned on the hitchpole while Bull gathered up the reins. He said, "I tole 'em we's man and wife, so you keep shut." He showed her a fist.

He tied the horses in front of the building; there was a black and white sign nailed slightly askew on the front over the door; *Sims Hotel, 25¢. Guaranteed Snake Proof.*

Bull pushed her. "Go on inside. I'll put the nags away and get us some grub."

She was weary to death and not inclined to argue. Inside was a tiny rectangular space with a black stove for heat, and a desk. There was a small window, and four chairs crowded about the stove, but no one in the room except the scarecrow behind the desk, leering at her with no teeth in his mouth. He was skinny as a lath, wearing a shabby coat over red longjohns, and he pointed to an open door.

"You go 'long there, Miz Smith. Jus' take any open one. Any one a-tall."

She nodded and tottered down the hall, her stomach grumbling. She turned in at the first door standing open; it was a room hardly big enough for the iron bed and the washstand. There was no chair and no window. The walls were rough wood planks and she could plainly hear someone snoring in the next room. She sat down on the bed, feeling the lumpy mattress, and closed her eyes.

234

Things *had* to get better. They couldn't get any worse. She sagged sideways on the bed and was asleep in seconds.

Bull awakened her when he scratched a match and lit the lantern. He had brought some bread and meat and half a dozen hard apples. The meat was fried and cold, very tough, but she chewed it and ate two of the apples. Bull would sleep across the hall, he told her, and he took her boots with him when he blew out the lantern.

When she opened her eyes again it was dawn. She blinked at the opposite wall, coming awake slowly, feeling sore and unwashed. Someone was talking in a muttering voice nearby, then footsteps moved along the hall outside the door. She turned onto her back, wondering where Frank was. Was he actively searching for her?

Of course he was. She must never let herself think anything else. It was a huge country and she could be anywhere. Maybe Ira had already completed whatever deal he was making—he had been gone a long time—and soon she would be free. She must hold that thought.

Then Bull opened her door and growled at her to get up.

Out of sight of the store, Frank halted and faced them. Before he could open his mouth, Karl said, "I vote we surround the place and keep watch. What you say?"

"I vote with you," Joel snapped, and Tim nodded.

"And soon's it gets full dark," Karl continued, "we close in."

Frank smiled. "We don't have to surround it, we can go two and two for company. It's going to be a long watch."

"There's two doors, one front and one back," Karl said

235

in an even tone. "Me'n Tim will watch the back, you take the front. That all right?"

"That's fine." Frank turned to gaze at their backtrail. Ira Brown might have followed them to see if they retreated as his instructions stated, but it would be a chancy thing for him to do in this open country. Frank would have liked to be across the river, but there was no way to get across save by swimming the horses, and it did not look like a promising idea; the river was too fast and treacherous except in front of the store.

They went back slowly, Tim and Karl riding off to the south to circle and come up to the rear of the store. Frank and Joel picketed the horses in a hollow and went forward on foot, separating and moving slowly, watching the skyline. When they came in view of the store again, they halted, lying flat. Frank could see the entire front and one side. He chewed grass stems, watching the light diminish; there were no shadows, but gradually the light faded from the land and it began to grow dark. Once Jamie Wright came out and looked at the sky, gazed around the horizon, and went back inside. A thin thread of smoke rose from the chimney, whirled along the roof into nothingness by the wind. The smoke increased after a bit, then was lost in the dusk.

Frank searched the prairie with his field glasses then, when Joel came up beside him, passed them over. "Can't see a thing."

"He'll wait till later," Joel said confidently. He watched Frank put the glasses back in a leather case. "Whyn't we move in and grab 'im, Frank? Make him tell us where Faith is?"

"I've been thinking the same thing—only if we show ourselves and he gets away—what'll happen to her?"

Joel grunted. "What'll happen to her if they get the money?"

"Yes, there's that." It wasn't much to bank on the

236

promises of a kidnapper. His impulse was the same as Joel's, to move in close. If they could get their hands on Ira Brown, it was a cinch bet they could make him talk. No matter what it took. Indians sometimes put a captive's feet in a fire, just for the hell of it. Ira might talk after the threat alone.

He looked behind them; the horizon was dark as the inside of a beaver. If they moved they wouldn't be silhouetted. The dark bulk of the store had disappeared when he stood up, and Joel jumped to his feet, chuckling.

Frank said, "No noise at all, hear?"

"You talk too much."

Frank grinned and moved toward the store. It was no trick to move silently; the wet grass deadened their footsteps, and they wore nothing that clinked. Frank halted several times to listen, hearing nothing out of the way. As they came closer there were faint sounds from the horse corral behind the store, and once a door opened and closed. Frank turned to look at Joel, a shadow beside him, but Joel shrugged. Maybe someone had gone to the privy.

Ira Brown would certainly go in the front door. He might not want to chance bumping around in the dark to find the rear. When the building loomed up, Frank halted again and knelt. There was a light on inside the store. If anyone opened the front door they'd see him clearly.

But no one did.

They saw no one and heard no one. An hour passed, then another. Joel was swearing softly under his breath. Frank rose to his feet, feeling stiff. Something *felt* wrong. Ira Brown should have appeared long ago.

Joel whispered, "Maybe he got past us."

Maybe he had.

Frank said, "Stay here." He moved off toward the back of the store. His eyes had long ago become accustomed to the dark and he could make out the poles and uprights of the corral several feet before he touched them. There was a space between the back of the building and the corral under an overhang. It was darker here and he inched along, feeling his way, feeling for the back door. Several horses in the corral snuffled and moved, sensing his presence.

He found the door near the far side, a plank door with a latchstring. Putting his ear to it, he could hear nothing. He pulled the latchstring gently and pushed on the door. It squeaked slightly and he slipped inside, pistol in hand. It was warm inside; smells crowded him—stale cooking, rancid odors, and smoke. He was in a kind of storeroom, he guessed, able to see very little of it, but there was a walkway toward the front, where a lantern was burning. Standing perfectly still, he cocked his head, listening.

No sound . . . nothing. It gave him an eerie feeling; Jamie and his wife should be here, talking, muttering, moving about—something. Unless they had detected his entry and were waiting for him to show himself and get in the first shot. That was a sobering idea.

He waited, listening, for ten or fifteen minutes, waiting for someone to get tired and move. But no one did. A tomblike silence hung over the store . . . an unnatural silence. He began to feel there was no one in the building but himself. Frank moved forward at last, the pistol out in front of him. He moved as quietly as possible, hardly breathing.

And then, as he came close to the large front room of the store, his foot touched something. He bent down, exploring with his hand. A woman lay face-down on the puncheon floor. His fingers found a pulse in her neck, fluttering and weak. She was still alive!

He stepped over her and rounded the counter, sure that he would find Jamie Wright lying on the floor.

There was a man on the floor—but it was Ira Brown!

Ira was dead, flat on his back, staring at the ceiling, a

terrible wound on one side of his head. A foot away was a length of iron bar, bloodied on the end. Frank swore out loud and looked for the package he'd left behind the bar. It was gone.

He opened the front door and beckoned for Joel, then ran back to the woman and lit a second lantern that was sitting on a box. When he moved the light close, Joel said, "Jesus! she's an Indian!"

"Yes. She must be Jamie's wife."

The Wrights' living quarters were behind the partition that divided the store, and they lifted her and placed her on the bed. She had been struck a glancing blow, and the wound had swollen enormously; the woman groaned as they moved her, but did not regain consciousness.

"Why the hell did he hit her?" Joel asked, frowning at the prone figure. He pulled a blanket over her.

"It looks to me like Jamie got curious about the package and opened it."

"So he got away with it!"

Frank nodded, moving back into the store. "But he waited till dark, and then Ira Brown showed up." He stood over the little man's body, hands on hips. "He killed Ira, and when he tried to run out maybe she wanted to stop him, and he hit her."

Joel said, "Hmmmm. Good's any, I guess." He took the lantern and went to the door. "I'll signal Karl and Tim."

Frank knelt and searched Ira's pockets, finding a little money, flint and steel, and nothing much else. There was no clue to Faith's whereabouts. The room was growing cold, and he opened the door on the stove and tossed in some shavings from the woodbox. When they flared up he added wood. What would he do now? If Ira didn't show up, would his partner come looking for him or would he lose heart and take to his heels?

He went around the counter and helped himself to a

cigar from a box, and lit it. Joel came back into the room and a few moments later Karl and Tim entered, frowning at the body on the floor.

They went through the story again, and Karl nodded approval. "With all that money, Jamie prob'ly decided to go without her, and he had to slug her outa the way."

None of them knew what to do for the woman, except make her warm and comfortable. There was no way they could go after Jamie Wright till morning, so they made themselves as comfortable as they could, sleeping on the floor.

Frank lay awake for hours, thinking it over. Killrain was at least two hundred miles north; it was a railroad stop, but so was Sunray, a good deal closer. Santa Fe was a long way south, and there were probably towns here and there with stagecoach connections. Stagecoaches were slow. If a man wanted to get out of the country fast, a train was best. Of course Ira Brown and his partner might have planned the kidnapping in advance; they might have a secret hideout provisioned where they could hole up till spring, when the hue and cry would have died. They might not have planned to get out of the country at all.

But what would they do with Faith? That was the big question. What he feared most of all was that the two had let her overhear too much. They might be afraid to let her live.

What would Ira's partner do if he discovered Ira was dead?

In the morning the woman seemed much the same. Her breathing was better but she did not remain conscious long. They made soup from a can and tried to feed her, but she moaned and dropped off in the middle of a swallow.

240

An hour after dawn, as they warmed themselves at the stove, the door opened. Joseph, the Indian boy, and an older man walked into the store to face four pistols.

They were both astonished and the man turned as if to run, but the click-clack of a hammer being pulled back stopped him.

Karl said, "That's the Indian kid!"

"Hello, Joseph," Frank said. He slid the revolver away. "We didn't expect you."

"You with them Indians camped down by the river?" Karl demanded.

The boy nodded, wide-eyed. Both were staring at the body on the floor, covered by a threadbare blanket.

Frank said, "We found 'im like that last night. D'you know him?" He pulled the blanket off Ira's face.

Joseph shook his head. "Not know him." He glanced around. "Where is Mr. Wright?"

"Gone away," Joel said, snapping his fingers. "Lit out."

The boy stared at him.

Frank beckoned and led both Indians around the counter to the woman's bed. "Do you know her?"

Joseph made an exclamation, both rushed to her, talking very fast in their own tongue. The older man examined the wound and said something to Joseph.

Joseph translated, "Who did this?"

"We think it was Jamie Wright. Do you know her?"

Joseph indicated the older man. "He is her father. She was married to Jamie. Why did he do this?"

Frank sighed. "Because of money." He explained the matter simply and Joseph translated, obviously stumbling over the conception. The man asked questions and finally seemed satisfied.

Joseph said, "He say he will go after Jamie and bring him back."

"Damn me," Joel said. "I sure like the sound of that."

Chapter Twenty-four

The older Indian, whose name, Joseph said, was White Horn, wanted to set out immediately. Karl said, "I'm going with him. This here is a law matter and I'm not a-going to let that Indian kill Jamie. He going to stand trial."

"It ain't your county," Joel said.

"I don't give a damn. Law's law. You coming with me, Tim?" He looked at Frank. "What you going to do, Frank?"

"I don't know yet." He went out to the back of the store. White Horn and Joseph were talking by the corral. He said to Joseph, "Ask him how many went away from here last night."

Joseph translated and the older man looked at Frank, then walked out beyond the corral looking at the ground. He walked away a hundred feet, paused, then came back and said something to Joseph.

Joseph said, "Only one."

"Only one horse?"

Joseph questioned White Horn who replied sharply. Joseph said, "He say only one horse. If two people go, why not take two horse." He pointed to the corral. "More horse there."

Frank said, "Thanks." He went back into the store and said to Karl, "I'm going to Sunray."

"Why the hell—?"

243

"She's got to be somewhere. White Horn said only Jamie left the store last night, so she wasn't here with Ira Brown. That means Ira left her with his partner, and the closest railroad stop is Sunray. I'm going to try there."

"What if she ain't there?"

Frank sighed. "I don't know. I'll worry about that when I have to." He watched Joseph ride off toward the Indian camp while White Horn sat by the corral and smoked his pipe. Joel put some food in gunny sacks and tied them on both horses, and in a few minutes Joseph returned with three men who went inside and lifted the woman, mattress and all, and carried her off to the camp, leading the horses.

Frank mounted and raised his hand. "See you back in Roseberry, I expect."

"Good luck," Karl called after them.

Sunray was probably two days' ride in a northwesterly direction. The only trail was along the Crowfoot River, not the direction they wanted. As they left the store behind, it began to drizzle again; they crossed the river and struck out over the prairie.

By nightfall a cold wind had sprung up and they rode hunched over, looking for a spot to camp. They found none; the prairie was devoid of trees and brush and the arroyos were running full. Frank nodded in the saddle, letting the horse take him. It was probably as comfortable as lying on the wet ground at the mercy of the rain.

He woke at intervals during the night, once when the rain was pelting down. His horse stopped, turning tail to the storm, and Joel's did the same. In the morning they were soaked and both irritable. There was no way to make a fire so they didn't try, but rode on under leaden skies, chewing cold, tough meat.

Toward nightfall they began looking for the town, though Joel was sure they'd passed it. Frank said, "We ought to run across the tracks if we passed it."

Joel grumbled. "We ought to see them goddamn tele-graph posts too."

Halting on the highest rise, Frank searched the country with his glasses, seeing no posts or town. It occurred to him they might have gotten turned around in the storm and were paralleling the railroad tracks; his sense of direction, usually unerring, might have suffered a reverse. He was about to suggest it to Joel when his ear caught something. Reining in, he cocked his head.

"D'you hear that?"

Joel glanced around the horizons. "What?"

"I don't know . . ." A moaning sound seemed to come from a long distance away, far to their right. Then it was gone. "You didn't hear anything at all?"

Joel shook his head, looking curious.

Frank turned toward the right. "Let's try this way."

"But you're going too far north!"

Frank didn't pause. "We're lost, is what we are. I think I heard a train whistle."

Joel spat. "You heard the damn wind."

"Then close your mouth and come on."

Joel sighed like a man enormously put upon and turned his horse's head.

They came to the railroad tracks in the next hour. It *had* been a train whistle. "Whistling for Sunray," Frank said with conviction. He pointed down the tracks. "That way."

Joel followed without argument, and they reached the cluster of huts and shacks soon after dark. The buildings were all on one side of the tracks, a water tower for the train on the other. Two boxcars stood idle and dirt-streaked on a siding and lights glimmered from a dozen windows.

Frank eased his revolver from the holster and held it under his coat as they rode in and halted in front of the hotel; *Sims Hotel,* the sign announced. There were no other horses at the hitchrack. Frank pointed and Joel rode around to the corral as Frank got down and stood in the deep shadows of the building.

Joel returned. "Two horses and a mule, all with the same brand."

Frank grunted. He put the pistol away, opened his coat, and went inside with Joel at his heels. There was a tubby old-timer dozing with his feet on the stove ring, and a skinny man with a patched eyeshade behind the desk busily writing on a sheet of foolscap with a pencil. The skinny clerk looked up and smiled as they entered.

"Evenin', gents. You-all wanting a room?"

Frank looked them both over. The clerk wore the dirtiest red underwear he'd ever seen, under a shabby gray coat, and he had no teeth. "Rather have information. You got a woman staying here?"

The clerk shook his head. "Nope. Not now."

"Not since when?"

"Was one, damn perty gal too—when she got cleaned up a mite. She'n her husband was here, but they went yestiddy."

"What'd her husband look like?"

The clerk grinned. "Big feller." He put his arms out.

"That's him," Joel said. "Where'd they go?"

The clerk looked from one to the other. "You fellers the law?"

"It doesn't matter what we are," Frank said. "D'you know where they went?" He reached out casually and took hold of the clerk's coat, pulling him halfway across the desk.

"No, I sure don't," the man said, squeaking the words.

Frank released him. "Did they say anything?"

The man shook his head. "The big feller, he went out for eats, that's all. They wasn't here long. I seen him a-standin' over there by the water tower starin' at the prairie a few times, like he was waitin' for somebody . . ."

246

"He was waiting for Ira," Joel said.

"Did they meet anybody here?" Frank asked.

The clerk shook his head quickly. "Not nobody I seen. They come in at night, got two rooms and—"

"Two rooms?"

"Well, them beds ain't big enough for but one person. The big feller took a room across the hall. Anyways, in the morning he brought her eats and moseyed around some, but he stuck pretty close. Like I said, seemed t'me he was waitin' for somebody. They stayed the next night and lit out in the afternoon. I didn't go out t'see which way."

Frank stared at the man who fidgeted and bit his lip under the steady gaze. Then he shook his head. "That all I know, mister."

Turning, Frank looked at the man by the stove. He said, "I didn't see 'em at all. I come in this mornin'."

Next to the hotel was a small mercantile store, and back of it a saloon. They looked in both, looked at all the horses and all the shacks. Bull and Faith were certainly not in Sunray.

They took rooms in the hotel and bought food in the store. There was a small café attached to the saloon, run by a Mexican woman, but the grease smells drove them away. Frank preferred to eat beans out of a can than greasy fried meat.

The cot bed was miserable, sagging in the middle and smelly. The tiny room gave him a terrible feeling of being squeezed by walls, and he was glad when dawn came creeping in to show him the washbasin where he could splash chill water on his face. Joel was up, and in half an hour they had saddled the horses and were riding out of Sunray.

"Forever, I hope," Joel said with feeling.

The gray skies were moving and shredding, and occasionally a ray of sunlight stole through, but not enough to warm them. There was no wind, and no drizzle, either, which was a blessing. Frank rode with a heavy heart; not knowing where Faith was, or how she was, did not contribute to his well-being. The fear that Bull would discover Ira's death and kill Faith clogged his mind.

They were following a faint track—someone had driven a wagon this way several times, and at one point had used a shovel to widen a saddle between sand hills. This was probably the path used by Jamie Wright, Frank thought, to get supplies to his store. There seemed to be fresh tracks too, horses going both ways in the last few days, and he thought it was certain that Bull would go toward Wright's to find Ira Brown.

Bull would be itchy because of the money Ira was to receive, and maybe he did not trust Ira.

It was all so completely logical that Frank feared to believe it. People were not always logical, especially a man like Bull.

It did not rain again that day and the prairie gradually began to dry out, helped by a cold breeze that ruffled the grass.

"Cold enough to snow," Joel said, rubbing his gloved hands. "We going to have a cold winter."

They halted at noon, made a small fire, and boiled coffee; the hot liquid was welcome and made cold meat more palatable. Frank ate, staring in the direction of Wright's Store. What would they find there? It was frustrating trying to outguess outlaws.

Two hours later they were riding along the banks of an arroyo filled with rushing brown water, seeking a way across. The hoofprints of other horses preceded and led them to a narrow place where they were able to jump their mounts over the torrent. As they did so, Joel said, "*Hsst*—what's that?" He pointed ahead.

Frank stood in the stirrups, trying to catch movement, and in another few seconds a man came riding up the far lope of a ridge and over it. He was followed in a few seconds by a smaller rider.

Faith? It had to be!

Touching spurs to the horse, Frank started for them with Joel at his heels. The distant man saw them at once and reined in. Frank motioned, yelling to Joel, "Move out!" Joel swerved, yanking his rifle from the boot.

The stranger was a big man, riding with a rifle across his thighs. He lifted the weapon, levering it, and his companion instantly turned away, put head down and dug in heels. The horse jumped and ran flat-out away from the big man. Joel headed that way, holding the rifle high.

The big man's first shot cracked sharply and the bullet flicked by as Frank drew his pistol. He was racing across the prairie turf and a handgun was as good as a rifle. He knew Bull would aim at the horse, and the second shot kicked up dirt and grass ahead of him. Bull was moving too, firing again and again. The bullets cracked viciously but only one came close.

Frank thrust his arm out and fired, thumbing the hammer. He had no hope of hitting Bull, but howling lead would distract him and spoil his aim. Stomach contracted, Frank ducked low, conscious out of the corner of his eye that Joel had reached the second rider. One of Bull's shots tore along the crown of his hat, ripping it off, and he thought he saw a grin of triumph on the big man's face. Bull was coming close as they raced toward each other, firing from the hip and levering the rifle as fast as he could pull the trigger.

Frank veered away, led the other's horse, and fired once, twice, three times. He saw Bull drop the rifle and slump. Frank headed straight for the man and, as Bull jerked himself erect, sent one more bullet into his chest. He was close enough to see the dark stain appear. Bull fell sideways and hit the ground hard as his mount pranced away, eyes rolling.

249

Reining in, Frank leaned down, staring at the unmoving figure. Automatically he began to punch brass from the pistol, turning the cylinder. This was the second of the men who had caused him enormous travail. The impulse to send another bullet into Bull for good luck was nearly overpowering. Then Joel shouted.

With an effort, Frank turned away. Joel and Faith were loping toward him, Faith had thrown back the poncho and her face was radiant.

"She's all right," Joel shouted. "Just hungrier'n hell."

Frank dismounted and, as Faith came up, pulled her from the horse, hugging her.

She was crying, tears streaking her face, unwilling to let him go, wanting to cling to him like a frightened child.

"It's all over," he said gently. "We can go home now."

She nodded her head quickly and gave him a wan smile. "They didn't hurt me . . ." She began to sob again as he held her tightly.

Joel had dismounted and was rummaging through the dead man's belongings. "Hell, no wonder she's hungry." He held up a grubsack that was practically empty. "They didn't have nothing at all!"

Faith did not look robust, but maybe it was the layer of dirt she'd accumulated. The reaction was beginning to wear off—the reality of him and his strength seemed to flow into her—and she closed her eyes, content to stand within the circle of his arms.

Frank said, "Bring her horse, Joel."

She said, "All I want is to sleep. I've never had enough sleep. Oh, God—those terrible nights!"

He put her on the horse, smiling as she clutched his sleeve. "Hang on," he told her. "We'll just walk over to that ridge and get down." He pointed. "Then we're going to fix you something hot to eat, and after that you can sleep."

She smiled at him and bit her lip.

Chapter Twenty-five

Preacher Logan Rossiter was a man with a heavy heart. He greeted his congregation on Sunday morning, and when it was his turn to stand in front of them to deliver the sermon, there were tears in his eyes. People gazed at him in astonishment.

"I've got a thing to say," he said in a voice very unlike the sermon-voice they were used to. "I been a fool, listening to gossip, preachin' against a good man, and preachin' a lie. I'm talking about Frank McCarty."

Preacher clasped his hands together as a gathering murmur ran through the assembled crowd. Bowing his head, Preacher said, "I'm askin' for the Lord's forgiveness for what I done, and I'm askin' Mr. McCarty the same. 'Whatsoever a man soweth, that shall he reap.' " Preacher raised his hands. "I'm willin' to take what's coming to me, Lord, because I forgot to listen to Your precious words: 'Be swift to hear, slow to speak, and slow to wrath.' I wronged this man in Your house—"

Someone said, "You didn't know, Preacher."

Preacher shook his head. "I ain't a fit man t'stand here and preach the Lord's message. That's what I got to tell you-all. Come mornin' I'll be far away, because I ain't got the right to stay. I'm goin' to—"

There were loud cries of "No—no!" Men surged up

from their seats, and in a moment the church was filled with protestations. People pressed toward him, and Preacher burst out sobbing.

Frank sat in Karl Welch's office, sipping bitter coffee, listening to Karl's account of the tracking. White Horn had led them with unerring persistence directly to Jamie Wright's camp.

Jamie had run south, probably hoping to swing west later to head for the coast, but he had holed up in the mountains the second night to get much-needed sleep. His horse was exhausted, and when they crept in to him, Jamie was hard to waken.

It had been a near thing, Karl said, to keep White Horn from knifing the sleeping man. They had merely tied Jamie up and let him sleep, and the next day had started back to Roseberry. The money was intact. Jamie was lying in a bunk in the jail awaiting trial.

When he got back to the office, there was a letter waiting for him, bearing the return address of the Tascosa & Tahlequah Railroad. Frank tore it open and read it, one foot up on his desk. It was signed by Horace Gromley and stated in rather stilted phrases that Gromley had submitted Frank's facts and figures to his superiors, as he had agreed in their meeting, and that Mr. Hightower requested a further meeting to discuss the proposed spur line to Roseberry.

Grunting, Frank tossed the letter to his desk top. He would sleep on that request and probably talk it over again with his father and Amos. The railroad was coming, he was sure of that, and it would bring more "progress," the same kind of progress that was building dance halls and saloons in the east end of town. It would bring other hings too, of course, more people and more enterprise, more jobs and money . . .

And it would make Roseberry a city.

He got up, took his Stetson off a peg and went out, calling to Ken Larkin that he'd be gone the rest of the day. On the boardwalk a dozen tipped-back-chair loungers gazed at him as he strode past to the livery stable. The weather was chilly, but the sun was shining and a man in the tailor shop strutted and turned, cocking his head, looking at himself in a mirror, clad in a new serge suit.

Old Sam greeted him with a smile, scratching his beard. "Howdy, Frank. Paper says it's goin' to snow come Thursday."

"Which paper?"

"Why, Noah's." Sam followed him into the stable. He pulled a saddle blanket off a pole and slapped it down on the back of Frank's sorrel. A coach went by outside with a rattle of doubletree chains and a rumble of hard tires.

"Then it'll snow," Frank said solemnly. "Noah won't play fancy with the weather. Too many folks depend on him."

Sam laughed. "Hell, Noah don't know." He cinched the saddle and gave an extra tug on the latigo. "Folks reads the paper all right, but they looks at the sky too. I seen the North Star a-flickerin' last night, so they's a storm on the way."

He stepped back and Frank swung up as the sorrel pranced.

"Gentle down," Frank said. He raised his hand and walked the horse out to the street, turning west. The sky was a powdery blue, paling toward the horizon with the curled feathers of saffron clouds beginning to steal southward.

He went out the River Road, watching the deep green river eddying and swirling, silent and cold as a beaver's

253

nose. Much of what he saw was the same as it had always been—since he could remember. But vast change was coming, and when he took Faith to Philadelphia next year for the Centennial, they would see the real beginnings of it.

He turned in at the house, pleased to see her buggy in front of the stable with Billy unhooking the horse. She came out on the back steps as he got down and dropped the reins to the ground, returning Billy's greeting. She was still dressed in a dark green coat with a lacy yellow dress underneath. She had removed her hat, and held out her hand to him as he crossed the yard.

"I'm glad you're home early, darling."

He kissed her and they went inside where it was warm.

Epilogue

In the early spring Billy Quinn was set to work raking and spading around the trees, cleaning out the dry leaves and grass and piling them in heaps so they could be burned. It was then that he heard the metallic clatter against his rake and, on peering down, saw the silvery flash of something. . . .

It was a brooch with a grimy but glittering stone, and when he took it to Frank and they washed it off together, the script letters "EL" were apparent on the back. Billy was very pleased because Frank gave him a dollar.

Karl Welch, when he examined it, said at once, "That's the Ledwidge brooch, Frank. Where the hell did you get it?"

"Billy found it in the yard near the fence. D'you remember the time I had a burglar who never took anything?"

"I still don't understand that." Karl shook his head. "What's this brooch got to do with it?"

Frank sat down, staring at the gem on the desk between them.

Karl said, "You want some coffee?"

All Time Bestsellers

☐ THE AELIAN FRAGMENT— George Bartram	08587-8	1.95
☐ THE BERLIN CONNECTION— Johannes Mario Simmel	08607-6	1.95
☐ THE BEST PEOPLE—Helen Van Slyke	08456-1	1.75
☐ A BRIDGE TOO FAR—Cornelius Ryan	08373-5	1.95
☐ THE CAESAR CODE— Johannes M. Simmel	08413-8	1.95
☐ THE CAIN CONSPIRACY— Johannes Mario Simmel	08535-5	1.95
☐ DO BLACK PATENT LEATHER SHOES REALLY REFLECT UP?—John R. Powers	08490-1	1.75
☐ THE HAB THEORY—Allen W. Eckerty	08597-5	2.50
☐ THE HEART LISTENS—Helen Van Slyke	08520-7	1.95
☐ TO KILL A MOCKINGBIRD—Harper Lee	08376-X	1.50
☐ THE LAST BATTLE—Cornelius Ryan	08381-6	1.95
☐ THE LAST CATHOLIC IN AMERICA— J. R. Powers	08528-2	1.50
☐ THE LONGEST DAY—Cornelius Ryan	08380-8	1.75
☐ THE MIXED BLESSING—Helen Van Slyke	08491-X	1.95
☐ THE MONTE CRISTO COVER UP Johannes Mario Simmel	08563-0	1.95
☐ MORWENNA—Anne Goring	08604-1	1.95
☐ THE RICH AND THE RIGHTEOUS Helen Van Slyke	08585-1	1.95
☐ WEBSTER'S NEW WORLD DICTIONARY OF THE AMERICAN LANGUAGE	08500-2	1.75
☐ WEBSTER'S NEW WORLD THESAURUS	08385-9	1.50
☐ THE WORLD BOOK OF HOUSE PLANTS—E. McDonald	03152-2	1.50

Buy them at your local bookstores or use this handy coupon for ordering:
